THE BROKEN HUNTRESS

THE BROKEN HUNTRESS

BOOK 2 IN THE CAPTRIX CHRONICLES

SHELBY MCCRALEY

ISBN-13: 978-1-7378242-2-0 (paperback)
978-1-7378242-3-7 (Ebook)
ASIN: B0BZG1LJ8X (Kindle)

Edited by Whitney Morisello at Whitney's Book Works
Cover Design by Stone Ridge Books

www.shelbymccraley.com

First edition

For Shawn

CHAPTER ONE

I STOOD IN THE dark clearing, feeling the waterlogged ground of the swamp beneath me. Trees surrounded the meadow like a cage with no exit in sight. A sharp breeze whipped through the trees and my oversized t-shirt, making my teeth rattle. I wrapped my arms around myself, chilled to the bone as my bare legs and feet froze in the night air. The full moon remained high in the sky, illuminating one particular spot in the clearing. I blinked and focused my eyes on the highlighted spot.

In front of me, a long wooden table laid in the moonlight with shackles and chains tumbling over the sides. I stared at the chains, wondering what they were for, and got the overwhelming sense I had been in this clearing before. I was supposed to know what this table meant.

I walked closer to the table, cold water squishing between

my toes, and tried to remember what I didn't know. In a blink, my mother, Artemis, appeared with her blonde pixie cut, shackled to the table, peering into my confused eyes. She wore her huntress outfit made of black leather pants, a corset, and a white undershirt, so it made little sense to me why she was on this table and not fighting witch creatures.

Then, I remembered why I had been in this clearing before. This was the place she was going to die.

"Atalanta, help me," said Mom, reaching her chained hands out to me. I broke out into a run as she pulled at the shackles in an escape attempt.

In the corner of my vision, I saw a silver pen knife floating in the air and racing toward her, faster than I could run. I panicked and quickened my pace, even though I realized there would be no way to beat the floating blade. The knife reached her first, leaving me petrified almost a foot away. The shackles pinned my mother's hands to her side as the blade touched her throat. I tried to close the distance, but couldn't move.

"No!" I tried again to close the gap, but my feet remained stuck in the ground.

The blade pierced Mom's throat and slid across, creating a huge gash. Blood began spurting out everywhere, almost reaching me. Her hands suddenly came loose from her chains, allowing her to grasp her neck as her blood flowed over her fingers, dripping red dots onto the table.

"Mom!" I fought harder to get loose. I had to save her.

She fell over onto the table, her body growing lifeless as the bleeding slowed. My feet came loose, but before I could move, a hand grabbed me from behind and pulled me backward. I screamed, needing my voice to change the outcome.

"Atalanta, wake up," said a familiar voice. They continued to pull me toward them. "You're having a bad dream."

I snapped awake, almost colliding with Bridgette's face. She leaned back just in time to avoid the collision. She held my sweaty hand and looked at me with sorrow in her eyes. I felt tears form at the corner of my eyes, a consequence of having a nightmare, and wiped them away with my free hand. Perspiration mixed with salty tears as I tried to slow my panicked breathing with deep breaths.

"I'm sorry. I didn't mean to wake you." I leaned up on my makeshift couch bed and ignored the aches overcoming my body.

I had been staying with Bridgette, my mom's best friend, ever since Mom died in the swamp battle six months ago and witch creatures turned my life upside down. With no home to go to and no family, Bridgette invited me to stay in her cottage as long as I wanted. She didn't have a spare room, so we turned her couch and part of the living room into my bedroom. Unfortunately, my "bedroom" was also next to Bridgette's room, meaning my terrible nightmares also kept her awake.

"It's okay. Were you having the nightmare again?" Bridgette rubbed my hand as she sat on the edge of the couch.

She secured her long, brown, wavy hair into a knot on the top of her head with a black elastic. Little pieces of gray frizz stuck out on the edges, showing the hairstyle had a few hours of sleep before I woke her. However, Bridgette's brown eyes with silver flecks were shadowed by her dark circles. She looked about as tired as I was. I felt guilty for keeping her up.

"It was a little bit different this time, but yeah." I squeezed her hand back. I wanted her to feel like I was okay, so maybe she would go back to sleep.

"That's the third time this week." Bridgette let go of my hand to rub her eyes. "You've been having the same dream for six months."

"I know. I'm sorry." I closed my eyes, trying to figure out something better to say.

She was wrong about it being the third time. I had endured a similar version of watching my mother die every day this week. Evidently, the past few times, I was quiet.

I tried numerous times to not end up in a dream hellscape where my mother kept dying in front of me, but every time I drifted to sleep, I was in the swamp where she died. Most of the time, I couldn't reach her before the knife due to freezing or my lack of speed. Sometimes, I spent the dream fighting witch creatures and got to her right as she took her last breath. No matter what I did or tried, she kept ending up as dead as she remained in reality.

"I didn't mean I was upset. I'm worried about you."

Bridgette looked at me with so much concern that it reminded me of how my mom used to look at me when she had the time to. Most of her life was spent in and out of the house hunting witch creatures rather than being a doting mother. Even though our relationship was strained, an ache throbbed inside of me.

I missed her. And I was the reason she was dead.

I swallowed hard to keep the tears contained.

"What time is it?" I asked, trying to distract myself. I pushed my fingers through my medium length blonde hair and combed the nightmare induced tangles out.

Bridgette raised an eyebrow and handed me my phone from the coffee table, deciding to let my diversion pass. Then, she slid my feet closer to the back cushion so she could sit further in on the brown leather couch. I clicked on my phone screen and squinted at the bright light. Through squinted eyes, I read three am, as known as the witching hour. How convenient. I laid the phone down on the couch and glanced back up at Bridgette. She still watched me with concern.

"I'll be fine. I promise. You should go get a few more hours of sleep." I gave her a weak smile.

"Are you sure?" My facade didn't fool Bridgette. Even though she wasn't my mother, she could see through me better than I gave her credit for.

"I'll be fine. I might read some before I go back to sleep."

"Maybe you should text Tristan. Isn't he normally up now? With the whole flipped sleep schedule to help hunt witches?"

I stifled a laugh. The witch creature world had been quiet for the past few months, so Tristan, Bridgette, and I weren't hunting much of anything. His sleep schedule would still be flipped for me. That is, if Tristan continued staying up late for no reason.

"I'll think about it. Go get some sleep. We can talk some more in the morning," I said, gesturing toward Bridgette's bedroom.

She yawned as she tried to come up with something else to say, but after a second large yawn, Bridgette decided not to fight me anymore. She lifted herself off the couch and walked half asleep back to her bedroom.

I glanced at the phone again, trying to decide if I wanted to text Tristan. If someone asked me about a month ago, I would have immediately said yes. He was my best friend and had been there for me ever since we fought the swamp battle that killed both of our mothers. We even tried dating, even though I was missing a chunk of my soul, so I couldn't love him romantically.

I broke it off a little over a month ago because it got too complicated and decided to keep my distance for a while. We hadn't seen each other in weeks. Before, I would text him every time I dreamed this nightmare. This was the actual reason he had started staying up this late, but it seemed unfair of me to expect him to always be there.

Rubbing my eyes, I tried to convince myself I wasn't tired anymore. I knew I needed some more sleep, but I couldn't bear to watch my mother die again in my dreams tonight. Pulling my knees to my chest, I laid my tired head on them. I hated my stupid brain for forcing me to live that nightmare over and over. My eyes stayed closed for a few moments, and I felt myself drifting off back to sleep.

I jumped off the couch, jerking myself awake, and went over to my trunk next to Bridgette's fireplace. I turned the key I left in the lock and began rummaging through all of my witch creature books. Being a witch huntress required a lot of back studying that I had refused to do before one attacked me. Since taking up the duty, I decided it was time to learn as many creatures as possible. With my voice inside my head, also known as my intuition, to guide me, I had been researching a ton of creatures while hunting was slow. I touched the books and asked my intuition which one I should read. My mind's voice was silent for a second, and then said, "*Sleep.*"

I huffed and picked a book on my own. Pulling out the

Captrix encyclopedia, I decided to continue reading more entries from my ancestors about their own hunts. I returned to the couch with my book and opened it to a new letter I hadn't read before. I glanced at the Latin names of the listed witch creatures, but they all ran together due to my tired eyes. My head drooped again as I focused on a bare entry without many Captrix comments. I bolted upward, rubbed my eyes, and tried to read the first sentence. Before I could read past the beginning sentence, I felt drawn back to sleep. This time, there was no fighting it.

CHAPTER TWO

I WOKE WHEN THE sunrise beamed in from Bridgette's bay windows into the living room. The sun shined off of the dark wood floors and furniture, creating blinding sunspots my eyes squinted at. My only source of relief was the enormous stone fireplace and the dull books on the built-in shelves that didn't reflect light. I glanced toward the largest window to check for Bridgette's movement in the recliner she had facing outwards, but the seat remained still.

The Captrix encyclopedia still laid open on my lap, so I shut it and put it on the coffee table. Wiping a bit of drool from my mouth, I tried to ignore the fact that I felt dead. I had some dreamless sleep for a few hours, but it only caused neck pain from falling asleep in a weird position and a headache. I rubbed the pain spot in my neck and tried to get my bearings. As I kneaded my temples to get my sleep deprivation headache to go away, the sound of coffee dripping in the kitchen brought me to attention. Thank God, Bridgette was awake, already brewing me an elixir of life.

I threw off my blankets and folded them up neatly on one side of the couch, so we could use it as daily seating, and trotted down the hall to the kitchen. As I entered the kitchen, smells of eggs, fried bacon, and coffee infiltrated my nose, causing my stomach to growl. The small cottage kitchen had a way of containing all the delicious smells Bridgette created in it. I had grown used to her always cooking or brewing homemade salves and potions. The brightly colored salves and potions lined an open rack shelf on the back wall of the kitchen and was her pride and joy. My favorite part of the kitchen was the sun catcher Bridgette had in the window over the sink. When the light hit just right, a rainbow would cascade on the hardwood floors.

I reached into the cabinet by the sink and the coffeemaker to pull down two white coffee mugs. Placing them next to the coffeepot, I went to the fridge, carefully avoiding Bridgette. I opened the small white fridge and grabbed the coffee creamer to make a delicious, sweet, and creamy cup of life.

"Did you get any more sleep?" I asked Bridgette, as the coffee pot finished.

"A little bit." She placed the last strips of bacon on a plate to drain. "What about you?"

"I think so." I poured the coffee into the mugs and topped it off with the creamer.

Bridgette took the creamer bottle from me and put it back in the fridge. Then, she looked me up and down to take in the horrid shell of a person I had become. My blonde hair was stick straight, but matted with grease from forgetting to wash it properly. The darkness under my eyes had developed into a permanent fixture on my face that I didn't think I could cover up, even if I wanted to. The rest of my body was pasty due to the season and because I remained inside except when visiting Mom's grave at the corner of the cottage's woods or during combat training. Needless to say, I avoided mirrors as often as possible.

"You look—" Bridgette placed the breakfast foods on the wooden table.

"Tired," I said, finishing her sentence as I brought our mugs of coffee over.

"I was going to suggest sad, sullen, and exhausted."

I cringed at the words. I knew she was right, but it still stung hearing them. She pulled out her chair and sat down. We passed the breakfast in silence and pushed the food around with our forks, trying to figure out what to say. Bridgette took a small bite of eggs, followed by a sip of coffee.

"I'm just worried about you." She gave me a big sigh.

"I know. You told me last night." I took a gulp of coffee, praying for a caffeine boost. "But I promise you, I'm fine."

"You're lying."

"No, I'm not. I swear—"

"Atalanta, there hasn't been any witch creature activity in over a month. You haven't left that couch for weeks, yet you aren't sleeping because of recurring nightmares."

"I can't help—" I tried to get a word in on Bridgette's speech.

"Not to mention you haven't talked to Tristan in weeks."

My fork scraped across the plate, making a screeching

sound that hurt my own ears. Bridgette looked taken aback and gave me her full attention.

"You know we broke up," I said, keeping my voice as deadpan as possible. "I broke up with him."

"You never really told me why, though," said Bridgette softly.

I bit my lip, trying to think of how I wanted to explain it, or even if I wanted to at all. Telling her about it wouldn't hurt me since my heart wasn't broken. The deterioration of our friendship hurt me more. I couldn't love Tristan, but that didn't mean I couldn't still care about him. Mainly, I was afraid if I told Bridgette the whole story, she would look at him differently, and I didn't want that.

Bridgette stared me down, waiting for a response.

I picked up a piece of bacon and chewed it slowly, weighing my options. My problem was I couldn't lie to Bridgette about something important, but I could tell her part of the truth.

"Do you really want me to tell you?"

"Yes. That's what I'm waiting on." Bridgette stared at me harder.

"I didn't want him to get hurt. Being with me was never going to end well with my soul and witch hunting. And I knew I couldn't protect him from either of those things." A small weight lifted, and I felt a bit lighter.

Bridgette ate a few more bites of breakfast until she was done and slid the plate away, lost in thought. Then, she rose, gathered the empty plates, and took them to the sink. The warm coffee mugs remained on the table with the last few sips of coffee in them. Bridgette stayed there, rinsing the dishes for an obnoxious amount of time until I couldn't stand it.

"Bridgette?" I raised my voice to capture her attention. "What is it?"

She turned the water off and took a deep breath, then returned to her chair, looking torn.

"I'm going to tell you something, and I need you to really hear me." Bridgette waited for me to nod. "You can't protect everyone. It's impossible and not an expectation you should have for yourself."

I looked down at the table, studying the shapes in the wood.

"Second, what happened to Artemis was not your fault. You can't spend the rest of your life feeling guilt over her death. You did nothing wrong."

"But I should have been able to save her. I should be able to protect people as a Captrix, and I clearly can't." My voice cracked, and I rushed the coffee cup to my lips.

My grief felt massive, like a beach ball expanding in my chest with no more room to grow, constricting my throat as I experienced the pang of losing my mother all over again. It was like I couldn't breathe, but I also couldn't gasp for air. This combined with the sinking depression I suffered every time I thought about my relationship with Tristan was too much.

I held in a panicked scream.

My chair squealed as I forced it back, making a scratch line onto the floor. I ran out the front door, trying to force myself to breathe as the air slapped me in the face. The tightness in my throat constricted more as I tried to swallow air, saliva, anything to calm this pain in my throat. I ran, not caring about the dew covering my feet, until I reached her grave.

I crashed to my knees at the edge of the settled dirt

and released a scream that transformed into a sob. My body rocked with all the tension I was releasing, and I felt the ball of grief deflate a bit. I gasped for air, trying to remind myself how to breathe normally.

Bridgette was crazy to think all of this wasn't my fault. If I had never failed my first hunt or failed to save my mother from Morgana, she would be here in front of me, not this mound of dirt with a wood cross at the end. I failed to save her, so I was determined to make sure no one else I cared about would reach the same fate.

Even if I knew I couldn't protect them.

My hands did little to wipe away the moisture drying on my face. Exhaustion consumed me, unfazed by the cup of coffee I inhaled, and I considered laying my head on the wet grass to rest. But training was more important. I had to be better to make up for my failure. So, I pulled myself off the ground to return inside like nothing was wrong.

The creaking of Bridgette's recliner welcomed me back in, but instead of turning into the living room to face her, I darted into the bathroom to take a shower. I didn't want her to see me tear stained and muddy when I was supposed to be improving. Back to a new normal even. With six months passing, I should feel better instead of having this weight upon me.

I, of all people, knew grief wasn't linear, but in my world now, it had to be.

Instead of focusing on how I felt, I scrubbed all the dirt away and took extra care to wash my hair twice. It was the most self-care I had forced my body through in weeks. When I stepped out of the shower, I looked like a new person and got dressed into a t-shirt and pajama shorts from a pile of clean clothes left in the bathroom corner. Bridgette and I still hadn't figured out the storage situation of the few clothes I possessed, so I kept them on an end table Bridgette stuffed by the door.

Bridgette's rocking stopped when I entered the living room to read. I considered doing some combat training, but my exhausted limbs demanded otherwise. She said nothing when I selected a random brown book from her shelf on medicinal herbs and forced herself to stay focused on the embroidery project in her lap. The stitched outline looked to be a rabbit matching the creature featured on my family crest, but Bridgette brought it closer to her chest before I could get a better look.

Sitting down with the herb book, I laid my phone on the coffee table and forced myself to focus on the reading at hand. Medicinal herbs didn't interest me at all like they did Bridgette or Tristan, so I found my eyes glazing over within five pages. My lack of concentration broke when my cell phone began buzzing on the coffee table. I set the book on the coffee table and exchanged it for my phone. Tristan's face lit up the screen with his shaggy black hair and warm brown eyes.

"Tristan's calling me," I said, dumbfounded at the surprise.

"You should answer it." Bridgette added another stitch to her embroidery, not looking up from her project.

I nodded at her, taking a deep breath. I rose from the couch and started for the front door to go outside. With my hand on the doorknob, I swiped the screen to answer the call.

"Hey," I said, opening the front door.

The sunshine blinded me as I shut the door. I squinted my eyes, allowing them to adjust as the crisp Georgia November air smacked me in the face. The day seemed brighter and colder now that I wasn't pumping with adrenaline like earlier. Luckily, it was still mild enough for me to be outside in my t-shirt and pajama shorts since I hadn't dressed for any morning calls.

"Hey. How are you?" said Tristan's smooth voice on the other end of the line.

"I'm fine. How are you?" The small talk between us felt odd, but it was also deemed necessary by the fact that we hadn't talked in weeks.

"I'm good. Have you been getting any sleep?"

"Umm, I'm managing." I wondered where this conversation was going to go. Surely, he had a different reason for calling than asking about my sleep patterns.

"That's good."

Dead silence filled the air as neither of us spoke. I waited for him to make the next move because I didn't know what to say.

"Are you going to be busy tonight?" said Tristan, breaking the awkwardness.

"Nothing is really coming up right now, so probably not."

"I'm having a couple of friends over at the apartment tonight I want you to meet."

"Uh, you want me to meet people?"

"Yes. It's not like you know that many."

That line stung a bit, but he was right. I only knew two people in this world that were alive, Tristan and Bridgette. I honestly didn't even know how to interact with people my own age, since I never had the chance after being stuck at home for eighteen years.

"I don't know, Tristan," I said, indecisiveness filling my voice.

"Please? I promise it will be super chill. Just a few friends I know from high school. I really want you to meet them."

"Why?"

"Because you need to get out of the cottage. Plus, I haven't seen you since—" He paused at the hard part. "You know."

I did know, but I didn't want to fill in the blanks.

"I'll think about it, okay?"

I could almost hear Tristan clench his teeth through the phone. I understood this had to be difficult for him, yet here I was, still giving him a hard time. I didn't mean to, but what was I supposed to do at a gathering of his strangers when I broke up with him?

"Okay. We're meeting up around nine if you decide to come by," said Tristan.

"Tristan, I'm—"

He hung up the phone.

I continued holding my phone to my ear, waiting for the silence to end and for him to say something, but he was already gone. I swallowed hard, hating myself, and stared out into the woods, trying to not think about the night I broke Tristan's heart.

$

It was just another night; there was nothing special about it except the fact that I was tangled in Tristan's arms in his bedroom. We had returned to the apartment after canvassing the neighborhood for witch creature activity. Nothing had turned up, so Tristan suggested we return to his place before taking me home to Bridgette.

I was used to being in his room, and it didn't bother me. I enjoyed looking at the echoes of his high school days plastered on the wall with polaroids of old friends and band posters. It was a way for me to see what a normal teenage life looked like. But the echoes also seemed to haunt the room, as it was a memory of the way things had been before Morgana, his mother, went on a deadly power trip. I leaned back onto the bed to have a discussion with my best friend like we always did because I enjoyed looking at the plastic glow in the dark stars Tristan kept on the ceiling. He laid beside me, looking at me like I was the most beautiful girl in the world, while twisting my hair gently around his pointer finger.

"Do you think the witch creatures are gone?" Tristan picked a new strand of my hair to twirl.

"That would be too easy," I said.

The witch creatures hadn't acted out in weeks, seemingly scared by the swamp meadow incident and my growing Captrix confidence. Right after the swamp, a few tried to test me, but my training with Bridgette and my unlocked intuition proved to be a force. The witches had fizzled out slowly, leaving me with untapped energy and almost too much alone time with Tristan.

"From what I know, they are never truly gone. This is the calm before the storm."

"It's a long calm." He grew bored with my hair, and the strands tumbled back onto my shoulder.

He gave my face a light stroke that made my skin tingle from the ticklish touch, not emotion. Tristan leaned in and gave me a small kiss that I accepted, even though I knew I shouldn't let it happen. Every time he desired to kiss me, though, I couldn't resist the hope in my heart that maybe this time would be the one time I felt something. My hopes, however, always led to something worse. When I let him in, it felt like I could sense the love inside me brew for a second, but then it drained to my lost soul piece. The more I let him touch me, the emptier I became. This time was no exception.

"Tristan, I—"

He cut me off with a small shush and went in for another kiss. This one was forced deeper and hungered for more. He moved on top of me, and I bore the weight of his lust and love for me. My body arched to him, and a spark erupted for a moment, but fizzled into a deep emptiness. The emptiness took my breath away and left a deep grave of hopelessness inside I couldn't escape.

Fear choked me.

I pushed Tristan off in a combination of fear and anger. I scampered out of the bed, catching my breath, which I had realized had become panicked in the fray. My palms grew sweaty as I tried to calm down, but this was all too much. I couldn't feel that empty again while I barely felt whole. The grief of losing my mother and this empty feeling were too much for me to deal with anymore.

"Atalanta, I didn't mean..." said Tristan, embarrassed at getting too caught up in himself.

I had never told him exactly how romantic encounters made me feel, even though he knew I was unable to love him back. But we still tried, clinging onto the wish that maybe we could put my soul back together by forcing me to feel love.

"I can't do this anymore," I said, choking out the words. "I don't love you."

Tristan leaped from the bed and grabbed my hands.

"I know that. I got carried away." His thumbs grazed the back of my hand in a pitiful attempt to calm me down.

"I can't do this to you anymore. It's wrong." The emptiness still swirled inside, threatening to swallow me. "It's not fair to you."

"We're going to fix it. Things are calm now."

My anger took over my fear. Bridgette and I had been searching for months for a way to put my soul back together with no lead in sight. Tristan was foolish to think that he was going to be able to fix it.

"I'm broken. There is no fixing this." I threw his hands away from me and endured the angry tears that began streaking my face. "I'm done doing this."

He stared at me hard, and I could see the passion he had for me moments ago crumbling behind his eyes. We stood together, me with my angry tears, and him trying to figure out words to say. I wanted him to say something, but I knew nothing would satisfy the pain and frustration I felt.

"Please, just take me home. Then, I'll leave you alone." I moved to the bedroom door.

Tristan pressed his lips together and grabbed his keys.

CHAPTER THREE

After a few moments of painful reflection, I decided to give in and go back inside for Bridgette's one hundred questions. I clutched my phone hard, trying to force the tension out of my body in a safe way. I wasn't angry, but the guilt from hearing his pleas did me in. Tristan wasn't asking much from me, but it was still a lot to make a socially ignorant person show up to a gathering with her ex-boyfriend's friends that she never met.

His friends probably thought I was a heartless psycho anyway. I knew I would. Tristan couldn't have explained that I was missing a piece of my soul. This meant he spun another story to his friends about why he was broken up with, leaving my imagination to run free, pondering what he came up with.

I pushed open the front door and found Bridgette sitting at the edge of her recliner having stowed her embroidery into the basket next to her where she kept all of her current craft projects. She looked eager, but seemed to be trying her best to hold back any excitement. I shook my head at her and sat down on the couch.

"Well, what did he say?" Bridgette leaned more toward me, narrowly avoiding falling out of her chair.

I took a deep breath and sighed. "He wants me to come over to his apartment tonight and meet his friends." I forced myself to not let out another sigh of despair.

"Is that not a good thing?" asked Bridgette, thoroughly confused.

"No...I mean, yes. Ugh, I don't know."

"Why don't you want to go?"

"Because I don't even know how to act around people. Let alone people who know I murdered their friend's heart."

"Murdered their friend's heart? Don't you think that's a little much?" The eagerness was wearing off, so Bridgette slid further back into her chair to assume her mother mode.

"No, I really don't. I don't even know why he wants me there." I considered chewing on my thumb nail to distract me from my thoughts.

"Maybe he misses you and wants to see you. Is that so bad?"

"I guess not."

"I think you should go."

My head snapped up to look directly at Bridgette.

"What?" I said, flabbergasted.

Bridgette held her hands out in a defensive pose and then moved them down in reassurance.

"Hear me out," she said, trying to calm my reaction. "It would be good for you to get out. You can think of it as patrolling."

I raised my eyebrows and turned my head to the side.

"Things have been really quiet lately. You can take this chance to go around the shops and make sure nothing suspicious is going on. So, a little bit of social life and a little bit of hunting." Bridgette seemed content with her idea.

"Uh huh." I controlled the urge to roll my eyes.

"I also need a few things from Tristan's store. I could give you a list?"

"Fine, you got me."

"Yay." Bridgette added a little clap for good measure.

"But if I'm going to go patrolling, I need combat practice."

Bridgette groaned, rolled her eyes, and made her way out of the front door.

We kept a basket of dodgeballs squeezed in at the end of the porch where a bush hid them. Bridgette took her place in the yard, waiting for me to bring the balls to her. The method we came up with wasn't the best combat training ever, but it worked by helping me perfect my reflexes. I lugged the basket to Bridgette's feet and took my place in the middle of the yard. She reached into the basket and threw a ball toward my face.

I imagined the ball as a fireball hurling straight at me and allowed myself to tune into my Captrix intuition, waiting for its movement command.

Right.

I darted to the right as the ball whizzed past me. The voice in my head faintly sounded like my mother still, even though I had been working on making it sound like more of my own. I wasn't sure how the voice worked, but I assumed it took the tone of mentors. Before it was my mother, my intuition sounded like my grandmother with a robotic edge.

Duck.

This ball flew over my head, but Bridgette used a bit of her telekinesis magic to bring the ball back toward her, so I dodged the ball again. She was taking the extra time to make the ball react like an Ignis's magic, a fire witch who used tracker fireballs to attack. The fireballs acted like a boomerang until making contact with their target or being extinguished. I evaded a few of Bridgette's balls until she took a break from throwing.

"You know, I'm glad you're going out tonight," she said, taking a moment to catch her breath.

"Why?" I walked to grab some dodgeballs left behind me.

"Because you're getting good at this. You need to have some fun."

"I don't need fun. I need training to perfect my skills."

"You sound like Artemis," mumbled Bridgette.

I bit my lower lip, giving my brain something else to focus on. I realized Bridgette didn't mean to say it loud enough for me to hear, but the line still echoed in my brain.

"Maybe I could use a bit of free time that doesn't involve witches." As soon as I said the words, I didn't know if I believed them.

"That's the spirit! I'm sure it will be nice to meet people your age."

"Yeah, if they don't hate me." I placed my gathered balls into the basket.

"I'm sure it will be fine." She gave me a beaming smile.

"If you say so."

"Now, what will you wear?"

My eyes widened in fear.

§

One replaced basket of dodgeballs and a few hours later, Bridgette tossed me combinations of her clothes mixed with the few I owned. Dresses, skirts, and tops piled high, covering the fluffy white duvet and the light blue throw pillows on her made up bed. Bridgette's bedroom looked to me like it belonged in a home magazine showcasing cottages. Dark wood tones ran on from the living room as the hardwood flooring continued into the bedroom. Bridgette complimented the hardwood by choosing a matching wood for her bedroom suite that included one nightstand, a chest dresser, and queen bed frame. On the nightstand, she kept a thin white cloth meant to be used as a napkin to protect the wood. Holding the cloth down was a white lamp and a glass vase holding freshly picked wildflowers and springs of rosemary, along with her car keys and a note. The vase's smell was intoxicating and rounded out the quaint bedroom.

But the giant pile of clothes on the bed was not helping the peaceful vibe. I grew overwhelmed looking at all the clothes, while Bridgette went along gleefully, preparing like she was dressing a Barbie. I lifted a skirt from the top of the pile up in the air and scrutinized it.

"How am I supposed to fight witch creatures in this?" I flipped the navy pleated midi skirt around, admiring the airy fabric that looked like an accident waiting to happen.

All I could imagine was being flipped upside down in a back alley and my underwear shining to the entire world. I would still kill the witch creature, but I would also kill all my decency in the process.

"Why would you be fighting witch crea—oh right, the patrolling after the party," said Bridgette.

I blinked at her, realizing she forgot the tale she spun to get me to go to this hangout. She hadn't planned on me patrolling at all.

"You're right." Bridgette recovered from her slip. "But you can't wear the huntress outfit, either. It doesn't blend."

She was correct, but I still crossed my arms in annoyance.

"I still need to wear pants and something I can use to hide weapons."

I grabbed a pair of my stretchy dark wash skinny jeans from the bed pile and slid them on. I glanced back at the pile to see if there was something I could wear as a top, but nothing looked good for hiding weapons. Massaging my temples, I regretted my decision to go.

"Wait before you get all frustrated, I've got it," said Bridgette.

She handed me a long line black tee and a dark gray duster cardigan. I took them from her and put them on. The black tee skimmed past my hips and the duster cardigan went past my knees. It was lightweight, still warm enough for late fall, but perfect for concealing my dagger, so I appeared normal.

"This is perfect!" I considered where I would put my weapons.

"I thought it would be." She handed me her herb shopping list and the keys to her car from the nightstand. "Be safe, and trust me, it will be fine."

I nodded at her and prepared to leave. Exiting the bedroom, I walked to my Captrix chest and opened it to get some gear. I had to travel light to avoid any awkward questions, so I needed to choose wisely. I grabbed my mixed metal dagger, admiring the six different types of metal swirled into the blade. It was predominantly silver, but the lines of gold and copper gave it a beautiful sheen. Since using different types of metal was the easiest way to kill a witch creature, I knew this would be the most strategic choice. I dug out a black leather pancake style knife sheath to hide it beneath my shirt in the small of my back. I also wanted to take a fire bomb and some blessed water for more distant fire power, but that would be tricky. The vials we had were large and made to be worn on a belt, not concealed.

"Bridgette, do we have anything I could use to carry some potions?" I said, yelling toward the bedroom.

Bridgette walked out of the bedroom, holding a long silver necklace with two vial shaped crystals on it. One crystal appeared to be a purple amethyst, while the other appeared to be a black obsidian. A small hook closure kept them secured to the necklace.

"I figured you would ask." Bridgette handed me the necklace. "You can fill these with some potions. To the plain eye, it will look like a crystal necklace."

I examined the necklace in my hand and took the time to look at the hook mechanism and learn how to open the faux crystals. After removing the crystal from the necklace by using the hook, a small bit of pressure at the top of the crystal popped open the hidden vessel. I opened the glittering amethyst and began pouring a small amount of blessed water into it. We raked fire bomb spices in the obsidian crystal, and my mini weapons were complete. Then, needing a fire source to light the fire bomb spices, I took a silver zippo lighter out of the chest and placed it in my back pocket.

"Thanks. This will work great." I put the necklace on and admired how they laid perfectly on the black t-shirt past my chest.

"Now remember, that isn't a lot of potion. It may be enough for a distraction or a small flame. It's not going to take anything out like you're used to," said Bridgette.

"Got it."

The outfit wouldn't be complete without my lucky penny, so I rummaged through my chest again until I pulled out the shiny copper coin. The penny had been my good luck charm since my grandfather had given it to me before he died and added a layer of protection since they actually made it with copper, unlike modern pennies. Tonight, I hoped it gave me luck not only against witch creatures, but also with meeting new people. I slipped the penny in my back pocket with the lighter before giving Bridgette a hug to tell her thank you again by giving her a hard squeeze.

"Be careful. Call me if you need me, okay?" Bridgette returned the squeeze.

"I will. I'm just going to pick up your list, meet some people, and I'll be back soon." I tucked the list she had given to me into my other back pocket.

Bridgette rolled her eyes at me like she knew better, and I shook my head at her to confirm I wasn't planning on actually staying long. I jingled the keys at her as I told her bye and left to go to Tristan's apartment.

CHAPTER FOUR

The drive didn't take long, but I spent plenty of time trying to figure out what this gathering was going to be like. I wondered what type of friends Tristan had and if they would like me. Imagining these things didn't help my anxiety at all, and I almost turned the car around twice. The knife holster also irritated my back, so I was almost glad to see the herb shop and apartment that held my impending doom. I parallel parked in front of the shop and stepped out of the car, readjusting the pancake holster back to a suitable spot on my back.

The hair on my arms immediately stood, creating goosebumps, and I listened deeply to my intuition as a force of habit. I enjoyed being able to sense the area because it gave me a sense of comfort. I stood next to the car, allowing myself to feel the area, but nothing dangerous perked my intuition. My arm hair calmed, and my skin returned to smooth.

I walked down the alley behind the herb shop until I met the stairs for the apartment. Walking up the metal stairs, I listened to the clanging noise my feet made until my ears focused on the music pouring out of the apartment's door. Then, I froze.

Was I supposed to knock? Or was I supposed to walk in like I knew what I was doing? Would Tristan leave the door unlocked for me, or would I endure the awkward weight of a door handle that wouldn't move?

I bit my lip, feeling stupid for worrying about such small things, and continued up the last few metal steps. When I reached the metal door, I decided to gently turn the knob to test it. The knob didn't budge, so I knew it was locked. Now, the door forced me to knock. I gave the door two hard knocks, to be heard over the music, and waited for what seemed like hours, until the door opened.

"Hey, come on in," said Tristan, swinging the door open wider.

He looked calm and relaxed in his gray v-neck shirt and light wash skinny jeans complete with black high top converses. Laughter spilled from inside the party, causing his grin to grow wider. It was the happiest I think I had ever seen him before. The idea of infiltrating that happiness caused me to panic. I quickly reached for my back pocket to grab the herb list Bridgette gave me, holding it up like it was the true reason I was here, not because he invited me.

"Hey," I said, pushing the list toward him. "Bridgette gave me a list of things she needs."

Tristan looked at me, surprised, but took the note. He

gave the list a quick glance and looked back up.

"Yeah, I've got all of this in the shop. I'll get it for you in a few minutes," said Tristan, handing back the list. "Why don't you come in and meet everyone first?"

I gave him an apprehensive nod and inhaled a deep breath, unhappy to go inside, but happy to have avoided awkwardness so far. I followed Tristan into the apartment to see it was almost exactly how I had seen it last, minus Morgana's various books and knickknacks that used to lie across the mantle. Her vial of ashes was also missing, probably moved to keep them safe from the partygoers. Someone dimmed all the lights except a small light box in the corner that strobed colored lights on the white walls. The TV was playing music videos at a volume loud enough to vibe with the music and dance if you felt the need to, but also quiet enough to carry a conversation with friends.

A few guys stood in the kitchen to the right while two girls sat on the couch, enthralled by the band on TV.

Tristan went straight toward the kitchen where the guys stood. When we approached, they were immersed in a conversation I couldn't make sense of, but stopped when I appeared. I made a small, awkward cough to clear my throat.

"Hey, guys. This is my friend Atalanta I've told you about," said Tristan, motioning to me. "Atalanta, this is Derek, Xavier, and Austin." He pointed at each one in the order of their names.

Derek was a tall, short-haired blonde with a lean basketball player build, but his outfit was a carbon copy of Tristan's. Xavier dressed in a red long sleeve, expecting the night to get cold, but it popped off his dark complexion. He looked me up and down, not making any moves, while Derek seemed uninterested in my presence. Austin leapt forward, though, extending his hand for a handshake. I gave him mine, and he took it for a gentle shake before dropping my hand.

"Austin. Charmed, I'm sure." He did a small twirl to show off his all black ensemble of a v-neck tee and skinny jeans, complete with combat boots. He had shoulder-length brown hair that he was clearly trying to grow out since it looked shiny and well taken care of. I let out a small laugh, amused by his antics.

"Atalanta, my liege," I said, feeling normal for a moment.

Austin returned my comment with a small bow.

"Let me go get the girls," said Tristan, leaving me alone in the kitchen with the three guys.

I watched as he walked away while the uninterested Derek and Xavier returned to their previous conversation. I moved a few steps back, excusing myself from their circle, but Austin followed me.

"Atalanta is a cool name. How'd your mom come up with that?" He gave me a warm smile.

"It's the name of a goddess, actually, or at least that's what she told me," I said, trying to ignore the sting of talking about Mom in the past tense.

"That's cool." He pondered another question to make small talk. "Have you ever played beer pong? The guys and I are about to play a match, and I need a partner."

"I'm not sure if I'll be any good." I hadn't planned on staying long. Meet people, get the list, and get out.

I turned my head to the left to see the redhead from the couch giving Tristan a kiss and holding him close. He laughed at something the redhead said as the brunette from the couch rose to walk away toward me. I observed Tristan give the girl another peck and realized this was why his eyes looked so happy.

A pang of jealousy stirred inside me as I stared harder. I wasn't jealous of the fact that she was with Tristan. However, I was jealous of the fact that she could be.

"That's Sarah you're staring at," said Austin, breaking my trance.

I looked back at Austin and gave him a smile to appear unbothered.

"She seems nice. How long have they been dating?"

"A few weeks now. She seems pretty cool. We went to high school together, but I never talked to her much."

The brunette reached Austin and me. She looked pleasant enough, but I could tell she was trying to hide her irritation.

"Tristan is a little preoccupied right now, so I figured I would introduce myself," said the brunette, struggling to hide an eye roll. "I'm Angie."

"Atalanta," I said, admiring her outfit.

Angie wore a brown sweater dress with riding boots. I thought it looked cute on her, and the outfit felt like something I could wear if I didn't have to carry weapons all the time.

"I like your dress." I hoped the compliment would come across as genuine.

Angie gave me a small nod and murmured a thanks as Tristan arrived with Sarah in tow. I took another glance at the redhead before she arrived into the circle and realized she was everything I wasn't. She was shorter and curvy in all the right places. Her red hair fell in loose waves past her shoulders and her freckles outshined my icy blonde hair and pale skin.

Standing next to her, I felt like an awkward beanpole while she looked like a pixie type seductress with piercing green eyes. I was in awe of her and ventured a thought, wondering if she was Tristan's normal type.

"Atalanta, I would like you to meet my girlfriend, Sarah." Tristan wrapped his arm around her waist, tugging her in close.

Sarah smiled at me, gleefully and pure. It would be hard to hate her if she kept this up.

"Hi," said Sarah, her voice coming out like a chirp. "I'm so excited to meet you! Tristan has told me all about you!"

A sinker fell into my stomach. I immediately locked eyes with Tristan, wondering if I should mentally inquire about how much she really knew. The power remained inactive because I hadn't stretched that part of my intuition since the swamp. I was afraid to use it, though, in case it came across as too strong. The past times I tried it, I left Bridgette and Tristan crumbling to the ground. I settled, deciding I would have to ask like normal later.

I returned my gaze back to Sarah.

"Funny, Tristan hasn't told me much about you." It came out a little more forced than I wanted, but Sarah seemed oblivious to the tension.

"That's Tristan. Always leaving the good stuff out." Sarah gave him a loving pat on the chest. The gesture kind of made me want to vomit. "We talked in high school, but rekindled our relationship a few weeks ago."

"That's amazing. I'm happy for you two."

I produced a forced smile. Tristan would know it was fake, but I hoped the rest of the group wouldn't detect it. The music video on the TV changed again, and the entire group reverberated with excitement, rushing toward the TV. I realized that this must have been a common band they shared and followed to get a glimpse of the excitement.

Most of them piled on the couch except Austin and I, who stood on the side. Austin glanced around and found a chair and motioned toward it to offer it to me, but I shook my head. I wasn't ready to be comfortable in this environment and still wanted an easy escape route. He plastered his eyes to the TV screen, along with the others. I looked around and watched the rest of the group's interest, but my eyes settled on Tristan and Sarah.

She sat in his lap to make extra room on the couch, vibing to the music, but also enthralled with Tristan. He rested his head on her shoulder and began whispering things in her ear, causing a small giggle to erupt. He planted kisses on her neck until she made him stop because the rest of the group stared at them for interrupting the music with their affection.

I should have been happy for him. He looked so dang happy. But all I could do was wish that it was me in his lap experiencing all the emotions Sarah felt. The butterflies, the giggles, the sense of new love where everything in the world was perfect. I wished I could actually feel things rather than the emotional drain they caused every time I tried. I didn't want to be stuck like this forever, wishing my soul was whole. It wasn't fair.

That should be me feeling Tristan's love.

Instead, I was a broken girl with no life who broke his heart. I had wasted months of his time, only for him to find this much joy in a few weeks. Anger brewed inside me, threatening to bubble out. I looked at the TV, trying to focus on the song lyrics, but I didn't hear anything because of the steam coming out of my ears. After a few minutes, the song concluded.

I turned away from the TV and locked eyes with Austin. He held my eye contact for a long moment like he could sense the pain I was in.

"Sure you don't want to join me for that game of beer pong?"

I pondered the idea. I knew it wouldn't be the smartest thing I'd ever done, but Tristan invited me to this party to have fun and make friends, right? Why shouldn't I meet new people if he was going to make out with his new girlfriend all night?

"As long as you're not planning to win," I said, giving him a small smile.

"Derek! Xavier! You guys ready?" Austin motioned toward the long plastic card table set up in the kitchen covered in red solo cups.

We walked together to the table, trailed by Derek and Xavier. They went to the far end of the table, closer to the stove, while I took my place at the end closest to the door. I stared down at the empty solo cups, confused. I, of course, had never played beer pong before, but I had the vaguest memory of seeing it in a movie once. There should've been something in these cups for us to drink. I didn't have the courage to admit confusion, but before I thought about it any longer, Austin slammed the refrigerator door. He brought out a case of Natural Light beer and set the large box in the center of the table.

"Where did you get that?" I said, letting the words slip out as I realized how naïve I sounded.

I thought for sure we all had to be under twenty-one, but these were normal teenagers with connections. Why did I have to be so awkward? I placed my hands in my back pocket, gliding one over the zippo lighter, feeling the design of the metal. It was something to distract my attention for a moment.

"My brother works at the corner store. He buys it for us," said Derek, lifting his hands up to make air quotes. "For a finder's fee, you know?"

I nodded, stroking the lighter's cool metal. I didn't really know, but I could pretend. Austin ripped open the cardboard box of beer, dispersing cans on either side. Xavier grabbed one of the cans and cracked it open, creating a soft fizz sound in the air, and began pouring it into the cups. Austin slid a can toward me.

"About halfway." Austin gave me a large grin as he continued unpacking the box.

I let go of my lighter, grabbed the can, popped the tab, and went along filling the solo cups. After about five minutes, the boys and I had all the cups filled. Derek pulled a white ping pong ball out of his pocket, blew off the pocket lint stuck to it, and put it in the center of the table. The beer pong game was ready to commence.

Xavier grabbed the ball to take the first shot, and I followed his hand closely, trying to figure out the best way to toss the ball. The ping pong ball left his long fingers, bounced perfectly in the center of the table, and leapt into a middle cup in the triangle. The beer inside made a splashing sound, and I watched as droplets jumped out of the cup. Then, my breath hitched. I had never drank before. I didn't even know what beer tasted like. Austin glanced over at me, but I remained frozen in place.

"Uh, I'll drink after Xavier. You can have Derek." Austin reached across the table for the cup the ball landed in. "Derek is better to drink behind anyway. He kinda sucks."

I let out a small giggle as Derek flipped him off. Austin removed the ball and guzzled down the cup of beer. He sat the cup down on a folding chair next to the table, dried the ping pong ball off on his shirt, and handed it over to me. I took it from his hand, feeling the leftover moisture from the beer on my fingertips.

"Are you sure you don't want to throw first? I've never really done this before." I passed the ball from my left hand to my right.

Derek smirked, probably anticipating that he wasn't going to have to do much drinking.

"Nah. You got this." Austin shot a look across the table to Derek who stopped smiling.

I took a deep breath and aimed toward the center of the table. If I hit it just right, this ball had to go in a cup somewhere. I let the ball go, giving it a light overhand toss. The ball bounced in the center, but lost direction and went to the right. It barely landed in the cup on the back far right, but somehow it spun around on the lip and plopped in. Derek immediately reached for the cup, removed the ball, and downed his beer. I screeched, jumping up and down. The boys all laughed as Derek added his cup to the chair.

I turned to glance at Tristan and Sarah on the couch. She was still sitting in his lap, but Tristan didn't seem interested in her as much. Instead, he stared at me with one of his "what are you doing" looks I grew to recognize in the past few months. I gave him a big smile and shrugged. All I had to do was fake that I was fine. At this moment, I didn't want him to know how much it bothered me that he moved on so quickly.

"See, I told you. You got this." Austin gave me a small thumbs up.

"About time you were on a winning team," said Derek, as he wiped the ball on his shirt.

He did his toss, and the ball sank into the cup at the tip of the triangle. I grabbed the red cup, removed the ping pong ball, and brought it to my lips. I hesitated for a moment, remembering how many shirts the ball had been wiped on. This ping pong ball was a germ infestation that cleaned off pocket lint in beer. I held my stomach and tilted the cup back.

Cold, fizzy liquid hit the back of my throat, enveloping my mouth in the taste of watered down Mountain Dew. Somehow this Mountain Dew was worse, though, because it was sour. I held in a gag at the flavor, realizing the rest of this game was going to suck if every cup tasted like that.

I handed my cup to Austin, and the game rotated back to Xavier. Angie migrated from across the room and sat down in the chair, holding the spare solo cups in her lap as we continued to play. After four cups of beer, I started not caring what it tasted like. By the time the game cups dwindled to four on Xavier and Derek's side, a light buzz took hold of my head. I felt light and airy—like I could do anything. It was the first time I felt free in months, and I was enjoying it. When only a few cups remained on both teams, Tristan and Sarah moved from the couch to stand in the kitchen and watch the final showdown.

Austin did a strategic toss, landing the ping pong ball in the last back cup we had left. Xavier reached out and drank it, leaving only one cup left in the first row behind where the tip cup had started. I gave Austin a little clap as Derek shot his ball to our side. He missed, and the ball rolled off the table to Sarah's feet. She leaned down, picked it up, and handed it to me.

"Show them what girls are made of." Sarah gave me a wink as she returned to her position next to Tristan.

Tristan wrapped his arm around her waist again, and I struggled to not flinch. I told myself it didn't matter. I was free, and my head felt like it was floating off my shoulders. Wiping the ball on my shirt, I took my final toss. The ball landed perfectly in the cup, creating a winning splash. I cheered and took one of the remaining cups left on our side as a victory guzzle. I slammed the cup down on the table and jumped up and down before giving Austin a high-five.

My airy body betrayed me, and I giggled as I stumbled. Austin reached out and caught me, strategically placing his hand around my waist. I let out another uncontrollable laugh as I saw Tristan return to his place. He had reached out to grab me too but didn't make it in time. I ignored the anger flaring in his eyes. At this moment, I couldn't understand why he was mad at me. I felt good, and I was having fun. This fun had nothing to do with witch creatures or dealing with my mother's death. This fun didn't end in crazy nightmares where I had to watch her die over and over again. However, this fun gave me the overwhelming urge to pee.

"Sarah, are you up for a game? Let's make these dudes loose twice," said Angie, as she brought the discarded solo cups back to the table.

"Of course. I like making them cry." Sarah left the arms of Tristan and pointed her musical laugh at Derek.

Tristan's face continued to sour as he crossed his arms in front of his chest. Clearly, he wasn't having as much fun at this party as everyone else anymore. Austin and I stepped away from the table as Angie and Sarah took our spots, arranging the cups. Once he was content that I had my balance, he let go of my waist. I trailed off, walking down the hallway to go to the bathroom.

"Don't worry, I got it," said Austin behind my back.

"Fine." Tristan sounded like he uttered the word through gritted teeth.

For the first time in my life since I was a toddler, walking became difficult. I bounced along the walls, even though I tried to maintain a straight line to the hall bath. Austin followed close behind, and I felt his hands hovering an inch behind, always waiting to catch me if needed. When I finally reached the bathroom, he allowed me to go in alone and do my business. However, when I returned to the hallway, he stood there shaking his head at me.

"What?" Even though I still felt the buzz in my head, he offended me.

"You're just a mess." Austin leaned back against the wall.

"How am I a mess?"

"You're clearly upset about Tristan dating someone new, yet you're trying to cover it up by being a party girl."

I swallowed hard. He was right, but I didn't think it was a fair accusation.

"I'm not upset. Just surprised." I stumbled closer to him and put on my best "I don't care" face.

"It's okay. I recently ended things with someone too." Austin reached up and tucked a loose hair strand behind my ear. His hand was warm and soft, with no calluses to be felt.

"I don't enjoy being the bad guy." I frowned and looked back down the hallway. At least I couldn't see the others from here. For some reason, an open hallway felt intimate. Cozy even.

"Not to mention things are more complicated than they seem."

"Yeah, I understand complicated." Austin ran a hand through his hair, combing a tangle out.

I raised an eyebrow and motioned for him to continue. He let out a sigh.

"My girlfriend and I recently broke up too. It was a long distance thing." Austin's eyes shifted, checking for people coming down the hallway.

"Oh." I didn't have much to say. I probably should have offered a comforting line to make things better, but I didn't have the energy to invest in other people's problems.

"But you're not here to talk about that or Tristan, are you?" said Austin, turning his attention back toward me.

He was clearly not as intoxicated as I was, but he had to be going through some effect of the booze. Right?

"I honestly don't know why I'm here." My buzz started to fade since we were talking about serious stuff.

The last thing I wanted to lose was the ounce of happiness I felt. I moved back slowly, ready to turn away, when Austin grabbed my hand.

"Before we go, can I try something?"

I opened my mouth, but no words came out. He tugged my hand and pulled me closer. I tripped a bit, but caught myself by pressing up against Austin's body. He was so thin, but I felt the presence of muscles beneath the v-neck shirt. Before I stepped away, Austin's lips crashed down upon mine. They were warm and slightly dry as they gave me a questioning peck.

I should have pushed away. I had no feelings for Austin, nor could I have feelings for him, but I decided to take my fractured soul on a joy ride to see what would happen. Leaning in closer, I kissed him back, deepening the kiss. Our mouths moved in sync, and unlike every time I kissed Tristan before now, this kiss didn't make me feel empty—or really anything. But it felt nice to do something normal teenagers did without my entire body rejecting the moment. I wrapped my arms around Austin's neck as he slid a tongue across my bottom lip, requesting entry. I parted my lips to let him in.

"What the hell is going on?" said Tristan, stomping along the hall.

My head snapped back, breaking the kiss, and I let Austin go. My cheeks flushed as I wiped the smidge of salvia left on my mouth.

"I...umm..." I continued adding careful distance between Austin and I.

"Nothing," said Austin, unfazed at Tristan's arrival.

Tristan reached and grabbed my forearm too hard. I tried to snatch it back, but he held firm, dragging me toward the bedroom. He flung the door open and forced me to follow him in. Tristan let me go and turned to shut the door.

"What the hell was that?" Then, he looked at me in disbelief, shaking his head.

"It was nothing." I rubbed my arm, trying to soothe the pain away.

"He's my friend, Atalanta. What are you doing?"

"I didn't do anything. He kissed me!"

"I didn't invite you tonight for you to screw around with my friends." He rubbed his temples and took in a sharp breath.

"And I didn't come here tonight for you to mack on the

girlfriend I had no idea about and shove it in my face," I said, giving him the same look of disbelief.

Tristan stood there silently and took another deep breath. I watched his body relax slightly, but he tightened his hands into fists.

"I'm sorry—I really didn't mean to."

"Sarah seems nice," I said, cutting the apology short. "How much does she actually know?"

"Everything," said Tristan without hesitation.

"Witch creatures, my soul?" I was shocked at the fact he would reveal all of this personal information to her.

"Yeah, I told her when I invited you over tonight. Plus, I wanted us to start hanging out again. I didn't want her to think there was any competition."

"How can there be any competition when she's constantly in your lap? You haven't talked to me for more than five minutes this whole time." I started pacing around the room, trying to work out the energy bubbling up inside me. "You revealed a whole magical world to her, including my most painful secret? All so your girlfriend doesn't get jealous?"

"It wasn't like that."

"I don't care what it was like! You told her everything! Captrixes don't run around telling people who they are and what they do." My breath hitched as I tried to work through the emotions. "I trusted you."

Tristan remained silent, watching me walk small circles around his bedroom. I avoided the bed and instead remained closer to the closet where the various punk rock band posters lived. I stopped, shaking my head at him.

"I didn't tell her much that she didn't know. She already seemed to know a bit about witch creatures," said Tristan quietly.

"You didn't think that was weird, either? What is wrong with you?"

He didn't reply, making me stew more.

"I'm glad she makes you that happy," I said, filling my words with venom.

"Is that really what you're upset about?" said Tristan, rubbing his forehead with his right hand.

"No. I'm glad you can move on so quickly."

"You can't be mad at me about that. You can't even love me, remember? You're the one who broke it off and stopped talking to me."

Anger threatened to erupt in him too, causing the powder keg of the bedroom to light between both of us. I could feel the sizzle of the fuse, but decided not to hold it back.

"It was supposed to be me," I said. I yelled at him so hard my chest hurt. I immediately started crying out of guilt, jealousy, and betrayal.

"Is everything okay?" said Sarah, entering from the back room. Her eyes settled on Tristan's back as she tried to read him.

"Everything is fine. I was just leaving to get some air," I said, unable to hold back the tears that had already begun flowing. I began speed walking out of the bedroom, pushing past her.

"Atalanta, wait! You're drunk," said Tristan to my back.

I forced myself to walk a straight line to the front door, past all of Tristan's friends. Austin tried to stop me, but I dodged him too, slamming the door behind me.

CHAPTER FIVE

The cold air smacked me in the face, chilling my tears, so I wiped the moisture away with the sleeve of the duster cardigan.

I continued stalking down the outdoor stairs, expecting Tristan to come out of the apartment, but I remained alone, sniffling as I took each stair with care. By now, my entire buzz had completely worn off. I noticed a small bit of fun hanging at the back of my head, but it was nothing like the elated feeling I had after winning the game of beer pong.

I sighed as I reached the last step, looking up at the sky, wondering what I had done. I broke up with Tristan so he could be free. It was only right to expect him to move on. But I hadn't expected him to move on so quickly. Now I was here, making myself into a fool in front of the people he trusted me to meet and making out with random strangers.

Coming here was a stupid idea. I should have stayed away.

Walking further into the alley, I tried to decide what I wanted to do. I didn't know if I could legally drive home to Bridgette's, but there was no way I could face going back into that party. The embarrassment alone would probably kill me. The longer I kept walking toward the car, the more goosebumps rose on my arms under the cardigan, but I wasn't cold. The cardigan was doing its job of keeping me warm, but my goose bumps got stiffer, as if it was freezing outside rather than a mild sixty-seven degrees. There could only be one reason my body was responding this way.

I questioned my intuition, trying to understand what it was reading, and heard the faintest whisper of a witch. My body tensed, preparing for an attack, but the alley looked empty. Before I could ask my intuition another question, it screamed at me to jump.

Roots flew out of the pavement underneath me, leaving cracks everywhere. My jump allowed them to miss my ankles, but the roots fought on the asphalt as if they were searching for me. I reached under my shirt and cardigan, grabbing my dagger from the back holster as I landed on an empty patch not covered by the roots.

I turned around to discover a Radix, otherwise known as a root witch, in a brown sack dress, holding her hands out at me. I learned the proper term for her soon after the swamp battle, but never planned on having to think about it so soon. She was rare to see in the middle of the city. Radixes relied on plant life to work their magic. Concrete and buildings weren't their friend.

My intuition fell into its battle mindset, ready to let me know when she was going to attack. The roots behind me circled and came at my hand, but I slashed them in midair with my knife. As the roots kept coming, I kept slashing them away, creating a sort of battle dance rhythm, allowing me to move in her direction. I needed to get closer to stab her in the heart and hope one of the metals in the dagger would be enough to maim her.

I continued moving forward, but the closer I got the more confused I became. Singe marks covered this Radix like she had been burned before. Even her sack dress appeared torched. Her head fell toward the side at an angle, leaving her staring at me with black eyes, covered in a cataract film. I blinked a few times, trying to correct the picture my eyes gave me as I continued slashing roots. One root managed to trip me, but I skipped closer to the witch, preventing myself from falling.

When I was a few feet away, the root witch stopped trailing my ankles with roots. Instead, she turned her attention to my face, forcing taller roots to come out of the concrete and direct their sharp points toward my eyes. I listened to my intuition's commands of dodge, stab, sway, and blink until I made it to the witch. When I met her face to face, I realized she was the exact same root witch I killed during our journey to the meadow during the swamp battle. There was no mistaking that she was the exact same person, and now it donned on me why singe marks covered her. I burned her before. She was supposed to be dead.

Lost in thought, I ignored my intuition and was met with a sharp root to my cheek. The root burrowed itself, trying to pierce its way through my whole cheek, so it could worm its way down my throat. I screamed, but fought the searing pain to lift the dagger up and cut a portion of the root out of my face. A small triangle of the root remained like a thorn.

The root witch groaned in pain, not enjoying her tools being ruined. I took this small moment of distraction and pivoted my dagger to her chest cavity, and thrusted the knife in. The witch yelped like she barely felt it, but I knew I hit something because a black sludge began leaking from where the knife entered. She fell back, slamming her head onto the pavement with my dagger still stuck inside. I rushed down to straddle her and broke the obsidian crystal open from my necklace. Forcing her mouth open, I dumped the firebomb spices down her throat.

I threw the fake obsidian away from me and pulled the knife from her chest cavity with my free hand. Tossing the dagger away in the same direction, I hoped my plan would work. Otherwise, I would be defenseless. I pulled the lighter from my back pocket and struck it, laying the burning flame on the witch's tongue where I noticed a few of the spices remained. I rolled off the witch as her mouth exploded into a small fire that began burning her roots on the inside. She writhed on the ground, but still made no sounds of pain. She burned slowly, so I took this moment to catch my breath before crawling toward my dagger and the obsidian.

"Atalanta," said Tristan, screaming from the back of the alley as he trampled down the staircase.

I turned my head as I crawled to see Sarah and him running down the staircase. The witch finally caught into a strong fire, similar to a small bonfire. Since I didn't have many spices, instead of immediately becoming engulfed in flames, she was burning low and slow like a sick barbeque.

The smell of burning rot caused my stomach to churn.

Tristan and Sarah reached me, gasping for air, and he held out a hand to help me up.

"Oh my god!" Sarah covered her nose and took a glance at the burning witch. "That smell is awful."

I picked up the dagger and the obsidian, placing the obsidian back on the necklace, and returned the dagger to the pancake holster. Then, I took Tristan's hand and rose.

"Are you okay?" said Sarah, her singsong voice plagued with worry.

"Was that a root witch?" said Tristan, overlapping Sarah's question.

"Yes, and yes," I said, beginning to feel the root still stuck in my face. I reached up to touch it and flinched. "Someone's going to have to help me get this out."

Tristan's face looked alarmed as Sarah visibly gagged under her hand at the protruding root piece. The root must have looked a lot worse than I thought it did.

"Let's get you inside the shop." Tristan pulled out his cellphone. "I'm going to call Bridgette and let her know what's going on."

I followed them both back to the herb shop, praying that I wouldn't have to watch them touch each other all over while the root came out. We filed into the dusty backroom as Tristan flipped on the various lights in the shop. When we entered the main store area, the spot on my face began throbbing in pain as my adrenaline wore off. The sensation was strange. The root burrowed every time I moved my face, but it also felt like it belonged there. I didn't enjoy that feeling.

Rip it out, screamed my intuition.

"Shhh," I said aloud to the voice, as I took my seat on the metal stool at the register counter.

Sarah raised her eyebrows at me as she gathered items from around the store that Tristan rattled off at her. Even though it was dark, the herb shop glowed from the lights Tristan had turned on. Lines of teas and various spices lined the main wooden store shelves. To the average consumer, the shop looked like an upscale chef and tea drinker paradise, complete with large storefront windows and framed pictures of leaves on the walls. The average witch creature, though, knew about Tristan's secret spice stash with ingredients ready to be used in rituals or potions, even though he wasn't helping that part of the cliental since Morgana died. His secret spice stash of late had been more of a personal store for Bridgette.

Sarah continued to grab items from the shelves, but I didn't know if Tristan had told her about the informative voice that lived in my head, so to her, me talking to myself probably made me seem crazy. Great, now my ex's new girlfriend was going to think I was even more of a psycho.

"What is it?" said Tristan, knowing who I was really talking to.

"My intuition is yelling at me to get this thing out. Something isn't right with it," I said.

"Your intuition is never wrong. We need to get it out."

I had read about Radixes a lot after the attack in the swamp, but I remembered nothing about their roots becoming embedded in their victim and causing harm, like my intuition seemed to believe. Roots piercing the skin was a popular occurrence in the countryside for my ancestors, so I was sure if getting a piece of their root stuck inside you was bad, they would have reported it by now.

Sarah laid all the requested supplies on the counter, including a pair of tweezers Tristan grabbed immediately. Among the pile were various ointments, crafted by Tristan himself, and a few bandages. He pressed on the bulge of my skin where the root had forced its way in and prepared the tweezers for entry. I closed my eyes, not wanting to see a metal object come that close to my face.

The cool metal point of the tweezers entered the wound, and I flinched. Tristan pressed the tweezers in deeper, but couldn't find the root fragment at first. However, the closer he got, I felt the root burrow deeper and yelped. I lifted my tongue and slid it across my cheek, feeling a solid piece almost in my mouth.

"It's freaking moving," I said, opening my eyes. I pushed myself up off the stool in panic, not enjoying the sensation of something being alive in my face, trying to wriggle its way into my mouth.

I heard the back door of the herb shop fly open and slam against the wall. Bridgette rushed into the store, looking frazzled and tired.

"What's going on?" she stopped next to Sarah, panting from wherever she ran from.

The root in my face moved again, seeing her arrival as a threat. My gag reflex lurched inside of me, forcing me to swallow bile down my throat. This thing was trying to become a part of me and grow. My intuition sounded all of my head alarms, making it hard for me to even think. I pressed my hands into my temples, trying to relieve the pressure building from the voice.

"This thing is moving into my mouth." I looked back at Tristan. "Get it out!"

Tristan glanced at the tweezers and then at me again in confusion. I forced myself to sit back down on the stool and grabbed his arm, pulling him toward me. Bridgette moved to look over his shoulder, and I closed my eyes. I felt the tweezers enter the wound again, but this time I didn't care about the pain. The root continued to frenzy in my face, getting closer to entering my mouth. I pushed against it using my tongue as a final defense until Tristan finally caught it with the tweezers. I gasped at the searing pain of the root's exit and opened my eyes as he tossed the root piece on the glass counter next to the ointments. Sarah came to the other side of the counter and we all watched the piece of root tremble as it swelled to the size of a small stick, then shrivel into nothing but dust.

"What even was that?" Sarah rubbed her eyes in an attempt to force the image out.

I looked up at Tristan and Bridgette, seeing the same confusion on their faces, and then back to the dust. I considered reaching out to touch it, but feared that the small particles would burrow their way into my fingers. Grabbing a random ointment off the table, I handed the jar to Tristan, not taking my eyes away from the root dust.

"Wait," said Bridgette, stepping in front of Tristan. "The skin is turning black. It's..." she hesitated at the word, "...decaying."

Out of impulse, I reached up to touch the spot, but felt tanned leather rather than my usual soft skin. I pressed down, feeling no pain even though I knew I should have from an open wound like that. Especially after how badly it hurt to remove it.

"What's happening to me?" I said, looking to Bridgette for answers.

"It's going to be okay." She leaned in closer, studying the wound. "I need a knife, some gauze, and a healing salve. Something with yarrow in it"

"Are you going to cut off her skin?" asked Sarah. "I can't watch that."

Sarah murmured to Tristan about going back upstairs, and he nodded. They gave each other a small kiss, and she left out of the back of the shop to return to the apartment of friends. I breathed a small sigh of relief when she left, but quickly reminded myself that this was not a time to be calm.

"Are you really going to cut my skin off?" I asked, as Tristan handed Bridgette a paring knife he kept for chopping up herbs.

"Yes, but you won't feel a thing. There's some sort of death magic happening here," said Bridgette.

My stomach clenched at the words death magic. A piece of root from a dead witch tried to kill me. I closed my eyes as Bridgette cut off the decaying skin from my face. She was right, because I didn't feel a thing except the metal touching the nerves in my face that were still alive. After she finished cleaning up my face, Bridgette applied the salve and placed a thick, square bandage on my cheek. I reached up to touch the perimeter of the bandaid, touching the smooth texture that extended from my cheekbone to my jaw. Leaving my hand there for a moment, I wondered just how much skin Bridgette cut off, but before I looked, she and Tristan had already collected it along with the dust in a brown paper bag.

"Am I going to be okay?" I opened my eyes to catch her expression before she could hide it from me.

"The salve will regenerate the skin. Tomorrow night, we should be able to take the bandage off," said Bridgette, wiping her hands clean with a towel Tristan had brought over. "Tristan said you were attacked by a root witch?"

I readjusted myself on the stool as Tristan brought over chairs for himself and Bridgette. They both sat down, ready to listen to my account of the fight. I told them about how I felt something was off after I made it past the stairs, but didn't determine what it was until the Radix began attacking. I skimmed over the battle since they didn't need to understand the nitty gritty of how the punches were thrown, but explained how the root went into my face before I killed the witch creature.

"There was something weird, though. I swear to you that was the same root witch from the swamp. She was singed like she had been burned already."

"That can't be right. We blew that witch up," said Tristan in a skeptical tone that made my eyes roll.

"He's right. I saw it myself." Bridgette nodded in agreement.

"I know that, but that was the same witch. She even seemed dead."

"Witches don't come back to life like that," said Tristan. "I'm sure she just seemed dead because you had too much to drink."

"Too much to drink?" Bridgette raised her eyebrows at me.

"I wasn't drunk when I saw that witch. I barely even had a buzz." If looks could kill, I would have killed Tristan with the one I laid on him.

"You played a game of beer pong and were having issues

walking straight. I know that was your first time drinking. It's okay, Atalanta."

I wanted to punch him and his condescending tone right in the face. I was already having a hard enough time getting Bridgette to understand what I was trying to tell her, and he was making me look like a drunk floozy.

I rose from my stool and began pacing. "I know what I saw. Beer or not." I flashed a look at Bridgette. "Explain to me how a dead witch attacked me and there was death magic in her roots."

"Maybe you only thought you saw the same witch. You've been having a hard time recently, plus the alcohol probably didn't help," said Bridgette, taking on a caring tone that I found almost as condescending as Tristan's.

I knew what she was implying. My lack of sleep and the increased dreams of the swamp battle were clouding my judgment. I was materializing these nightmares into real life. My grief had given me a whole other level of denial. The stress of seeing Tristan with someone new was making me more erratic, along with the effects of the alcohol. For a moment, I wondered if she was right, but I knew exactly what I saw and felt in my face. Something wasn't right with that Radix.

"I understand that," I said, refusing to make eye contact with Tristan. He hadn't known I was having a hard time recently and now Bridgette had put me on blast. "But I know what I saw and what I felt. That was the same witch."

"Maybe you just need to sleep on it," said Tristan. This time he might have meant well, but it still came off as patronizing.

They really didn't believe me. I couldn't understand how they didn't trust what I had seen. They knew how strange witch creatures could be, and they didn't believe me. My heart sank.

"Guys, I know what I saw," I said, pleading with them to agree.

"Tristan's right. We should sleep on it." Bridgette rose from her stool and grabbed the paper bag containing my skin bits.

"What is there to sleep on? That was a zombie witch who put a death magic root in my face." I pointed to my face bandage for emphasis. "Last time I checked, Radixes don't do death magic. Or rise from the dead."

"The death magic was strange, and I'll see what I can do to test it further," said Bridgette. "But there's no sense in jumping to conclusions. It's late."

"I need to get back upstairs before they notice anything weird," said Tristan, single-handedly ending the discussion. "I'll let them know you caught a ride home."

I stood there, my mouth agape, staring at them both. I felt like the boy who cried wolf, yet I hadn't done anything for them not to trust me right now apart from having a bit of fun. Did they really think my mental state was that bad? Was I really so broken, I couldn't identify a zombie-like witch creature?

I considered striking the argument back up, but the look on their faces told me it wasn't worth my breath. I gave Tristan the warmest smile I could manage, so I didn't rip his face off.

"I'll talk to you later then," I said, conveniently sidestepping to Bridgette to avoid a hug.

"Later." Tristan nodded.

He clamped his hands in front of him as I walked through the shop back into the alley. My flushed face felt better when the night air hit it again, but the relief quickly drained when I saw Austin standing next to the dead witch's embers. Luckily, by now,, she had broken down into some coals that could be swept away and the smell had dissipated, but Austin still stood there, mouth agape.

"What's this?" He looked at Tristan, Bridgette, and me. "Who's she?" Austin pointed at Bridgette.

I took the lead, walking in front of them as Bridgette sauntered in the direction of her car I brought to the party earlier.

"I have no idea what that is, but she's my ride," I said, stopping in front of Austin.

"Yeah, Atalanta's leaving. Let's go back inside." Tristan trailed toward the stairs, hoping Austin would follow.

"I'll be there in a minute." Austin locked eyes with me before looking back down at the coals. "That is strange, but if you want me to ignore it, I guess I can."

"I'm not trying to force you to do anything. I just really need to go," I said.

"I'm sorry if I put you in an awkward situation back there." Austin left the coals and walked closer to me.

"It's okay. It was awkward to begin with."

"Are you okay?" He seemed genuinely concerned about my well-being, which was refreshing considering the exchange that happened in the herb shop.

"I'm fine." I cracked a weak smile. "I really should get going. I've done enough for one night."

Getting drunk, making out with a stranger, killing an undead Radix, and arguing with my ex-boyfriend was enough for me to be done doing things for a while.

"Wait." Austin pulled a cell phone out of his pocket. "Can

I get your number?"

I hesitated, wondering what the correct choice should be. "Are you sure you want it?"

"Yeah, I'm sure."

I took a deep breath and held my hand out for the phone. He handed it to me, and I added myself as a contact into his phone.

"Text at your own risk. I'm really bad at responding." I wanted to go ahead and set him up for disappointment. After my last relationship and the current events happening, I wasn't sure if I could bring another friend into my life. Especially one who didn't know what was going on.

"Will do. And like I said, I really am sorry." Austin slipped the phone back into his pocket and turned to follow Tristan back up to the apartment.

I walked toward Bridgette's car I parked on the street, eventually catching up with her as we exited the alley. I looked for another car, but saw none.

"How did you get here so fast?" I said, moving to enter the passenger side. I figured since it was Bridgette's car, she might as well drive it. Not to mention, I probably still wasn't legal to drive no matter how sober I felt.

"Uh, I kind of teleported. It's hard to explain." Bridgette walked to the opposite side and opened the driver's side door.

"You can teleport?"

"It's more of a locator spell, but I don't like to do it because it takes a lot out of me and needs a ton of ingredients. The more magic exhausted I am, the more...irritable I get."

I closed the passenger door behind me, understanding what Bridgette meant by irritable. Even though Bridgette was a Domum, a good house witch, she could transform into a Venefica if she did too much evil magic or lost control. She had almost killed me once during a transformation, so I knew if she got "irritable," it would lead to her tapping into her evil mojo she tried so hard to keep under wraps.

Bridgette cranked the car, and we began making our way back home to the cottage. When we got out of the downtown area away from blinding street lights and traffic stops, she glanced over at me.

"Did anything else happen tonight?" asked Bridgette, returning her gaze to the road.

"Tristan has a new girlfriend." I stared out the window, watching the trees pass by, and took a deep breath.

"Was that the girl in the herb shop?"

"Yeah. Her name is Sarah. She seems nice."

"What about the guy outside?"

"His name is Austin. We kinda made out for a second."

I turned to look at her as Bridgette's eyes bugged out, but she regained her composure, pressing her lips together hard.

"And how was that? I guess that's what I'm supposed to ask." Bridgette shook her head, tightening her grip on the steering wheel.

"The kiss itself was nice, sure. But I didn't feel anything. It was more of getting lost for a moment." I reached down and fidgeted with a chunk of hair, waiting for the judgment to come.

"I understand in a way. But why are you so upset about Tristan dating someone new, if you're also playing the field?"

The question stung a bit, but I understood how she was able to see it that way. It was never what I meant to do, so now I was even more embarrassed about Austin and my session in the hall. I even gave the dude my number. My head met my palms as I hid my face from her.

"It was supposed to me," I said, half mumbling the words from behind my hands.

"What?"

"It was supposed to me." I increased my volume as I lifted my face back up. "I'm supposed to be his girlfriend."

"But you broke up with him and kissed another guy."

"Yes, because every freaking time he touches me I feel emptiness and loneliness. I can't even love him, so he was wasting his time anyway. But I still want it to be me. And I'm jealous because she can freaking feel love with him while he tears me apart because I have no soul. So yeah, I got angry and wanted to see if it felt like that with everyone. I wanted to have a normal kiss without feeling my insides rip out."

The words tumbled out of my mouth before I could catch them. I immediately regretted putting them out into the world, but it felt nice to finally say how I was feeling aloud. Bridgette tapped the brakes a little too hard, taking in my comments, and I lurched forward into the dash. I caught myself as the seat belt snapped. She murmured sorry and turned into the tree line for the secret driveway of the cottage. The glittery protection veil rained down upon us as the car passed through. Bridgette kept the veil up to keep herself hidden from hunters and other witches, but the veil had magic woven into the spell that allowed people she wanted to enter.

"I didn't know that was how he made you feel. I thought you didn't feel anything," said Bridgette, parking the car.

"I didn't know how to explain it. Tristan doesn't know, either, so please don't tell him. I don't want him feeling guilty about it."

"Is that fair to him, though? Does he even know why you broke up with him?" Bridgette turned the key to turn off the car and stared at me.

"It doesn't matter now. I just want my soul back. We have to be able to figure out something." I pulled the latch of the door and exited the car before she could ask me any more thought provoking questions.

We walked the short path to the porch and went into the cottage. Bridgette was silent, and I could tell she was still absorbing my word vomit. She walked to the kitchen with the cursed paper bag, and I entered the living room to open my chest. As I put the gear back in my chest, I heard her come in. The silence was thick as I waited for her to say something.

"What is it?" I asked.

Bridgette avoided my eyes, which made me queasy.

"Bridgette?" I raised my voice to capture her attention. "What is it?"

"I read something in a book while you were gone about your soul. It was just a small paragraph, so I don't know how much merit it has."

"I still want to hear it."

"It said that you can only get a soul fragment back by killing the Venefica that took the piece."

"Wait. That doesn't make sense. Otherwise I would be—" I cut off my thought as I stood up from the chest, taking a seat on the couch. "Show me."

She walked over to her shelf where there were several

books about witch creatures that my mom had lent her over the years of their friendship. I was glad Mom had thought about diversifying the location of her collection since the rest of her books had burnt down in our house fire. Otherwise, I would barely have any reference materials to look at.

Bridgette looked through the books until she found the one she was looking for and pulled it off the shelf. She brought the medium size book over, with her finger stuck within to mark the critical page. I caught a glimpse of a green fabric cover reading, "All About Souls." If this book was all there was to know about souls, I was severely disappointed. Even though the book looked medium sized because of its cover, there could have only been 100 pages in between, making it not thick at all. Bridgette opened to the page she marked with her finger and handed it to me. As I scanned the page, she turned her recliner away from the window to face me and took a seat.

> *To repair a fractured soul, you first must identify how the soul was fractured. This will determine if you can repair it. In this case, let us say that a Veneifca ate a piece of your soul but couldn't finish the job. The piece of your soul still lives in the Venefica, providing it with substance and life force until the next soul is taken. If you manage to kill the Venefica before it attacks someone else, the piece of the soul will return to your body and realign itself with the other pieces of your soul. Therefore, your soul will be complete again.*

> *The main issue becomes apparent the longer the soul stays fractured. If fractured souls aren't repaired, side*

effects can include depression, hallucinations, and a missing element.

The book moved on to mention types of broken souls and missing elements, but I wasn't worried about that information since I already knew how mine was broken and what my missing element was. I took the time to read the entry about the Venefica again, confused by what it was telling me. After I read it the third time, I decided it didn't have any more information to provide. I was just trying to read into words that weren't really there. Closing the book softly, I sat with my thoughts for a few minutes to gather them. When I realized I didn't have much to gather, I looked up at Bridgette.

"This doesn't make any sense. The Venefica that ate my soul is dead," I said. "If this theory is correct, my soul should be whole."

"I know. That's why I didn't want to show it to you yet," said Bridgette, looking at me with regret.

"So, this is either completely wrong or missing a piece of information."

"I think so, but I don't know what it is. That's why I'm not sure if it's helpful."

There was a sadness to her voice now that I felt guilty for causing. It reminded me of how sad my mother was when I told her a piece of my soul was missing. What would she even think of me now?

"I know you don't believe me, but I swear that was the root witch from the swamp." I stood up and turned around.

"It's not that I don't believe you. I've never seen it before, and we have all been going through a rough time, which can make us see things differently. So, I think it's best to treat it as a strange root witch incident rather than assume necromancy or something crazy."

"And you think I'm suffering from fractured soul side effects?"

Bridgette said nothing, confirming my thought. She thought the zombie Radix could be a hallucination.

"I wasn't hallucinating."

"I know what you think you saw. I'm not denying that. But I think we should test the contents in the bag before jumping to strange conclusions. I'll test it in the morning to see what we can find out."

My heart sank. I could push the argument further and try to get her to believe me, but I realized it would be futile in my condition. Until she had proof validating my theory, Bridgette was going to second guess me because of my broken soul.

"Goodnight. I really hope you can get some sleep." Bridgette exited to her bedroom, shutting the door behind her.

I considered staying up late to do some research to avoid sleep, but my body was so worn out from the battle earlier that I wanted to give in. I reached up to touch the band-aid and hoped it was healing the giant wound on my face. Sleep would allow my body to work better with the magic, but I really didn't want to have a nightmare tonight. The couch bed called to me, though, knowing just how exhausted I really was. I sighed, deciding to give in, and got ready for bed.

CHAPTER SIX

A GUST OF WIND rattled the bay window in the living room, waking me up from my dreamless sleep. I groaned, wondering why my body couldn't ignore the wind since I was happily not having any nightmares. I stuffed my face further into the couch to ignore the pounding hangover headache forming and dry mouth from dehydration. My intuition nudged me to check on something.

Window. Check the window.

I begged the voice to let me go back to dreamless sleep before I started having bad dreams, but it was relentless. My intuition continued telling me to get up and check the window. I groaned again and reached up to turn on the side lamp next to the couch. My eyes tried to adjust to the light but remained in a tried squint. Throwing my quilt off my bare legs, I walked to the window behind Bridgette's chair in my usual oversized sleep t-shirt that went to my knees.

Rubbing my eyes, I forced the sleepy crumbs out and blinked fast to readjust the image. I reached the window, pushing back the sheer curtains and stared out into the darkness as I swallowed to get some moisture in my mouth. I rolled my eyes to let my intuition know that this was ridiculous, since there was nothing out there except blackness. My intuition seemed intent on me remaining there, so I stayed to appease it. It wasn't going to allow me to go back to sleep until I saw whatever it wanted.

A white figure with a flowing gown came out of the forest. It looked like it was floating, searching for a place to go. I blinked a few times, expecting the assumed floater to leave my vision, but it remained there, levitating closer toward the cottage. I pinched myself to check if I was dreaming and felt the pain. Well, that concluded I was awake. But how could I be when this figure was casually floating around the yard? Of course, I believed in witch creatures, but ghosts were an entirely different topic. There was always a logical explanation for things, even magic.

Pressing my face closer to the glass, I tried to see if I could make out the figure's shape, since it was moving closer to the cottage. When it got to the far side of the yard, I could start making out familiar features. Short, cropped blonde hair. Elegant, regal facial features. I thought I saw a neck gash as well, but it looked red and open, with no blood pouring out. I ran to the front door, unlocked it, and ran outside onto the porch.

"Mom?" I yelled toward the figure.

The figure that looked almost exactly like my dead mother paused and cocked its head as if it heard my yell. I walked further off the porch onto the steps, feeling the cold whip around my bare legs.

"Mom, is that you?"

I felt insane. There was no way that could be my mother. I saw her die. I went to her grave almost every day. She couldn't be walking around the cottage yard. The figure remained frozen, turning its head again like a dog listening to an owner say something in a high-pitched voice. I advanced more into the yard, careful to keep some distance since I was unarmed and not sure exactly what this was. However, the closer I got, the clearer her features became. I became convinced I was staring at my dead mother.

"Mom, are you okay?" I asked, feeling stupid the moment I said it. Of course she wasn't okay. She was dead.

My intuition got a queasy feeling, telling me that something didn't seem right. The figure moved closer, stopping halfway, and stared into me. Her eyes were black, her skin was pale, and her lips looked blue in the dim light. She resembled a Mortia through and through, except for the long red gash on her neck from where Morgana had slit her throat. I licked my lips, trying to think of something else to say, but no words would come to me.

The figure's mouth flew open and let out a blood-curdling scream, causing a pressure to build up in my head. I covered my ears, trying to deafen the sound, but it wouldn't stop. The air chilled even more around me, and my bare feet started to feel pinpricks from being too cold.

"Stop!" I pressed my hands down over my ears as hard as I could to shut out the sound.

The figure's mouth snapped shut and stared at me with the black eyes. In a blink, it vanished completely, allowing the air to return to normal. I removed my hands from my ears and stood there dumbfounded, not sure what I had seen or experienced. Was that a ghost? Was that actually Mom rising from the grave? I didn't know what to think.

"Atalanta are you alright?" I heard Bridgette running onto the porch.

I turned around to look at her, making my way back to the house. I wasn't sure if I was mentally alright, but I figured physically I was fine. Being fine was something I was used to saying anyway.

"I'm fine," I said, reaching her at the front door.

"I heard screaming." Bridgette motioned us both back inside the cottage.

"It was m—" I stopped myself. Bridgette didn't believe me about the root witch and already thought I was experiencing hallucinations. If I told her I just saw my mother screaming in the front yard, she would surely think I was off my rocker. "I must have been sleepwalking."

Bridgette rubbed her temples, trying to get a headache out before it took hold of her brain. She looked as haggard as me, and I realized she must have not been getting great sleep, either. I had no idea what time it was, but I felt guilty waking her up two nights in a row. She looked exhausted and didn't question my lie.

"Okay," said Bridgette through a yawn. "Let's try to stay inside for the next few hours. Please?"

I nodded, giving her a half smile and a yawn for effect. She returned to her bedroom and closed the door behind her. I sat back down on the couch, trying to process what I had just witnessed outside, but my intuition didn't have any answers.

Instead, it sent goosebumps that suddenly covered my arms, instructing me to be wary. I contemplated going back to sleep, but I felt wired from being woken up. Apparently, my brain wanted to dive into research instead.

Something strange was going on around me, and I felt like I had to lie to Bridgette so she wouldn't think I was crazy. It was an isolating feeling, not having someone believe you. She had never done this to me before, and I wondered how broken she thought I must be to believe I wasn't trustworthy. This would have never happened if I was whole with an entire soul. That had to be the problem here.

If I had a complete soul, I would be happy with Tristan, instead of always feeling empty and full of grief. I would be able to get my mind off things. I was so tired of feeling broken, but there had to be a way to fix it. My soul had to be the key to all of this. I was determined to figure out what was going on with this undead Radix and try to figure out a way to live with my fractured soul. I knew deep down that I didn't hallucinate the undead witch. Now, I needed to find the evidence to show Bridgette and Tristan to prove to them something was amiss that wasn't my soul. With a mystery like this, there was only one place to start.

I walked over to my chest and pulled out the Captrix encyclopedia of witch creatures. I wasn't sure what I was looking for, but I hoped maybe if I looked up death magic in the book, it would be a jumping off point. Sitting on the couch, I flipped to the D section. I skimmed the page looking for the word death, but I didn't find any specific entry. There were witches listed there that began with D, but it wasn't what I was looking for. What I needed was a book on death magic to learn more about the root that became embedded in my face.

I took a glance over at Bridgette's bookshelf, observing the spines of the books. Nothing said death magic, but I already knew that before I looked. Bridgette wouldn't want to read about that type of magic. It was too dark for her to absorb since it couldn't be used practically. One death magic spell, and Bridgette would be on a one-way ticket to Venefica hell. I had seen no death magic books in the small stash Mom left me in this chest, so I was at a dead end. I bit my lower lip, trying to come up with another idea.

I grabbed my phone off the coffee table and pulled it off its charger to check the time. The phone screen glowed with a crisp 4:00 am at the top of the screen. It dawned on me who would have a book on death magic, but after tonight's events, I really didn't want to ask. However, before we killed her, Tristan's mother, Morgana, was into finding out about all facets of magic she could use when she took power of all the witch creatures and wasn't confined to Domum friendly magic. I had a feeling death magic would have been on the top of her list.

I sent the message before I changed my mind. Closing the Captrix encyclopedia, I laid it on the coffee table and flicked off the side lamp. I pulled the quilt back over me, leaving my phone on my stomach. I expected it to stay silent, so I closed my eyes to give them some rest. Then, my phone vibrated and glowed with a text back from Tristan.

Umm maybe? I'm not sure. We would have to look through her stash.

It killed me a little inside seeing how he talked about his mother as her. Sure, she used to be an evil, crazy person who killed my mother and tried to kill me. But she was still a person who was his mother. As far as I knew, before her obsession with becoming the witch creature leader took over, she was a good mom. He was so disconnected with the idea of her now, where I reveled in everything I found of my mom, even with the rocky relationship we'd had. I began typing another message.

Can we do that tomorrow? If you're not busy.

Sure. I'm not busy after closing the shop if you want to come by.

Dots went across the bottom of the screen as Tristan must have typed a message and backed it out, stopping. The phone went silent. It was my turn to either continue the conversation or let it die here. I decided to try and continue since this was our first free moment without anyone around. Or anyone around I knew of. The image of Sarah lying next to him in bed asleep as he texted in the wee hours of the morning crossed my mind, but I shook it off.

Why are you awake?

You know I'm always awake now. You just haven't texted me like you used to.

My stomach lurched, the guilt rising in my throat, choking me once again. I decided to be honest.

I didn't think you would want me to after...you know.

Did I ever say that?

No. But...

I thought we were still going to be friends.

More guilt rose into my throat, and it felt like it was swelling from all the pressure. Had he really thought I didn't even want to be friends anymore? I closed my eyes, trying to figure out what to say to him. How to say it. Was it time to tell the truth about how he had made me feel? Probably so, but it wasn't something I wanted to do over text messages. I cringed harder thinking about what he saw tonight with me kissing Austin. That probably was a slap in the face to him too after I refused to engage with him for the past few weeks.

I still want to be friends. There's a lot of stuff I haven't been able to tell you.

Tell me tomorrow then?

Sure.

I shut off my phone screen and laid my phone face down on the coffee table. I knew if I kept messaging him, I would end up texting word vomit that needed to be said in person, along with a possible apology. At this moment, I thought that I may have the courage to tell him what was going on with me. To finally tell someone I wasn't as fine as I was pretending to be. That all I wanted was to actually feel fine.

I settled deeper down into my quilt to get some more rest. I figured I would be safe from the nightmares now since I had disrupted my sleep cycle enough to avoid dreaded REM sleep, which made my mental health even worse. Closing my eyes once again, I drifted off to sleep with images in my head of the floating figure, Tristan, and Austin's warm lips that made me feel fine for a moment.

CHAPTER SEVEN

Instead of running straight to the kitchen when I woke up around nine, I wanted to check the bandage on my face. I scurried to the small hall bathroom that Bridgette and I shared, along with some clothes to take a shower. Upon entering the bathroom, I went straight to the mirror to face my bandage.

The edges of the bandage lifted slightly from my tossing and turning on the couch, making it easy to slip a nail under it. I tugged at it, still feeling no pain as the adhesive loosened. I threw the bandaid in the trash can by the toilet once I finished removing it and gave myself a quick glance in the mirror. The chunk of my face that covered most of my cheek Bridgette had cut off looked strange, as if a professional skin graft had been done. It was pink, and angry looking with a clear wavy border on the edges where my normal skin began. In the center of the cheek was a three inch long gash with a quarter sized black circle around it. I took a deep breath and reached up, touching the wound. I flinched, expecting to deal with some sort of pain from the open gash, but nothing happened. Touching harder, I only sensed the pressure of my fingertips. My nerve endings were shot, and apparently, a whole chunk of my face was dead. Yet, Bridgette and Tristan didn't believe me that there was some death magic afoot.

I took a shower, avoiding getting soap in my cheek as much as possible, and got dressed in a pair of jeans and a grey t-shirt. After towel drying my hair, I ran a brush through it and left it to air dry as I made my way into the kitchen. Bridgette sat at the dining table with her hair in a low bun, surrounded by various open books. Her navy maxi dress had short sleeves, allowing me to see the light sheen that glittered across her skin in the morning light. In her shining hand, she clutched a purple mug full of coffee. It amazed me how she could always look so radiant in the little rainbows that kaleidoscoped across the kitchen.

"How's your face?" Bridgette tucked a loose wave back behind her ear and looked up from the book she was reading.

I turned my cheek to her to let her study the wound and then went to the coffeemaker to get my own cup of coffee.

"It looks gross to me, and I still can't feel anything in the whole area. Just pressure." I brought down a coffee mug and made my coffee with extra creamer. I needed the sugar and caffeine boost.

As I sat down, Bridgette peered at the wound harder and took a sip of her coffee.

"Yeah, we're going to have to put more salve on that. You'll have to wear a bandaid again today if you leave."

"I figured." I took a long sip of coffee and savored it. "What are you up to this morning?"

"Trying to do more soul research." Bridgette flipped the page in the book in front of her. "This is the fifth time I've gone through these books, but I still can't find anything."

I frowned. We needed more books to go through if we were ever going to figure this out.

"I was planning on going to see Tristan today and look through Morgana's old books for something on death magic. Maybe I'll see if I can find anything else on souls or Venefica." I took another sip of coffee, waiting to gauge her response.

"I think that will be a good idea. I've pretty much exhausted all the books I have here." She gave me a half smile of encouragement.

It surprised me she didn't comment on the death magic, but I took it as a good sign that she wasn't immediately dismissing it this time.

"Have you done anything with the bag yet?" I took a glance at the counter where the cursed paper bag from last night sat next to the sink.

"No, I was waiting for you to get up so we can look at it together."

I nodded and got up to retrieve the paper bag to bring back to Bridgette. Swallowing hard, I hoped it didn't look as disgusting as I thought it would. I didn't know what to prepare myself for whatever was on the other side of the sack. I handed Bridgette the paper bag, and she took her time rolling the top open. The bag crinkled when she looked inside, but she refused to reach her hand in.

"Can you clear some of the table?" Bridgette sat the paper sack down in her chair and rose to collect a bowl from the cabinet.

I closed all the books, making a neat stack on the far end of the table closest to Bridgette's herb stores, and took our empty mugs to the sink. She brought back a medium glass bowl and a bamboo skewer. After she placed the bowl in the middle of the table, she grabbed the bag and dumped it in. Little flakes of black and ash fell into the bowl. Bridgette reached for her skewer and used it to separate the whole pieces. She looked dumbfounded.

"Is my skin ash?" I reached up to touch my face to make sure it hadn't eroded more since I last looked at it. I felt the firm pressure of my fingers on leathery type skin causing even more panic. "Is my face going to turn to ash?"

"Of course not. Let me get some more youth salve and dress it. I'll need to craft something with cypress to help bring the skin back to life. The youth salve is just trying to keep your skin from deteriorating." Bridgette scurried to her shelves and pulled out the same salve we used last night along with another large bandaid.

She slathered the sticky balm on my face and covered the dead skin with the bandaid. I touched the bandage, taking extra care to smooth down the corners so it wouldn't come up. Even though I didn't understand her magical science of using a youth salve to keep my skin from dying, I needed to seal in whatever magic was supposed to be happening to my face.

"Have you ever seen anything like this?" I tried to keep my voice calm, but there was a small crack in it.

"No." Bridgette sat down and poked at the bowl of ash with the skewer again. "But something isn't right here."

"What do you mean?"

"I don't know a lot about death magic because I try to avoid it at all costs, but there is an energy wafting off this that isn't right."

"You can feel the spell's energy?" I raised my eyebrows at her.

"It's hard to explain. It's more like a sense that it was done wrong." Bridgette dropped the skewer next to the bowl.

"Like my intuition?"

"Something like that. This spell is falling apart which is why the skin and root turned to ash."

"Falling apart? You mean it wasn't done well?" I know the confusion showed on my face because Bridgette gave me a hefty sigh.

"I guess that's what you could say. The skin I cut off last night was completely dead, but it looked like it was regaining life." Bridgette dared a glance at the bowl. "When I opened this the skin leftover would be solid if this was true death magic. But instead, the spell dissipated instead of keeping the skin alive."

I realized where this was going. If I was to be believed about an undead witch attacking me, I needed this skin to be alive right now.

"So, either the death and resurrection magic was done poorly or the magic of the root died with the witch."

I squeezed my hands into fists, waiting for Bridgette's conclusion.

"Basically, we're no closer to being able to tell if you actually dealt with a resurrected witch. As far as I can tell, this is dead root magic. I've never had a piece of a witch embedded inside of me when they died to know how my or your body would react to it."

I stood up allowing myself to pace around the kitchen in order to choose my next words carefully.

"So, what you're saying is you believe I fought a regular Radix and felt death from the root because she was dying outside?"

"Maybe." Bridgette rubbed her temples with her hands.

"And how do you want to explain what's going on with my face?" I forced her into uncomfortable eye contact as I pointed to my bandage.

"I don't know."

"Why can't you believe I was attacked by an undead witch? I know what I saw!"

"Because necromancy is extremely rare and requires a powerful witch to do it. If a true necromancer raised a witch to attack you and that witch put something inside of you..." Bridgette pointed at the bowl of ash. "That bowl would be full of living skin."

My jaw dropped, and I froze in place, staring at Bridgette's confusion.

"You really don't believe me." It came out sadder than intended, but it hurt having one of your strongest supporters fail you.

"It's not that I don't believe you. I know what you think you saw and fought, but the evidence isn't there." She rose from the table and walked over to me to give me a hug.

I let her wrap her arms around me, but didn't reciprocate. She let go, looking as hurt as I felt.

"I think you're overly exhausted and have trauma from seeing what you saw in the swamp. It would be easy for you to imagine the Radix you fought as the same one. You're still trying to get revenge for Artemis," said Bridgette, giving me some distance.

"But I know what I saw. I know what I felt," I said, trying

to hold back the emotion encompassing me. "Why don't you believe me?"

I stormed out of the kitchen to the living room to grab the things I needed to go visit Tristan. Anything had to be better than this never-ending cycle happening with Bridgette.

"Atalanta, wait!" Bridgette followed me down the hallway.

I sniffled, dragging any tears threatening to begin back into my face. I gave her a deadpan look as I placed my cell phone in my back pocket and grabbed the same cardigan from last night to wear.

"Can I borrow the car again?" I reached in the chest to grab the mixed metal dagger and pancake holster, situating it again underneath my t-shirt.

"Sure. Let me grab the keys," said Bridgette, defeated by not having the right words to say.

She returned from her bedroom and handed the keys to my outstretched palm.

"Did you need anything from in town?" I pretended like nothing happened between us.

I was fine. I had to be fine.

"No." Bridgette shook her head. "I'll let you know if I need anything while I work on the improved salve."

I nodded and left to go to Tristan's shop.

§

I was a bit earlier than Tristan probably expected, but I took the same spot in front of the herb shop I used last night. After parking, I took a moment to eat a bagel I procured from a bakery the block before. The last thing I wanted was to be hangry when talking to Tristan about all the things he and I wanted to know.

Drying my crumb filled hands on a napkin, I took a moment to fix my hair in the rearview mirror, then exited the car. Two steps later, I opened the front door of the shop. Tristan sat at the front counter reading a book, but when the bell on the door rang, he looked up to see me. Immediately, he gave me a look of shock, but quickly changed it to one of his prize winning smiles. I sauntered past the tea section until I reached the counter.

"I'm sorry I'm a bit early." It dawned on me that I was supposed to be here late afternoon and it was about eleven.

"No, it's okay." Tristan grabbed a piece of receipt paper to use as a bookmark and closed his book.

I tried to sneak a glance at the book title, but he strategically covered it with his hands.

"How's the cheek?" he said, looking up at my fresh bandage.

"Disgusting, to be honest. Bridgette's working on crafting another salve to help finish its healing."

"Gotcha."

Awkward silence fell between us, and I yearned for when our silence was comfortable. I hated feeling like I was standing across from a stranger.

"I'm sorry about last night." Tristan slipped his book under the counter.

"Which part? The witch or the conversation before the crazy?"

"I shouldn't have told Sarah about you without asking. And I shouldn't have sprung the fact that I had a new girlfriend on you. I'd been waiting for the right time to talk to you, and you were avoiding me, and..."

"So, it's my fault you didn't tell me?"

"No." Tristan sighed. "I really am sorry. I didn't know me moving on would upset you the way it did. We should have talked about it."

I nodded. It wasn't fair for me to make him feel guilty when I was the one not telling him the truth and giving up on my soul. It was my fault for letting us pursue a relationship in the first place.

"So, about the books? I need to see if you have any on souls or Venefica too. We've run out at the cottage."

Tristan opened his mouth to reply, but the bell on the door rang out again. I turned around to watch Sarah walk into the shop like the ray of sunshine she was.

"Hey, babe. How's the shop—" Sarah stopped when she saw me standing in front of the counter. I thought I saw her face shift, but her smile reappeared before I had a chance to think about it. "Oh, hey, Atalanta! Are you feeling any better?"

"I'm fine." I turned back to Tristan, realizing why he hoped I would come in the afternoon. He was trying to avoid this exchange.

Sarah approached the counter, but instead of walking behind it like I assumed she would, she planted herself on neutral ground next to me. It seemed like a thoughtful gesture after last night's excessive PDA.

"So, what's up today?" Sarah looked at Tristan, then back to me.

"She came to go through Morgana's book storage," said Tristan, his eyes glued to me for my reaction.

I gave him a smile. "Yep, need to see if I can find some more reference material. I figured it would be a good place to start."

"Can I help?" asked Sarah.

"You don't have to do that. I'm sure I can help her out." Tristan looked at us both, not sure what side to take.

"No, silly. I'll help. You need to run the store." Sarah walked behind me, toward the back storage area. "I know where to look anyway."

Tristan and I locked eyes, telling each other of our discomfort. Sarah remained unfazed and motioned for me to follow her. I looked back at Tristan with a final plea and shrugged. I came here to talk to him, but now I sidestepped another argument, and I was going to be stuck doing research with his girlfriend. Karma really had it in for me today, so I followed Sarah to the back room.

We walked through the narrow hallway into the area where all the back stock shelves were. Sarah passed through them until we arrived at a corner stacked with various books. The book columns began on the floor and extended a little past my hip, but there were at least fifteen stacks of books here.

"Tristan stacked them down here a few weeks ago. I believe they were in her room before," said Sarah, counting the books to see how many we would have to look through.

I never saw the inside of Morgana's bedroom, so I took Sarah's comment as truth. What surprised me, though, was that Tristan never asked me to help him move the books out, but I tried to let it go.

"What exactly are we looking for?" Sarah approached the first stack, dividing it in half to make them shorter. I followed suit, splitting a stack next to me.

"A couple of things. Death magic, for sure. Possibly

something on resurrection." I hesitated, not sure what she would think about my next comment. "And souls or Venefica."

Sarah nodded as we sat down on the dusty floor together, seeking comfort over clean clothes.

"How much do you know about this stuff? Witch creatures aren't typical knowledge." I slid off my cardigan and balled it next to me.

"Uh, my mom has always been into the occult. Discovered this stuff when I was a kid and taught me ever sense." Sarah gave a nervous grin.

I made a mental note to try to see if Sarah's mom was a Domum or met a Captrix once. It was possible for regular people to have a run in and believe in witches, but knowing more than that was fishy.

"I'm not sure if we'll find anything on Venefica or souls," said Sarah, steering the conversation. "I think Tristan has most of those books by the register to read."

"Oh." I tried to hide my surprise as I took the first book off of the stack closest to me.

Sarah also took a book off the stack closest to her, and we opened our books at the same time to skim the contents. I tried to focus and tune into my intuition, but my mind kept drifting to the thoughts of Tristan researching souls and Venefica. I knew he mentioned looking into it when we first started our relationship, but it was something we never talked about when we patrolled for witches or hung out. I assumed he had given up ever putting my soul back together, which made breaking up with him even more necessary. Finding out he was looking this entire time was a punch to the gut I didn't need.

I finished skimming the contents of the book for the second time and realized it was a book on plants, so I set it to the side along with the few books Sarah had finished going through. We continued this rhythm of cracking open a book, skimming the contents, and placing it in a pile to the left if we found nothing. About twenty books in, my speed grew slower as I became more discouraged, but Sarah continued to look carefully through each book. The fact she cared enough to softened my opinion of her. She really appeared to be a genuine person. If she was the one to be with Tristan, maybe we could be friends. I never had any girlfriends before.

"So, what's the full story on you and Tristan?" I asked, deciding to build a connection.

"We had math together in high school, along with a few others you met at the party last night. We never really dated, but I always had a crush on him." Sarah placed another book in the pile and grabbed a fresh one. "A few weeks ago, we decided to all get together like we did last night, and we just had a spark, I guess."

I nodded, grabbing my own fresh book.

"Do you want to tell me about you and him?" Sarah clutched a book in her hands, refusing to look through it until I answered.

"What do you want to know?" I peered down at the book, studying the lines in the blue fabric cover.

"How you met. Maybe why you aren't together?"

I looked back up and took a deep breath.

"We met when Morgana sent him to scope out my house after her witch friends burned it down. I tried to kill him with a crossbow."

Sarah's eyes grew wide. I held in a laugh, not realizing

Tristan probably forgot to tell her the most important part of our meeting. I opened the book, checking for an interesting title and avoiding her second question.

"And why you aren't together?" Sarah pressed her question again.

"Why do you want to know that? He told me he told you about my—" I hesitated, trying to find a good way to describe my soul. "Condition."

"Yeah, he gave me his version, but I want to hear it from you."

"I broke up with him because it was too hard to be together. I can't feel the same way he feels about me, and no matter what the cosmos thinks about us being together, it can never be as long as my soul isn't complete. It wasn't fair what I was doing to him." I noticed the book title had something to do with potions, so I set it to the side for something to be looked at further.

Sarah remained quiet as she skimmed her book, tossing it into the reject section.

"Atalanta, I'm not here to compete with you or rub it in your face that he's the one who got away." Sarah brushed her fingers through her hair and sighed. "I really hate the way Tristan and I got together, but I do like him."

"I know. I can tell he likes you too." I gave her a small smile.

"Is there any way we can be friends while wishing we were with the same guy?"

I felt a pang in my stomach as the reminder of having to give Tristan away sunk its claws in deeper. It would be impossible for me to turn down her request if Tristan and I were going to be friends again, so I gave her the only response I could.

"Of course. I would like that."

"Thank you." Sarah grabbed another book off the dwindling stack.

I nodded and grabbed another book, feeling hopeless. I assumed by now we would have found something, but all I had was an awkward conversation with Sarah and a stack of currently useless books to stare at. The next book I pulled off the stack was titled *Amissa Anima Mea*. My intuition lit up liking the title, so I flipped open to the table of contents seeing topics on missing souls. I read down the page a little further to see topics on magics to do with souls. This was what I had been looking for. I held up the book for Sarah.

"It's a book about souls. Tristan must have missed it when he took all the other ones to read."

"I missed what?" Tristan entered the back room from the front of the store.

"*Amissa Anima Mea*, to be exact. I believe it means lost souls?" I said, holding the book cover for him also.

"Guess so. Any other luck?" Tristan looked over at Sarah.

"Not exactly, but I think this book might be about necromancy. It's discussing how to bring animals back to life." Sarah held the book across for me to look at.

I took it and scanned the same page she had finger marked open. She was right. The book contained a few rituals on how to bring pets to life. It wasn't full blown witches, but it would be a place to start when we didn't have much.

"Doesn't it take a special type of witch creature to do necromancy?" asked Tristan. He moved to peer over my shoulder at the same page.

"That's a good question. I think when I looked

necromancer up in the encyclopedia, the entry was blank. I'll have to look again when I get back."

The bell rang on the store door, and Tristan scurried away, back to the front, to see to the customer. Only a handful of books remained, so Sarah and I continued our routine to finish looking at them. I picked up another book and checked it out. Scanning through a few pages, I realized this book was a sort of rituals for dummies. I went to toss it into the reject pile, but my intuition buzzed with anticipation.

Keep.

I shook my head and moved to toss the book into the pile again.

KEEP!

I yanked the book and placed it back into my lap for another read.

"Everything okay?" asked Sarah, as she dumped her final book into the pile.

"Yeah. The voice in my head likes this one apparently." I looked at the book again to confirm that it was a ritual tutorial book and then put the book in my keep pile to take back to the cottage.

"The voice in your head?" Sarah gave me the "she's crazy" look, which she tried to mask soon after.

"I guess he didn't tell you about my intuition?"

She shook her head.

"It's kind of my Captrix superpower. The voice gives me warnings and helps me fight as long as I embrace it. It also helps me find useful information." I figured it was a good idea to leave out the whole "helps me send mental messages" part.

"So, like a fancy spidey sense?"

"I'm about as close to Spiderman as you can get in that aspect."

We laughed, and I stood up to stack the books back in the corner that we didn't need. Sarah followed suit, and in no time, the books were back in place like we found them minus the four I sat aside to take back to Bridgette. I picked up the books, and we walked back into the empty storefront where Tristan was finishing up with a customer buying a few artisan spices. I sat the books on the counter.

"Is it okay if I take these to read at the cottage?"

Tristan went through the stack, noting the different titles I picked up.

"Sure. I can help you go through them later if you want."

"Not tonight, though, right?" Sarah sounded like she was pleading, and I didn't understand what exactly I was interrupting.

"Oh, yeah. Maybe tomorrow then?" Tristan reached out to squeeze Sarah's hand as she took her place next to him behind the counter.

"What's going on tonight?"

"Oh! You should come," said Sarah, accepting Tristan's hand. "Tristan's taking me to Parksdale to go dancing at one of the clubs. We're going to meet up with some of my college friends."

"I don't want to intrude." The idea of going to a club in Parksdale sounded foreign since I spent most of my time reading or patrolling.

Parksdale was the first major town about an hour away from New Meadows. It wasn't anything super special but had a couple of bars and clubs people could hang out in. I personally had never been there before, but I remembered hearing about it on the news a few times since there were some petty crimes in the area.

"I'm sure she doesn't want to go." Tristan read my hesitation like a book.

"I insist. It will be fun! Remember, friends?" Sarah's smile grew larger as she referenced our pact from earlier.

"Friends. Right..." I pulled my books closer toward me, ready to pick them up and leave.

"It's settled then. We'll pick you up around nine, okay?"

"I can't wait." I plastered on the best smile I could as I picked up the books.

"See you later then." Tristan gave me a shrug mixed with an apologetic expression.

I tucked the books in my arms, gave them a small wave, and exited the shop.

CHAPTER EIGHT

"You're doing what tonight?" Bridgette looked back to me in disbelief as she washed up our dishes from a late lunch.

"Apparently, I'm going to a club in Parksdale, thanks to Sarah." I brought our remaining glasses from the table and set them next to the sink.

Bridgette giggled at my conundrum, but managed to reel it in after a few moments.

"I mean, I'm glad you're getting out. A change of scenery will be good to get your mind off things."

I ignored her comment, returning to the table to lay out the books I brought back for us to read through.

"I found a few books at the shop. One is on potions I thought you would find interesting. Then, I have a lost souls book, a rituals for dummies, and a book on death magic."

"Rituals for dummies?" Bridgette placed the last dish on the drying rack and came over to give the books a gander.

"Yeah, I don't know about that one, but my intuition insisted I bring it home."

Bridgette grabbed the ritual book first and looked through it before moving on to the others.

"*Amissa Anima Mea...* lost souls," said Bridgette, as she read the book title out loud.

She laid it down and glanced at the remaining books. Content with the selection, she sat down at the table.

"I think Tristan will want the potion book back, but I thought it might be helpful for my face." For a while I forgot about the bandage, but with my impending social activity the fact that my face was decaying weighed heavily on my mind.

"Let's take a look at it. I did work on a new balm today while you were out that we can try."

I felt around the edges of the bandaid, trying to find a loose spot. The bottom left corner had lifted itself slightly, so I took that as my in. I ripped off the bandage, feeling the tug on my skin and possibly a sting from the adhesive letting go.

"I think I felt that." I flipped the bandaid over to look at the white center. Nothing appeared there, so at least my face wasn't leaking anything.

"It looks a bit better. I'm still concerned about the black spot in the middle." Bridgette stared at the wound. "Let's try the new balm and a small bandaid over the black area. It won't be as noticeable as the large one in public.

I walked over to Bridgette's herb and salve shelf, looking for the newest tin. I saw a small silver one and unscrewed the lid.

An overwhelming woodsy smell with a hint of rosemary filled my nose as I touched my fingers to the balm. It was a bit thicker and stickier than Bridgette's normal salves, but I globbed it on my fingers anyway and smoothed it onto my face. A tingling sensation covered my face, and I thought I could feel my skin come to life to repair itself.

"Is it supposed to tingle?" I screwed the lid back on the tin and placed it back on the shelf.

"I didn't know if it would, but that's a good sign."

I retrieved one of the smaller circular bandaids she kept on her shelf and walked over to Bridgette so she could put it on the grossest area. Her nimble fingers peeled the backing of the bandage, and she placed it in the center of my cheek, taking extra time to smooth out the edges.

"Hopefully this will be the last time I have to wear a bandage on this cheek." I took a seat opposite of Bridgette, ready to look through a few of the books.

"Knowing you, I doubt it." Bridgette slid herself the book of potions and began thumbing through the pages.

I stared at the books before me, not sure which would be the right one to choose. Did I want to know more about the death magic I needed to prove or try to find hope for my soul?

My hand reached out for death magic, not wanting to disappoint myself with bad soul news. I scanned the beginning, looking for the helpful entry Sarah had found. My eyes finally spotted a few rules on death magic, so I flipped to them. My intuition liked this idea because it buzzed when my eyes saw the page.

The Three Rules of Death Magics

1. *Don't bring back anything you can't control.*

2. *Do perform in groups for a stable power source.*

3. *Don't bring back witch creatures.*

The avoiding bringing back witch creatures stumped me. The other rules seemed to make sense in the simplest of terms. Most rituals required multiple witches to be performed successfully. Often, a single witch only wielded a particular element or skill, so it was necessary for them to work together to work advanced magic. A single witch bringing people back from the dead would be difficult, even if they had that skill naturally. The control rule seemed to imply that risen creatures were servants that needed to be controlled, also known as fancy zombies. Not bringing back witch creatures, though, seemed counter intuitive. If a witch with this kind of power wanted to really tip the scales, bringing deceased witches back to life faster than Captrixes could kill them seemed like a solid plan.

"Is performing death magic a popular thing in witch circles?" I watched Bridgette peer up from the potion book to answer my question.

"I don't think so, but I also don't really have a group. Death magic requires a lot of power, though, which is what I was trying to explain earlier. One witch isn't going to be able to bring something back to life."

"Why is one of the rules not to bring witch creatures back?"

"Probably because it's too much and not something you want to mess up." Bridgette looked around the room for something to reference, then her eyes floated to the books. She reached out and grabbed the ritual book. "Imagine if the ritual took five witches to raise something this small from the dead. Now, to raise a full being, it would take at least double the power."

"So, if someone or even a small group resurrected something on their own, it would be like halfway doing a group project?"

"I mean, if that's how you want to simplify it, then sure."

"So, there isn't really a necromancer species of witch creature?"

"It's more of a title for someone who does it a lot and has a knack for it. As far as I know, a witch becomes a necromancer with a coven. She's not born that way."

My brain mulled over the idea of the possibility of an entire coven raising witches from the dead. The odds to me seemed unlikely given they had attempted to organize six months ago and failed. As far as I knew, most witches were staying underground or went back to their solo nature. Then, something in my brain clicked. I went to the passage in the death magic book and read the required items to do a death ritual. They appeared normal enough. Apple, sage, and Yew bark were common items, but the thing that made the difference was the combined powers. I reached out to the ritual for dummies book and scanned the table of contents for failed ritual information. The passage I was searching for appeared toward the front of the book.

Ritual went wrong? It's okay!

So you tried your first ritual, and it didn't quite turn out the way you thought it would. Don't worry! This happens to every witch, especially Domums. What's important to remember is you tried! But you're probably wondering, what will happen now? Good news! The ritual will continue to work, but it won't be as strong as intended and will fizzle out quickly so you can try again. Now, as the spell fizzles, crazy things may happen. Don't be surprised if things fall apart, or combust. It's all in the learning experience.

The rest of the passage went over techniques the book was going to teach you in order to help prevent failed rituals, but I didn't think that was important. My mind kept circling around the idea of what it would be like to fail death magics.

"Can I bounce another idea off you?" I closed the ritual book.

"I'm listening," said Bridgette, placing her hand in the book to mark her place.

"Remember how you were saying my face wound appeared like poorly done magic?" I waited for Bridgette to nod, then continued. "What would happen if a single witch poorly performed death magic? Say they screwed up the ritual?"

Bridgette rolled her eyes to the side as she pondered the question. It was like she was going through all the files in her brain, searching for the correct one to be the answer.

"I'm honestly not sure. I assume that whatever they raised would be messed up and not quite right. Their magic would dwindle quickly, though." Bridgette stared at me. "I'm not sure what you're thinking, but I'm telling you, a single witch doing that magic would be almost impossible."

"What witch type do you think could do it?" I had been considering this question as well, but I wanted to hear it from her.

"My best guess would be a Venefica. They are extremely

powerful fresh after a feed, but they still would not do a perfect job on their own Or a Beastia, but they raise animals, not humans. My bet would still be on a Venefica, though, because Captrixes have wiped all Beastias." Bridgette stared at the table, seeming to drift off into thought or an old memory.

This narrowed down my search. Instead of searching for any type of witch creature raising past witches from the dead, I was now looking for a feeding Venefica that I could find if she got sloppy. I was about to tell Bridgette my idea when my phone started buzzing on the table. I glanced down at it to see a text from an unknown number flash on the screen.

Hey, it's Austin from the party. How's your face?

An odd question, but at least he was thoughtful. I needed to make my decision if I wanted to cut him off or not. He seemed nice, and it would never go anywhere, but making another friend to drag on my Sarah and Tristan third wheeling seemed intriguing. I would just refuse to go out on a date and only hang out in a group setting. Most of all, no more hallway kissing.

It's fine. I'm healing.

What are you up to tonight?

Sarah invited me to go clubbing in Parksdale with Tristan and some of her friends.

Sounds fun.

We'll see I guess.

A few dots appeared on the screen but disappeared. I shrugged at the phone and put it in my back pocket, so I could feel if more messages came through without it vibrating off the table. Then, I dove back into the books, looking for any more useful information.

§

Hours passed, until I found myself wearing a spaghetti strap lilac bodycon dress that barely skimmed past my thigh that Sarah brought for me to put on for clubbing. I stood frozen in the bathroom's mirror, tossing my hair up in a sleek ponytail, feeling even more ridiculous than I had the night before. When I requested Tristan to ask Sarah if she could bring me something to wear, this was not what I expected. First, it was impractical—I was going to freeze wearing this. Second, I felt exposed, like every inch of my body was there for the world to see. It didn't help that I still had a small circle bandaid on the center of my cheek to cover up the black spot. Bridgette had reassured me the flesh colored bandage wasn't noticeable, but I remained self-conscious about it.

A knock sounded on the bathroom door, and I held in a groan.

"Does it fit okay?" said Sarah, behind the door.

I opened the door and resisted the urge to hide my body with my arms. Sarah stood on the other side with a huge grin on her face. She was wearing her own green bodycon dress, but hers had short sleeves to give her an extra fraction of warmth.

"You look hot! I was worried it would be too short since it's knee length on me." Sarah gave a small little clap of joy and went back down the hall to the living room.

"I'm going to freeze," I murmured to myself.

"Do you want me to see if I have something in the car to keep you warm?" Tristan came up on my left side from the kitchen, startling me.

I turned to look at him, and our eyes met. His sparkled

at the appearance of me in this girly fashion. He coughed and regained composure.

"I think I have a flannel out in the car. Let me check." Tristan passed by me in the tight hallway, and I inhaled the scent of pine trees and soap I loved so much.

No matter what, that smell took me to a place of comfort like nothing else did. I walked to the living room to put on my socks and huntress boots. Instead of choosing a holster this time, I stashed my dagger in my boot. It was a little tight, but I would have to manage it. There was no way I was going to Parksdale for the first time without protection.

Shortly after I got everything situated, Tristan brought in a green and black flannel that I tossed on over my bare shoulders. The final touch was my lucky penny that I tucked into my bra when no one was looking.

"It's kinda grunge, but I like it!" Sarah stood up from the couch where she had been sitting while waiting for Tristan to return.

Bridgette gave me a nod of approval while placing a hand over her face to contain her giggle. I gave her my best glare, but that only made her do a fake cough.

"We'll be back later tonight. Is it okay if Sarah and I crash here on the floor if it gets late?" Tristan dangled the car keys in his hand as he waited for Bridgette's response. "Sure. I'll be sure to set out some extra blankets and pillows. Y'all have fun, okay? And be careful." Bridgette extended her arms out into a hug, which I reciprocated. "It was so nice meeting you officially, Sarah."

Bridgette gave Sarah a hug as well, finishing up with a hug for Tristan. After we said our goodbyes, we made our way out to Tristan's prized Toyota Corolla. I immediately went to the passenger side door for my usual seat, but stopped myself short as Sarah opened the door first. I faked like I was walking to the back and slid into the backseat of Tristan's car for the very first time.

The back of the car was foreign to me, but I was determined to make the best of tonight and prove these new relationships could work. I remained silent most of the drive, staring down at my phone, waiting for a new text message from Austin to come in. None came as Sarah continuously changed the radio station to avoid the commercials and sing along to the songs she knew. Thankfully, her voice was pretty, so I didn't mind her singing at the top of her lungs to the radio. Tristan kept glancing up in the rearview mirror, checking on me, but as we got further into the city, his eyes remained glued on the road.

I looked at my phone again, still seeing no messages, so I figured I would try to get the scoop on Austin.

"Umm, what do y'all know about Austin?"

"What do you want to know?" Tristan reached across to the volume knob and turned down the radio.

"I'm just curious. He started texting me earlier."

Tristan's eyes flickered up to the rearview mirror, and I noticed the muscles in his face tense. I wasn't sure what he was angry about. Me giving my number to Austin or him texting me?

"He was dating another girl from our school, Lorelei, long distance. They broke up recently." Tristan neutralized his face as he turned into a parking garage.

"She was actually pretty nice. Everyone thought they were meant to be." Sarah searched for an open parking spot as Tristan rounded to the next level of the parking deck.

"Yeah, he was head over heels for her. He was taking the breakup hard." Tristan located his spot and parked the car.

That was all the information I needed. To Austin, I would be a quick rebound, which explained his forwardness at the party. He probably assumed I was heartbroken too and needed some company. Glad I dodged that bullet since he wasn't texting me back.

We exited the car and walked a few blocks further into the downtown area of the city where the clubs were. Parksdale reminded me of a much larger New Meadows. There were plenty of old buildings and lots of dark alleyways to get lost in. The main difference here was the sidewalks were crawling with people and the metropolis never seemed to end. Finally, we reached our destination, a club named Enigma.

I studied the dark bricks that towered upward into the neon sign of the club's name. Sinking backwards away from the crowd of people waiting in line at the door, I naturally clung closer to Tristan as we watched Sarah run off to meet a few of her friends standing outside the entrance. She was so extroverted, and I wanted to crawl back into myself and die. I felt my hands get sweaty, so I balled them into little fists. I thought about turning to run away, but I felt Tristan's warm hand unballing my left fist.

He gave my hand a soft squeeze, something we used to do to let each other know everything would be okay. I snorted in a quick breath of air as the surrounding atmosphere grew heavier. My adrenaline spiked, and instead of wanting to fight, my body prepared myself to fly away. Tristan squeezed again, this time interlocking my fingers into his. Another squeeze, and my heartbeat slowed a fraction.

"We don't have to go in there if you don't want to. I promise Sarah won't mind," whispered Tristan.

"It's something I want to try." I dropped Tristan's hand when Sarah turned around to come check on us.

"Are we ready to go in?" Sarah waved us to follow her.

I took a deep breath and flexed my hands, following her to the front door. Tristan paid our cover fees, and we all stumbled into the dark club. People covered the Enigma dance floor, jumping to an electronic dance music track. On the right of the club sat an old wooden bar lined with people holding up cash to get drinks. People herded us to the dance floor where the flashing lights blinded my vision at random times. Sarah reached out and grabbed my hand, pulling me deeper into the crowd of sweaty bodies behind her friends. I lost sight of Tristan as he faded away behind me. Sarah continued to hold my hand as she began dancing along to the music. I stood still, trying to get my bearings, but Sarah waved her free hand in front of my face. Through the random bursts of light across her face, I saw her mouth the word "dance."

I mimicked her moves for a few songs, finding my own beat in the music. Sarah's friends gathered around us, providing us a protective circle, so we could dance in peace. Eventually, one went off to grind on another man, but the remaining girls danced along with us. The heat of the bodies grew, and I felt myself sweating under the flannel as my face flushed. But I kept dancing, enjoying the catharsis the music provided. As the lights flashed, I was fine. I wasn't broken. I was a teenage girl dancing at a club.

A lie I told myself as the heat in my body grew warmer. As the light flashed again, I realized how many people were around me, touching me. Everyone was touching me, and I couldn't escape this mass of people. My heartbeat raced as I looked for an escape but didn't find one as bodies covered every inch of the floor. My throat gasped for cool air as every breath I took felt thick and heavy with no oxygen. I searched for Tristan in the crowd, but I couldn't find him. My eyes rested on a corner of the club for a moment, and in the light flash, I swore I saw a Ventus, staring at me with cold black eyes. Another light flash, and I stared harder at her, but she vanished into thin air. I gasped again, desperately searching for air in the mass of people. I needed to get out, but every time I tried to catch Sarah's eye, she continued dancing or grabbed a friend.

I pushed myself backwards, turning to face the enormous crowd. I pushed through as I began to feel dizzy from the lack of oxygen, looking for the main door until I found a piece of street light pouring into the club. My body needed that light, that fresh air of the outdoors, so I kept pushing, mixing other people's sweat with my own until I ran out the exit of the club.

Cold, fresh air smacked me in the face as I tried to control my hyperventilating. My dizziness had me spinning, making me stumble with each step I took down the sidewalk. I needed to sit down and breathe. But I swore I saw a Ventus in the club. How could I try to relax when there was a witch creature that close to people?

I stumbled, falling on the sidewalk. I caught myself with my hands, scraping them and my right knee. As I continued to gasp for air, I cried out, adjusting to the fresh pain. Footsteps ran up behind me and arms grabbed my waist, pulling me up. I thrashed, trying to escape this person too. I needed to be alone, away from all these people. The Ventus had to be found.

"Atalanta, stop! You're okay," said Tristan, holding me closer to his body.

A bouncer walked up to us as Tristan turned me to face him.

"Is everything all right, ma'am?" The bouncer looked Tristan up and down, analyzing his threat level.

"I'm fine," I said through gasped breaths. "Too many people."

"She's having a panic attack. I'm trying to calm her down." Tristan released me enough so I could stand on my own.

The bouncer peered at us harder, barely buying Tristan's story.

"He's telling the truth. I swear." I tried harder to slow down my breathing.

"I'll stand right here with her if that makes you feel better."

"You move away from this spot without her being calm, I'm calling the cops." The bouncer puffed his chest and walked back to his post at the Enigma entrance.

Tristan looked at my hands, checking for anything worse than scrapes from concrete. He grabbed them, careful to avoid touching my wounded palms.

"I need you to breathe with me, okay?" He looked me in the eye as he took a deep breath.

I mimicked him, taking in a shallower breath, but better than I had been managing. He exhaled, and I followed suit. Tristan continued this exercise for a few minutes until my breathing became controlled again. As more oxygen made its way to my lungs and brain, my dizziness subsided and the world became clearer.

"Now, can you tell me what's wrong?" Tristan took a

glance at my knee, evaluating its damage as well.

The knee stung sometimes when the night air hit it, but I assumed it wasn't too bad because I didn't feel any blood trickling down.

"I was fine and then I realized how many people were around." My breath quickened as I relived the initial anxiety. "And then I swear I saw a Ventus in the club." I teetered on the edge of hyperventilating again.

"Shhh. Slow down, and breathe." Tristan squeezed my hands. "There's no one out here surrounding you right now. We're in open air."

I slowed my breathing again, assessing the amount of space I had around my body. I squeezed Tristan's hands back, letting him know I felt better.

"And you saw a Ventus?"

"I think so. I can't be sure because of everything going on." I felt crazy like I was imagining witch creatures. Maybe Bridgette was right about my lack of sleep and possible hallucinations.

"If she is here, we can handle it as long as you're calm."

I nodded, thankful for the fact that Tristan wasn't accusing me of seeing things.

"I don't think I can go back in there." I motioned back toward the club. "I'm sorry for ruining your and Sarah's night."

"Don't worry about it. I think there's a park nearby we can hang out in. Let me text Sarah and let her know what's up." He took out his phone and began typing.

"I'm going to talk to the bouncer and let him know I'm alright, so you don't get arrested."

I walked back to the bouncer and explained the situation,

adding in that Tristan was safe and I wanted to leave with him. The bouncer still seemed skeptical, but allowed me and Tristan to walk to the open park one street up from the club.

The park was a spot of nature within all the buildings, and I liked how it had plenty of benches to sit on but also open space to run around. When Tristan and I got there, we were the only ones in the park, so we took a seat on a bench wet with dew that faced an alleyway. Tristan's flannel kept the water from sinking into my clothes, but one look at Tristan, and I knew his butt was wet. I giggled a bit at his uncomfortable face. He gave me a little arm push with his shoulder to stop.

Being away from all the people with Tristan felt like old times. Right after the swamp battle, we took to patrolling the swamp late at night, even though any signs of witches there had dissipated. I spent many nights in the cooler air, laughing with him like we were in our own world. One that had now been forgotten by him moving on. At least for me.

"Since we're alone, do you want to talk about what we were supposed to discuss in the shop?" Tristan wiped dew-covered hands onto his jeans as he focused his attention on the grass in front of us.

"I'm not sure what you really want me to tell you." I pulled down the sleeves of the flannel as far as possible, so I could fidget with the buttons that kept them closed.

"Why did you break up with me?"

The dreaded question I knew I would have to answer one day. Before now, I thought of a thousand excuses I planned to tell him rather than the truth, but the moment he asked me the question, they vanished. My mouth dried as I tried to push salvia in to re-wet it.

"It hurt to be around you." I fidgeted with the sleeve button some more. "It's hard to explain, but the closer we got, the more empty I felt. When I was meant to be falling in love, my soul was in more and more pain."

I bit my lip, trying to not remember the pain I felt before. Tristan turned to me, giving me a nonverbal request to continue.

"After my mom died, I've felt guilty and so empty, like I've been scratching to climb out of a dark hole, but I can't. Being with you was pushing me further into that hole, and I couldn't take it anymore."

"So, you let go instead of telling me what was going on." The hurt on Tristan's face was evident.

"What was I supposed to say? You didn't deserve to be with someone who couldn't love you like you should be loved."

"So, instead, you broke my heart."

I felt the tears brewing as the weight of what I'd done smashed further down on top of me.

"I didn't want you to feel guilty for hurting me when it wasn't your fault. I knew you would beat yourself up about it."

"You didn't give me the chance to choose. That's not fair, and you know it." Tristan bit the lower part of his lip, a telltale sign I recognized as a way he kept his emotions under control.

"It doesn't matter now." I gave him a forced smile as I felt tears slide down my cheek. "You're with Sarah now, and you're happy."

I lifted the sleeve of the shirt and used it to wipe away the tears.

Tristan nodded and stood up to pace a bit on the grass while I remained on the damp bench feeling even more lost.

My soul ached, dragging me down into the emptiness I tried to avoid. Inside, I felt the sensation of a pulse as my soul scrambled to reassemble. A sharp pain hit me, and I gasped when the soul forced itself tightly together without the missing piece. Tristan rushed back over to me.

"Are you okay?"

I pressed a hand to my chest as the pain subsided. My soul resettled, still discontent, but giving up for the moment. I stared at the ground before me wishing I wasn't broken. Even though I had grown in the past six months, no matter how hard I tried to be something, my broken soul reminded me that I was still the same stupid girl that got her mother killed.

"I'm fine. My soul does that sometimes when it wants to force itself back together." I looked around the perimeter of the park for something new to settle my eyes on, so I could ignore Tristan's expression.

I never wanted him to see me in that pain because of him, and here I was, showing it for all the world to see. There was no one else I could blame. I was the naive girl who went rounds with a Venefica when I shouldn't have. And I was also the ignorant girl who couldn't figure out a solution to fix the soul I messed up.

"I'm sorry, Atalanta," said Tristan in a whisper, as he sat down next to me again.

"I'm honestly fine," I lied.

He didn't call me out on my lie, even though I suspected he knew, and we sat there in silence. I peered at the alleyway and noticed a figure tossing something next to the dumpster and darted out of the alley. Then, a breeze blew by as little leaves skated on the ground at my feet. Another figure floated next to the body, admiring it in the alley. I stood up as all the hairs on my arms rose to attention.

"Do you see that?" I pointed to the floating figure in the alleyway.

"Do you think that's the Ventus you saw in the club?" Tristan stood up as well and squinted his eyes to look.

"There's only one way to find out." I leaned over to grab my dagger out of my boot, not caring who I possibly flashed my underwear to.

I hid the dagger up my sleeve as Tristan and I crossed the park to the alleyway. The closer we got to the alley, the more the figure came into focus. I paused right at the edge of the grass to get a better look as she turned around. There was no mistaking the Ventus, even though she looked so wrong. Her head hung a little to one side as a long gash of clotted blood ran the width of her neck. Her flowing cloak looked slashed from all the overkill stabs I did to her after she died months ago. Little specks of dried blood remained on her face near her once black eyes. Now, they were a dull-grayish black without the original life left inside.

We moved a few steps closer as she groaned at me in agony and floated away from the body toward us. She waved a limp hand, and I felt a gust of wind try to knock me on my butt, but I remained standing. She was no longer as strong as she was before. I closed the distance between us with my intuition's permission as I walked against the light breeze she produced. Pulling the dagger out of my shirt sleeve, I held it firm, ready to stab it into her heart.

"Kill me," whispered the Ventus. The wind carried her

words to me. "Kill me."

I hesitated as we became close enough to feel her breath. Her pale hands reached out to me, begging me to end her life. I obliged and stabbed the knife as far as I could into her heart. She fell to the ground in a mass of tangled limbs. Tristan and I stood over her, trying to blink the image away from our eyes. The death magic continued to wear off until the Ventus started turning into gray dust. I stepped over the dust and ventured to the alley with Tristan trailing behind.

When we reached the opening of the alley, I saw what the Ventus had been hovering over.

"Is that a—" Tristan stopped himself at dead body, but there was no mistaking what we were looking at.

A woman, possibly in her mid-twenties, laid face up on the pavement with a stillness only death provided. Brunette hair fell in a tangled heap around her grayish face, revealing green eyes covered in a film that dulled the once vibrant color. Her mouth looked forced open into a scream giving me flashbacks to the time a Venefica forced my own mouth open to devour my soul.

I clamped a hand over my mouth and turned away, catching my breath. Seeing dead witch creatures didn't faze me anymore, but dead humans that looked tortured in their last moments did. Tristan's phone buzzed in his pocket, and he pulled it out.

"It's Sarah. They are finishing up at Enigma."

"We have to call 911. It's a dead body," I said, pushing my shock and horror deep down within myself.

"And what about the dust mound and cloak?"

"I'll throw away the cloak. Hopefully the dust will dissipate." My eyes darted around the park, looking for a trash can.

"That's risky." Tristan typed an update back to Sarah.

"I know, but we don't have another choice. Stay here."

I ran back to where the cloak was and picked it up as I dialed 911. As I placed it in a nearby trash can at the opposite end of the park, the operator answered.

CHAPTER NINE

I STARED AT THE red and blue flashing lights reflecting across the yellow crime scene tape blocking off the alley. Shortly after I called, police swarmed the area and lined it with police tape. Investigators even put down the little number signs next to possible evidence to take photos, like in the movies.

Everyone seemed to bustle around like busy worker bees, each knowing their own role and how to complete it. I, on the other hand, was stuck sitting on a bench with Tristan and Sarah close to the alley, waiting for a detective to question us about the night's events. Sarah said goodbye to her friends right after Tristan sent her the text informing her what we found. She showed up a few minutes before the cops did. Tristan draped his arm around Sarah's shoulder to keep her warm since she didn't have a jacket to put on. I probably should have given her the flannel Tristan lent me, but I kept it wrapped around my body, so I could fidget with the buttons while I thought.

An undead Ventus asked me to kill her for the second time as she hovered over someone I was almost positive she didn't kill. Not because she couldn't have killed the mystery woman, but the Ventus didn't look strong enough. She was suffering from whatever brought her back. The person who did her ritual had done a poor job, enough that a witch creature begged me to kill her. Apart from that, the woman had been dropped off by whatever figure I saw in the alley to begin with. And the quick look I had of the body proved to me the Ventus didn't blow her around like a rag doll. Not to mention the open mouth that I witnessed over and over again when I closed my eyes.

What had killed her then? There were no obvious wounds on her, but I wouldn't be able to confirm that without seeing the body again. While I didn't want the woman to be shot, stabbed, or strangled, any of those things would have been better for me than a witch creature killing. The last thing I needed while dealing with zombie witches and lost souls was to track down a rogue witch. Instead, I needed to focus on who was bringing back witches from my past and why. But I wouldn't know for sure what my next move would be without seeing the body again.

I stood up and began walking over to the crime scene tape. Tristan called after me, but I ignored him. If I got caught staring too hard, I would figure out an excuse. But I had to have a second look, no matter what.

"You can't be that close to the tape," said a man in a dark brown suit.

A badge flashed on the corner of his belt, and I realized this was the detective I had been waiting for. I ignored his comment and stared at the body, analyzing it for any type of wound, but still seeing no obvious marks in the night.

"Please, miss, I need you to step back." The man touched my shoulder.

"I'm sorry. I've just never seen a dead body before," I lied and turned to face him. "Are you the detective?"

"Yes, I'm Detective Peterson. And you are?"

"Atalanta. I'm the one that found the body." I took another glance at the dead woman, as the medical examiner turned her over and still noticed nothing.

Detective Peterson pulled out a notebook and flipped it over to a fresh page.

"I was about to come talk to you. Can you tell me what happened?"

"There's not much to say that I didn't say to the first officer." I crossed my arms to protect myself from the cold as a breeze blew by.

"Do you mind telling me? I enjoy hearing it straight from the person." Detective Peterson clicked his pen, ready to write down any interesting responses I gave to him.

"I was in the park with my friend Tristan." I pointed at Tristan sitting on the park bench holding Sarah even closer to his body. "I was trying to calm down, so we were talking on one of the benches."

"You were trying to calm down?"

"Yeah, I had a panic attack inside Enigma, and I needed to get some air." I picked at a button tucked underneath my crossed arms.

"I see." Peterson scribbled something down on his notepad.

"We were talking on the bench, and I saw a dark figure drop something big in the alley. And then run out the end of it."

"Did you get a decent look at this person?" Peterson continued scribbling down more notes.

"Not really. We were on the opposite side of the park, and it's really dark over here." I uncrossed my arms, realizing I needed to appear calmer.

"Then, what happened?"

"We walked over to check it out. We saw the dead body, and I called 911. That's it."

Detective Peterson closed his notepad.

"Fair enough. I'll need to talk to your friend and get some contact information. Then, you can head out."

I nodded and walked back to the bench to retrieve Tristan. He let go of a shivering Sarah and began walking over to the detective. I pulled off the flannel and handed it to Sarah, allowing my bare arms to feel the chilly night air. She smiled at me as she took it and wrapped herself in it. As I walked to catch up with Tristan, I turned around to see Sarah had stopped shivering with the added warmth.

Rubbing my arms up and down to create heat with friction, I snuck past the detective and Tristan, trying to get as close to the crime scene tape as possible. The medical examiner was now zipping up the dead woman into a bag, so I tried a different strategy. Two cops stood off to the side, maintaining the perimeter, so I scooted closer to them to see if I could overhear any useful information. At first, the two male officers discussed a random sports game, but eventually, their conversation turned to the dead woman.

"Can you believe this is the third one this week?" asked the brunet officer.

"I can't believe they look like that with their mouths hanging open." The stockier blond officer kicked an invisible can with his shoe to deal with the uncomfortableness of the discussion.

"I wonder if we have a serial killer on our hands. Just weird coincidences, you know?"

Gathering all the information I needed, I walked away from the officers back to Detective Peterson and Tristan. Peterson was handing Tristan a business card and giving the obligatory "if you remember anything else, give me a call" speech. Tristan nodded at him, then turned to me.

"We're free to go home now. Let's grab Sarah and get out of here."

"Sounds like a solid idea to me."

We walked back over to Sarah to collect her to go back to the parking garage. Within a few blocks, while explaining to Sarah what exactly happened, we made it to the car. The drive back to the cottage seemed to take forever. Everyone was drained, and my brain was going crazy until we reached the protective barrier to turn into. Tristan passed through the barrier with ease, and we pulled into the yard a few minutes after midnight. We spilled out of the car and made our way into the cottage, ready to catch some sleep.

As quietly as possible, I opened the front door with Tristan and Sarah following closely. The lights were all dim except for the lamp left on for us in the living room. When we entered the room, Bridgette was nowhere to be found, so I assumed she already went to bed, grateful for some peaceful sleep without me. On the couch were extra pillows and blankets so Tristan and Sarah could make a small bed on the floor. We moved the coffee table out of the way, placing it next to Bridgette's recliner to allow Tristan and Sarah to make their bed. A few minutes later, we were all settled, staring at the ceiling, trying to scrub the expression of the dead woman out of our brains. Even though her face wouldn't fade from my mind, I eventually fell asleep.

§

I stood in the clearing a few feet away from the sacrificial wooden table. I had no chance to chase after the knife this time, as it already laid bloody in my hand. My mother's neck wound caused by the knife sprayed my black leather huntress outfit with blood. She had fallen back on the table, arms limp, with her eyes wide, staring at the night sky.

I dropped the knife onto the table and wiped my hands down the front of my corset, trying to make the blood disappear, but only got my hands covered in the red, sticky substance. Panicking, I tried to wipe the blood on the wooden table, hoping the coarse wood would scratch it off. Nothing came off onto the wood as the table remained pristine, except for the blood that had already gotten on it from the wound spray. I looked at the palms of my hands coated in the red blood as if I had dunked them into a stamp pad full of red ink. A permanent stain of what I had done. Reaching down, I touched my mother's arm, staining her skin with a red handprint. I shuddered.

No, no, no, I thought. I was ruining what was left of her perfect skin, but I expected it to be warm to the touch like there would somehow be some life left in there. She was ice cold, an impossibility given the fact she just died. I began to sob in the quiet clearing, snatching my hands away so I would stop leaving marks all over her. My body felt like it wanted to collapse into a tiny ball and die out there with her. The knife laid on the table, and the blood already was on my hands. What would it matter if I took another life?

Mom's eyes snapped open, black as the night sky. She leaned up on the table, touching the wound on her throat like she was checking to see how bad it was. The air became icy, and every time I breathed, I could see the clouds of my breath. Mom blinked rapidly, adjusting to the unfamiliar sights and sounds of the world. She removed the hand from her throat and did a flex of her hand to the sky, causing little snowflakes to rain down and catch onto our eyelashes. Then, she looked at me and screamed her piercing, sound-defying scream.

I hit the floor as I fell off the couch, landing with a soft thud, and woke up from the nightmare. I crawled, untangling my limbs as I went to the door, hoping no one heard me fall. My breath was heavy and shallow, so I needed to get some air in order to return to a controlled breathing state for my poor lungs. When I reached the opening of the hallway, I found the strength to stand before opening the front door and escaping out to the front porch.

The cold air hit me, giving me fresh air for my lungs to enjoy, so I sat down on the dirty porch steps to calm down. Using my hands, I rubbed at my eyes, trying to force out any crust from my disturbed sleep, when I heard the front door creek open behind me. I turned around to see Tristan exiting the cottage while holding my blanket from the couch. He sat down on the steps beside me and tossed the blanket over the both of us.

"Did you have a bad dream again?" asked Tristan, as he rubbed his own sleep crust out of his eyes.

"Yeah." I pulled the blanket closer to my chest, but not before I checked my palms for the blood I saw in my nightmare.

"Do you want to talk about it?"

"I don't know. It was the usual setup, except this time, I had blood all over my hands and Mom woke up as undead Mortia after she died." I paused, remembering my dropping the knife in my dream. "I think I killed her this time."

"Dang." Tristan shook his head. "Your subconscious really knows how to create some messed up stuff."

"Why did you wake up?"

"I heard you fall off the couch, so I came to check on you."

"What about Sarah?"

"She's still asleep. She sleeps a lot better than I do."

My mind drifted to the realization that Sarah and Tristan must have been falling asleep a lot together for him to know her sleep patterns. I rubbed at my eyes some more, trying to push the thought out of my head.

"I didn't mean to wake you up. I'm sorry." I pulled my knees up to my chest and laid my head on the makeshift pillow.

My mind was still heavy with the fog of sleep, and I wanted to go back so bad, but I hated the place my brain trapped me in.

"I can tell you're tired." Tristan placed a comforting hand on my back and rubbed it.

"I am tired," I said, muffling my voice with my knees. "But this is my punishment for what I did."

"What do you mean?"

"I got her killed. Her blood is on my hands because I couldn't save her, so my punishment is to be tortured by my mistakes when I try to sleep." I considered crying, but I was so exhausted my body couldn't produce the effort to make tears.

"That's not fair to yourself. You did everything you could."

"Did I? Why didn't I get her out of the shack faster or stay with her instead of walking away?" I clutched my knees harder. "Or why was I too lazy to burn my clothes after going to that stupid warehouse?"

"We can play the what if game all night, but it won't change what we are left with here. You did your best. You have to stop blaming yourself for her death, or you will never get any sleep." Tristan reached his arms around me and pulled me off my knees.

"It's not as easy for me as it is for you." I forced myself to look up at the sky rather than stealing a glance at the wood line where my mom was buried.

"You think this is easy for me?" Tristan flinched. "I have dreams about killing my mother. And I feel guilty for helping her screw up your life every day."

He slipped and used mother instead of saying Morgana. Now, I felt even more guilty for not considering what he went through.

"I didn't know," I whispered.

"You never asked, and I didn't expect you to." Tristan resumed rubbing my back, and I laid my head on his shoulder. "If anyone is to blame for what happened in the swamp, it's me. Not you."

"I forgave you a long time ago. I don't blame you for anything."

"If you can forgive me, then you have to forgive yourself."

"I don't know if I can. I didn't protect her, and I don't know if I can protect anyone."

He exhaled a puff of air as he tried to think of more words to say.

"I'm sorry for messing your life up too and for taking Morgana away," I said.

"You can't blame yourself for the choices she made, either." Tristan stopped rubbing my back and held me in a hug.

I closed my eyes while I tried to think of something else to say, but felt my body slowly float away back into sleep in Tristan's arms. Sometime later, I thought I felt Tristan carry me back inside and lay me on the couch, but I wrapped myself in the blanket and buried my face in the leather sofa, not giving it a second thought.

§

My phone buzzed on the coffee table where I left it the night before, forcing me to open my eyes to bright light. I rolled over, trying to grab it before the phone woke anyone else, and found myself staring at Austin's name flashing on the screen.

It was a phone call from him, unexpected since our text messages fell dry before. I assumed I might get another text, but a phone call seemed insane. My finger hovered over the screen, needing to swipe in order to answer the call. I launched myself off the couch and tiptoed out the front door, avoiding Tristan and Sarah's sleeping bodies. The phone buzzed in my hand until I had the courage to answer before the call went to voicemail.

"Hello?" I tried to sound perky, but my voice only came out surprised.

"Hey. How are you?" Austin sounded unfazed by my surprise.

I took a moment to think about how I really was and wondered if I should be honest.

"I'm okay. It was a long night."

"Seems like you have a lot of those, huh?" Austin let out a small laugh. "I get it."

"How was your day?" I asked, realizing I needed to be cordial.

"Fine, considering it's only nine o'clock. Apparently, not as bad as your night."

I cringed. Of course it was still early in the morning. I was honestly terrible at talking to anyone but Tristan and Bridgette.

"It wasn't terrible, I've just had better."

"Well, I don't know if this will cheer you up." Austin paused to clear his throat. "But do you want to have coffee with me today?"

"Like on a date?" I couldn't believe the words tumbling out of my mouth.

"I mean, if you want it to be. Or we could be two friends catching up over coffee."

I had to give it to him. He was smooth.

"I think friends catching up over coffee would be okay," I said. It would be nice to have a normal conversation with someone that didn't revolve around witch creatures or dead bodies.

"Amazing." I thought I could hear Austin smiling from behind the phone.

"Um, possibly weird question, but do you think you could pick me up?" I didn't want to have to borrow the car again in case Bridgette had errands she needed to run today.

"Yeah, no problem. Just text me the address. You want me to pick you up around two?

"That works great. Thanks."

"I want to chat more, but I have to make another call. Will you text me?" I felt like I sounded like a combination of a middle schooler and a businesswoman.

"Sure. Sorry I didn't text you back before. I got a little busy, but I will, okay?"

We said our goodbyes, and I thought about slumping to the ground before going back inside. I didn't know what I had gotten myself into, but something felt freeing about hanging out with someone that didn't know me.

Austin didn't know who I was or that I got my mother killed. He didn't know I was missing a piece of my soul. To him, I was just a girl he met at a party and kissed. However, using Austin as a distraction wasn't going to solve all the witch creature mysteries I was dealing with, so I headed inside to see if anyone else was awake.

After I got back inside, the rest of the crew had stirred, so we all gathered around the table holding coffee cups filled with energy, except Sarah, who opted to drink water instead. She had mentioned something about needing to hydrate before drinking other things, but I ignored that idea on the account of my restless night.

"So, let me get this straight, you are convinced that you saw the Ventus you and Tristan killed in the swamp in Parksdale last night?" Bridgette took a sip of her coffee.

"I'm dead serious. She asked me to kill her. Same wounds, but she wasn't strong enough to do anything." I took my own sip of coffee and rubbed my eyes for the fifth time since I sat down at the table.

"She's right. I saw it too, and we were completely sober in the park," said Tristan with his hands tight around one of Bridgette's largest mugs. He was as desperate for the caffeine as I was.

"Okay then." Bridgette's eyes went wide as she adjusted to

the new information. "So, what's the running theory?"

I took a long sip of coffee, trying to prepare myself to explain my theory to her. It sounded correct when I researched it before going to the club, and even more after what I saw last night, but I was still afraid it would sound stupid if I said it out loud.

"I think we have a necromancer who is very poor at her job. She's bringing the witches back, but she either isn't doing the rituals right or she doesn't have enough power to sustain them for an extended time." I reached up to touch my cheek, remembering the magic done to it.

When I checked it this morning on the way to the kitchen after talking with Austin, there was only a small black speck left with the rest of the healed skin, so I didn't have to wear a bandage with it. Based on my theory about the necromancer's abilities with death magic, my face would be completely dead if they were any good at their spells.

"You make a compelling case, even if it seems almost impossible," said Bridgette.

"Then, how does the dead alley woman play into that," asked Sarah from behind her water glass.

"I'm not sure. We saw her body get dumped, and she looked like she was possibly killed by a Venefica. But I can't be sure." I took one last swallow, finishing my cup of coffee.

My mind pondering, I remembered Mom's notes about Veneficas devouring only the heart when they removed a soul. She was tracking the witch creature, and I was sure she didn't deal with the bodies first hand. That wasn't the kind of thing most investigations released to the public, so that meant she had to have someone on the inside she got information from to determine witch killings.

"Bridgette, how did Mom get her information about killings? The only way to determine if a Venefica kills someone is to know what organs are removed, so how did she know?"

"You know now that you mention it, I think Artemis had a medical examiner she worked with. They would let her in on the notes from the exam, and from there, she could determine if a witch creature was present." Bridgette rose from the table and walked over to a drawer closet to the fridge.

In this drawer, Bridgette kept random pieces of junk, phone books, and bits of paper, among other things. She shuffled to the bottom of the drawer and grabbed a piece of paper that had been ripped from a notepad. Bridgette stared at the piece of paper, using her fingers to trace the handwriting I made out from the sunlight hitting the paper. Then, she looked up and blushed, realizing all of us were staring at her.

"The doctor's name was Rose." She handed me the paper. "I think she's assigned to mainly work in New Meadows, but she might be able to get some information from Parksdale. I'm not sure."

I looked at the paper, realizing Bridgette was studying my mother's handwriting. The note was nothing special. It said, *Be right back. I'm going to see Rose.* Something about it, though, made her have fond memories. I thought about pushing to see what exactly Bridgette was remembering, but she sat back down and seemed to clam up back into herself.

"Looks like I'm going to go see a coroner. How fun." I flipped the note over to check the back, but it was blank.

I handed it back to Bridgette, and she took another glance

at it before placing it in her lap for safekeeping. She looked so sad, and I heard her fidgeting with the paper under the table.

"Oh, I've got to go. I forgot I have class in two hours." Sarah stood up and pushed her chair into the table.

"I've got to take her back to my place to grab her car. Do you want me to go with you to the medical examiner?" Tristan stood up and pushed his char in too.

Sarah reached around him to collect his coffee cup and took their glasses to the sink. I considered if I wanted Tristan to go, but I thought this may be a nice adventure for Bridgette and me. Then, I remembered I had agreed to a coffee with Austin.

"No, you've got to run the shop today. Me and Bridgette can go later." I turned to Bridgette. "Right?"

"Of course." Bridgette still appeared lost in a far-off haze as if her mind poured through memories.

"But I'll shoot you a text and let you know what I come up with."

"Alright. I'll talk to you soon." Tristan followed Sarah out the kitchen to the car.

Bridgette's hands clutched her coffee cup, almost turning her knuckles white while the scrap of paper remained in her lap. I reached out and touched her hand.

"Are you okay?"

"I just miss her a lot sometimes." Bridgette gave me a smile, and I noticed the tears pooling in her eyes. "I kept all these notes she left as a joke because I used to say she could never sit still."

My mind wandered, remembering all the times Mom disappeared during the day while I was doing schoolwork, especially when my grandparents were there to watch me.

"Did she spend a lot of time here? Like during the day?" I keep my hand firm on Bridgette's.

"She did. Sometimes she would work her cases on this table like you, then she would find a lead while I was out collecting plants. I would come in to these scraps of paper, letting me know where she went." Bridgette loosened her grip on the cup, and her face covered itself in guilt.

She felt guilty for taking her away from me, and I understood. All those times I was left alone, Mom was either out fighting witch creatures, researching, or here with Bridgette. It was a hard pill to swallow, but it was hard to be angry with her about it.

"I'm glad you have some nice memories to think about. I miss her too." I pulled her hand off the mug and gave it a small squeeze.

"You remind me of her a lot." Bridgette's tears streamed down her face, and she sniffled. "I'm glad you're still here to remind me of her."

I held her hand until she dropped it to stand. She took the slip of paper as she continued to cry and placed it back into her junk drawer. Then, she dried her face on one of her long dress sleeves.

"We can go check out Rose in a little bit. I just need a few minutes to collect myself." Bridgette sniffled again, threatening herself with another crying session.

"Actually, about that...I have plans with Austin later."

"Oh?" Bridgette paused in the middle of the kitchen.

"Yeah, he asked me to go get a coffee this afternoon. Can we go see Rose tomorrow?"

"Sure."

I pushed my mug to the other end of the table where Sarah sat before as Bridgette exited the room.

Then, I pulled the books we had left on the table from the day before close to me along with a notepad and pen to take notes. On the piece of paper, I began listing the different witches we killed at the swamp in the order they died in: Ignis, Radix, Ventus, various Mortias, Morgana. I scratched a line through the ones I already saw—the Radix and the Ventus. If the necromancer was raising witches I already fought, I was slowly getting left with the worst ones. If I went out anymore, I needed to be sure to take my crossbow and some blessed water bolts to deal with the rest of the things on that list.

I stared at the name Morgana, knowing if she came back, she would be a Venefica.

I really hoped the necromancer would leave her alone if this was a way to get back at me or using the available pile of witch creatures we left. I didn't know if they could raise her since we turned her to dust, but I didn't want Tristan to have to witness his mother die twice. That would be too much for even me to bear.

I scribbled more things we identified on the pad like the shotty rituals, half alive witches, and the body dumping. Even though I couldn't connect the body dumping to the death magic, I still felt like I was missing something here. I chewed on the pen cap, lost in thought, before writing down "motive" in giant letters and adding tons of question marks around it. I had to figure out what was missing, but it would have to wait until after coffee.

CHAPTER TEN

After lunch, the pre-coffee jitters sank in as I put on a pair of jeans and a white t-shirt. It was one of the few things I had that was mine, and I didn't want to borrow clothes from anyone for a little while. I also didn't want to give Austin the cottage's true address, in order to keep the secret protection veil safe, so I told him to pick me up at the beginning of BeeBrush Drive, where it met the paved county road. While waiting, I typed out a quick text to Tristan to let him know I would go to the medical examiner tomorrow.

A Chevy Camaro drove down the road and stopped when the passenger door was equal to my body. The window rolled down, and I saw Austin sitting in the driver's seat with one hand on the steering wheel and a grin plastered on his face. He unlocked the car doors, and I jumped in after taking a quick glance in the backseat to make sure it was empty. Austin rolled the window back up and pulled off the shoulder of the road, turning the car back in the direction of New Meadows.

"You really didn't have to walk. I would have driven down the dirt road to pick you up," said Austin.

"I didn't want you to get your car dirty."

The interior of the car was immaculate, like it had been freshly detailed. The only dirt visible was the few specks of sand my shoes brought in from the dirt road. The dash was dustless, and the leather seats looked and felt recently conditioned. To complete the car's clean appearance, two black Christmas tree shaped air fresheners hung off the rearview mirror, covering the vehicle in the scent of male cologne as if it belonged in a car. The smell almost made my nose water from the intensity, so I cracked my air vents open more with the hope of fresh air spilling in.

"Do you always keep your car this clean? I'm impressed." I fiddled with the air vent some more until the breeze blew in my face.

"I mean, I try to keep it like this, but to be honest, I got it detailed before I came to pick you up."

"You really didn't have to do that." I was worried he was getting the wrong impression about what this coffee meeting really was. "Especially for a friend getting coffee."

"Don't worry about it. I try to get it done every few months. Plus, I can't have my new friend thinking I drive around in a messy car." Austin cracked a smile as he continued to drive into town.

He parked the car in the parking lot of Peaches & Steam, New Meadows's only coffee shop. It had been open for a few years now and was owned by a local who took an old restaurant and converted it to only coffee. A genius idea because the shop seemed to always be bustling with people in need of a caffeine fix. Austin held the door of the coffee shop open for me, and the smell of roasted coffee beans expelled the car air freshener scent out of my nose, which I was grateful for. We strolled up to the counter, ready to order our drinks and pastries.

I ordered a vanilla latte, and Austin ordered a mocha coffee and two croissants. I offered to pay for my own with some money I borrowed from Bridgette, but he insisted on getting it for me. We found a small table in the back of the shop and sat down with our coffee. I smiled at my latte because the barista had taken the extra time to do a heart on top. It was small, but it made me feel special since I didn't make coffee like this in the cottage. Austin passed me one croissant, and I took a bite, letting the flaky pastry melt in my mouth, followed by a small sip of my latte.

"Is it good?" Austin took a sip of his coffee, then grabbed the sugar on the table and added some to his drink.

"It's delicious. Thanks for buying." I gave him the biggest smile I could manage without coming off as weird. "So, tell me about yourself."

"Well, I'm taking some general ed classes at the college near Parksdale. Not really sure what exactly I want to do yet. Other than that, I party with my friends and sometimes watch tv." He took another sip of his coffee, this time liking the sweetness of the added sugar. "Kinda boring, I know."

"No, not at all. It seems normal. That can be good sometimes."

"What about you?"

That was a bit more complicated, and I hadn't thought out an answer before I got here, much to my dismay. I was determined to keep my happenings in the witch world from Austin, since he didn't know anything about it.

"Complicated, I guess. My mom passed away a few months ago, so I've been crashing on her friend's couch, not really sure what I want to do next. I've been working in the family business for the time being." I took a sip of my latte.

"Family business?"

"Uh, yeah." I put my brain in overdrive, trying to come up with a lie. "We research animal patterns for science. So, I hang around outside a lot."

Stupid, stupid, stupid. That lie sounded ridiculous.

Austin raised his eyebrows, not completely buying my lie.

"That seems interesting. A lot better than taking boring college classes."

"It has its moments, but most of the time, it sucks." I took another bite out of the croissant, thinking of a way to change the subject. "So, do we want to talk about the deep stuff or more small talk?"

"Deep stuff?"

"You know, how we failed our relationships, our lives are a mess, etcetera."

Austin laughed at my joke, and I breathed a little easier, hoping we could talk about something other than my strange profession.

"I don't know if I have much to tell in that department. I was with my girlfriend Lorelei for a couple of years in high school. I really loved her, but she decided to go to college far away, and we struggled to make the distance work. She cut it off before it got too hard." Austin's face fell, and I felt bad for making him tell me about his ex.

"I'm sorry. I shouldn't have pressed. I can tell you're still getting over it."

"What about your failed relationship? I know you've been third wheeling with Sarah and Tristan lately."

I cringed and took a final bite out of my croissant to stall. How could I explain the reason why Tristan and I weren't together?

"It's really complicated. I'm trying to be a good friend, and I like Sarah."

"Right. But that still doesn't answer my question." Austin tapped his fingers on his mug, waiting for a better response.

"I already told you before. I didn't love him like he loved me, and I broke it off."

"I don't buy that. Otherwise, y'all wouldn't be as close. You're still in the same relationship, but without the romance tag on it."

My mouth fell open. Austin cocked his head to the side, admiring the expression. He knew he struck a nerve.

"I didn't realize this was an interrogation about my relationship with Tristan." I drank the final sip of my coffee and sat the cup down with a clang.

"It's not an interrogation. More of an observation to see if you would actually go out to dinner with me on a real date. I needed to know how much you still cared about him."

I covered my mouth with my hand, trying to make it look like I was stifling a yawn, so I wouldn't give him the satisfaction of seeing my surprise a second time.

"But what about Lorelei? You obviously still love her," I said, muffled behind my hand.

"If I'm being honest, I do, but I'm trying to put myself out

back, assuming my dagger was going to be there, but then I remembered I hadn't packed any weapons. I figured since I was going out with Austin during the day, there would be no need.

The hairs on my body came to attention, solidifying my suspicion that there was something in the woods. I could wait to enter veil and try to run the creature out and see what was there, or step through the veil and disappear. Another slight movement, and the blob moved deeper back into the woods, stepping on another fallen tree branch. The blob was an animal trying to cross the road, but too afraid to, I told myself, but it didn't bring me any comfort. My courage waned, and I jumped through the protection veil, letting the glitter shower upon me, hiding me from whatever was watching me in the woods.

I turned back around, this time seeing nothing as if whatever was out there vanished. My intuition calmed, returning to a neutral state, so I speed walked up to the cottage and rushed inside. Bridgette sat in the living room, cross stitching in her recliner.

"Hey. How was your coffee time?" Bridgette smiled, taking a moment to tuck her needle into the fabric.

"Fine. Do you have a way of knowing if something gets past the protection veil?" I tried to say it calmly, but it came out a bit more nervous than I meant.

"Is something wrong?" Worry covered Bridgette's face, and I knew I was busted.

"I thought I saw something in the woods before I came through the veil. You would know if something tried to pass through, right?"

"Yes. I can feel the energy passing through my spellwork.

Kinda like how you feel stuff. Are you okay?"

"I'm fine. It was probably an animal." I took a deep breath, trying to show I was fine.

"Do you want me to make us some tea or something?" Bridgette took her cross stitch and set it in her basket, preparing to get up.

"No, no. I'm fine. I think I'm just going to read." I threw my jacket on the couch and went to the kitchen, trying to shake the shape in the woods off my mind.

Bridgette followed me, refusing to leave me to my own thoughts. As I sat down at the table, she filled the tea kettle and put it on the stove.

"What type of tea do you want?" She opened the cabinet where she kept the coffee grounds to look through her tea collection.

I pondered the decision, wondering what the right choice was to make. If I wanted to be up all night, I needed to drink something with caffeine to pair with the latte from the coffee shop. If I wanted something to put me to sleep, I needed to drink something with chamomile.

"Chamomile is fine." It had been a rough few days, so I thought it would be better to try and get some sleep later. Most of the time, chamomile knocked me out, so I wouldn't have any dreams.

Bridgette pulled down the appropriate box containing the tea bags for a chamomile tea that had a bit of fruit flavors to it. I knew it was one of her personal favorites, especially when she was stressed. She waited by the stove for the kettle to boil, while I reached across the table to grab *Amissa Anima Mea*, but something still bothered me about the veil.

"Bridgette, if you can feel things moving through the veil, why didn't you know Morgana came through?" I never asked the question before, but I wanted to be sure we wouldn't be attacked on our home turf again.

Bridgette stopped, setting the box of tea on the counter.

"Morgana didn't read as a threat. She found a small opening in the veil on the backside of the house and expanded it using Domum magic. I sensed the tear, but that is something that happens with the veil. It needs constant maintenance." She opened the box and extracted some tea bags. "I assumed it was something I could fix in the morning and didn't think we were under attack."

"So, you don't sense any tears in it right now?"

"No. And if I do, I repair them immediately now. Are you sure that you're okay?"

"I'm fine. I just wanted to be sure."

"I'll check it in the morning before we leave for town." Bridgette placed a hand on my shoulder. "Will that make you feel better?"

"Yeah. Sorry. Guess the woods has me a little more shaken up than I thought."

"It will be alright." Bridgette left to go grab the whistling kettle from the stove.

I pushed the black figure in the woods from my mind, determined to have a relaxing evening.

CHAPTER ELEVEN

Around five pm the next day, Bridgette and I arrived outside the medical examiner's office for Thackston County that served New Meadows. The outside of the building appeared normal. It was a red brick building with large windows at the front and seemed like a place you would go to check out a book or settle a tax bill, not a place to peer at dead bodies. Bridgette parked on the street and remained in the car. On the way over, we decided it was better for me to go in alone since Bridgette had never met Rose. I could easily explain away my arrival, but Bridgette and I might be more difficult to explain since I didn't know how much of her life my mother revealed.

I shut the car door behind me and strolled up to the front of the building. A plaque next to the door announced that this was the medical examiner's office, but when I checked for business hours, there were none. I assumed this meant it was always opened for business, so I pushed on the door and went inside.

Immediately, I was met with the smell of bleach and other harsh cleaning chemicals in an open lobby with no chairs. A small sliding glass window sat at the front with a purple twist up air freshener at one end of the tiny counter under the window. The air freshener produced a lavender scent the closer I got to it, but it still did nothing for the chemical odor of the place.

A thin man, possibly in his mid-twenties, stood behind the window, gathering his things to leave for the day. He was looking down at something under the desk, so I gave the glass a light tap to get his attention. His head snapped to look at me with an annoyed glare. He reached his hand out and slid open the glass.

"We're closing to the public right now. You'll have to come back in the morning."

Turns out, they had business hours after all. I decided to try my luck anyway.

"I'm looking for Rose. Is she here?" I put on my sweetest smile, hoping to appear innocent.

"Who's asking?"

I wondered if I should give my name, but I knew she wouldn't know me even if I gave it. If I gave Mom's name, she should recognize that, but did this guy know my mom? Would he recognize me as an impostor? There was only one way to find out.

"Artemis Capp. I need to speak with her."

"One moment." The man closed the window and dialed some numbers.

I caught hushed whispers over the phone that I couldn't make out, and then the click of the receiver when the man put it back. He gathered the rest of his things and came out a side door that led into the small office behind the window.

"She'll be out in a minute. Have a good night." He exited the front door and onto the street he went.

I took it as a good sign that he didn't throw me out of the building and assumed my plan had worked. The waiting felt like forever since there wasn't anything on the walls to look at or even anything on the counter to mess with. This room was clearly not meant for waiting very long. After a few minutes, I heard the shuffling of shoes coming down the hall, and the door on the left side of the lobby opened.

Out came a woman with brunette hair tied in a ponytail at the back of her head. She wore a white lab coat over light blue scrubs. Black glasses perched on her nose, giving definition to her makeupless face. Her round face was jarring with a strange beauty angular faces had, reminding me of Angelina Jolie. She also had an intensity behind her green eyes of someone that had seen too much early in life.

Rose closed the file she was reading and tucked it under her arm as the door slammed behind her. She looked me up and down, then crossed her arms in front of her.

"You're not Artemis." She rolled her eyes. "Swear I can't get any good help these days," mumbled Rose. "Did he not even ask to see a form of identification?"

"I'm sorry to bother you," I said, trying to remember the speech I rehearsed in my head during the drive over.

"I'm sorry too. It's after hours, and I'm not showing any bodies right now." Rose came closer to me, trying to usher me out the door. "You can come back during business hours and show a proper ID to whatever new office person I have."

I stepped around her, avoiding being pushed out the door and made my way toward the door she came out of.

"Please let me explain."

"There's nothing to explain. You aren't Artemis Capp. Now leave before I call the police. I don't have time to deal with this today." Rose grew more irritated and pointed at the front door.

"You're right. I'm not Artemis, but I am her daughter, Atalanta Capp. And I need to ask you some questions."

"Artemis is the only person who is allowed to come talk to me."

My mind stumbled on the word *allowed*. I didn't know anyone "allowed" my mother to do anything. She tended to forge her own path like it or not. How much did Rose really know?

"Artemis is dead. I've been taking over for her." I hoped this would be enough of an explanation.

"She can't be dead. I never saw her body." Rose straightened, and I noticed her reach for the phone in her scrub pants pocket.

"Because she was killed by a witch creature, and I didn't know how to explain it." I facepalmed myself, realizing how crazy I sounded.

"What killed her?" Rose loosened her grip on her cell phone.

"Technically? A Domum slit her throat before transforming into a Venefica after they turned my mom into a Mortia."

Rose's eyes bugged out, and she dropped her hand. The other readjusted the folder held in the crook of her arm.

"We can talk in my office for five minutes. If I don't believe what you say, you're leaving. Understood?"

"I got it."

Rose moved to open the door she came out of and held it for me to pass through. We walked down the sterile white tiled hallway that reeked of the same bleach scent of the front lobby. After passing a few doors, Rose stopped at the door with the Rose Saunders, MD nameplate nailed to it. She opened the door, motioning me into a room with an old low pile green carpet and beige walls. Her desk sat to the right side with a white desktop computer on top and had a large bookcase behind it full of what looked like medical books. The walls were relatively bare except for the wall by the door that had framed diplomas of her degrees. She pointed me to the two green pleather guest chairs that matched the carpet. I sat down in one, mortified by the sound of the chair deflating. Rose took her seat at her desk in a cloth computer chair that didn't make a sound at all when she sat down. She pushed the file she had been carrying to the far side of the desk, away from her computer, and crossed her hands in front of her. Then, she stared at me with those piercing green eyes.

"Let's hear it," said Rose, staring at me harder.

I pushed myself up higher on the squishy chair by pressing against the wooden chair arms that matched Rose's desk.

"Hear about my mom or what I came to see you about?"

"Artemis."

"I told you the summary. She got kidnapped by a Domum looking to rule the witch creatures and killed after being used for a transformation ritual." I realized I didn't know how much Rose really knew about witch creatures. "If that makes sense."

"Not much sense, but I guess it could track. Why hasn't the Captrix council told me about this?" Rose relaxed her hands a little, but her stare remained.

Captrix council? I had no idea what she was talking about, but I couldn't let her know that or I was sure she would throw me out. It was time to craft a lie, something I'd grown better at in the past few months.

"I'm not sure why they had waited since it's been a few months. Maybe they were waiting for me to come tell you and I didn't realize?" I kept my eye contact steady to cover up my lie.

"Swear, that's just like them. I mean, one day, they turn up and tell me about witch creatures and how I'm supposed to help them. Yet, they have the audacity to not tell me when the Captrix I worked with has died." Rose rolled her eyes and sighed.

"Were you close?" I was curious to know just how many friends my mother had she neglected to tell me about.

"In a business sense, I guess. I didn't know her personally. You said you were her daughter?"

I nodded and pressed my lips together.

"I'm sorry for your loss then. Anytime I worked with her, she seemed nice. Hard, but nice." Rose shook her mouse and did a quick scan of her desktop. "You said you needed to see me for something other than telling me about Artemis?"

"Yeah, actually. I think a witch creature could be responsible for a string of killings, but I needed to know about what their deaths were like." I assumed these were the types of questions Mom would ask, so I went for it.

"Gotcha. Which ones are you looking into?"

"I saw a dumped body over in Parksdale that didn't look right and overhead the officers talking about it looking like some other murders they'd seen recently."

"My jurisdiction technically isn't Parksdale, but I think I

know what you're talking about. Woman in her twenties with her mouth wide open?" Rose moved to a stack of files on her desk next to where she placed the other one.

She shuffled through them until she pulled out the file she was looking for and opened it. Rose read something off the file and typed on the computer to bring something up.

"Exactly the one I'm talking about. Have you heard about or seen any other bodies?" I leaned forward, hoping for a solid lead.

"Yes and no. I saw one with a similar pattern on the outskirts of town a few weeks ago near the park, but the type of killing you're describing is happening mainly in Parksdale." Rose punched some buttons on a keyboard. "I'm friends with the examiner over there, and she tells me if something strange pops up. So far, she's sent me files for three other victims."

"Where exactly was the New Meadows body found?"

"If I remember correctly in the back corner of the recreation park near the playground."

"What's strange about these bodies other than their mouths being forced open?"

Rose scrolled on the computer and glanced down at the open file on the desk.

"Well, first of all, the victims all died of a supposed heart attack. That's what the body is showing, but their hearts are missing during the examination. Poof, but there's no evidence of them being extracted."

"That's on all of them?" I thought back to what Mom had said about Veneficas versus Brujadans.

If it was a Brujadan, all of the organs would be missing. A Veneifca only ate the heart whenever it was devouring the soul.

Rose read over her file again and looked at her computer.

"Yep, that's all of them based on what my colleague in Parksdale told me."

"So, I'm hunting a Venefica." I struggled to hold in a groan.

A Venefica was all I needed. I had a hunch before I came here, but I didn't want it to be true. It added a whole extra layer to my problems, and I had no idea if all of these things were related.

"I would think so based on the little bit Artemis told me about them." Rose closed the file. "Does that help any?"

"Yes, this means I have a Venefica to hunt down." I stood up from the guest chair. "Thank you so much for your help."

Rose stood up as well to walk me out. When I went to push the door open to leave, she stopped me.

"Atalanta, If you need to come back for any other questions, feel free to. I'll have the office guy add your name to my special persons list."

"I appreciate it." I gave her a smile and pushed open the door.

When it shut, I heard the sound of Rose locking it behind me. I exhaled a deep breath, happy to have made it through my first official Captrix meeting and sauntered my way back to the car. When I opened the passenger door, Bridgette tucked the book she was reading in between her seat and the console.

"Well, what do we have?" Bridgette cranked the car and shifted it into gear.

"We're hunting a Venefica. All of the women the police guys were whispering about were missing hearts and their mouths were stuck open." Even though I knew this was a valuable piece of information, I felt no closer to the real truth.

"I guess if you wanted some action, you got it." Bridgette

drove through town, making her way back to the cottage.

"Nothing makes sense, though. Looking past the undead witches, the Venefica killings are confusing as well."

"What do you mean?"

"Tristan and I saw someone dump that body and run down the alley before the Ventus appeared. If that was a Venefica dumping a body, I feel like I would have been able to sense it."

Bridgette nodded, following my line of thinking.

"Venefica don't care about where they leave their victims as far as I know, so why would one take the extra time to move their kill after devouring the soul?" The idea bothered me to no end.

"What if a Venefica didn't dump her kill?" Bridgette rounded a corner, putting us only a few minutes away from the cottage.

"So, you're saying a human or another witch creature dumped the body for the Venefica?"

"I mean if we're following what you're thinking, then yeah." Bridgette shrugged, perplexed by the mysteries as well.

"So, we have a necromancer raising witch creatures and a Venefica on an eating binge that has her own body dumper." I looked out the window in frustration as we pulled into the cottage driveway. "Does this make any sense to you?"

"If you asked me a week ago, I would have told you that you were crazy and going down the wrong path." Bridgette parked the car. "But with the way things have been stirring, I'm inclined to believe you're completely right."

I was happy she believed me, but it stung a little since she thought me crazy before.

"So, it took Tristan telling you we saw a dead witch creature to believe me?" I said it before I could catch the words falling out of my mouth.

Bridgette remained silent and opened the car door, ignoring my statement. I exited the car behind her.

"You didn't believe me until he said it was true." My lip trembled as I realized how deep the wound really went. "I saw the first undead witch days ago, and you told me I was seeing things."

"I'm sorry. I didn't think it was possible." Bridgette sighed and left her back to me.

"But you still didn't believe me. Even if it was unlikely, you should have believed me." My voice broke down into a soft whisper. "We're supposed to trust each other."

"I'm sorry, I should have believed you." She fiddled with the key until the front door unlocked.

"And now you won't even look at me."

Bridgette turned around and walked back to me.

"I swear I'm sorry. Please." Bridgette held her arms open for a hug of forgiveness, but I stepped back away from them.

"You thought I was hallucinating. Going crazy from my soul. You didn't even stop to think I was telling the truth."

"It's not that simple. I believed you saw what you thought you did. I had no idea it was real until after you and Tristan saw it again."

"So, you don't trust me then."

"I do trust you. I'm allowed to make mistakes too." Bridgette lowered her arms.

"I need a minute to call Tristan." I walked away from her, toward the woods.

Bridgette remained frozen in the yard for a moment before going inside. The sun was almost below the trees now, making it too dark to visit Mom's grave, so I stood in the yard on the far side of the house alone.

I fumbled my phone out of my pocket to call and give Tristan an update. I told him yesterday I would keep him in the loop, but I honestly didn't feel like talking to anyone. Bridgette's betrayal hurt my spirit, even if she didn't see it that way. I knew I would get over it sometime, but right now, I wanted to wallow in the hurt. I made the dreaded call to Tristan anyway. He answered it within a few rings, and I began detailing to him the events of the day. I felt him nodding through the phone as he listened, but when I got to the part about the Venefica, he inhaled sharply.

"We're hunting a Venefica on top of everything else? Wonderful," said Tristan.

"That was pretty much my reaction as well." I sighed.

"Are you going to go hunting tonight?"

"I don't think I have any other choice. I'm tired, but we have to get something under control." Some extra sleep sounded amazing given the events of the previous nights, but it was a luxury I couldn't afford.

"Where are you going to go hunting?"

"I was going to start on the edge of town in the park, possibly near some of the subdivisions. There was a body dropped there on the way to Parksdale a few days ago according to Rose."

"What time do you want to go? I'll pick you up." Tristan sounded firm, ready to go.

"Are you sure? I can go alone. I know you've had a rough few nights too."

"I'm not letting you hunt a Venefica by yourself. End of discussion."

I huffed a breath, but Tristan didn't waver.

"So, what time am I picking you up?"

"I guess around one." It would be a couple hours before the witching hour, giving us enough time to get situated before witch creatures would be on the move.

"I'll pick you up then. Bridgette going to go?"

"I'll ask her." I didn't really want to, but this was the type of hunt I wanted her to be around and have my back on.

We hung up soon after, and I decided now would be a good time to return inside and face Bridgette. I planned on acting like nothing was wrong and maybe avoiding the discussion all together.

I entered the living room and found her sitting in her recliner doing a random hoop of cross stitch. Whenever she didn't want to read, this is what Bridgette tended to do when she wanted to wind down. This signaled to me she had enough of witch creatures today, but I decided to ask anyway.

"Tristan and I are going to go hunting for the Venefica tonight." I took a seat on the couch. "Do you want to come?"

Bridgette stopped pushing her needle through the fabric and secured it, so the thread would stay taut.

"I don't think it's a good idea for me to go tonight. I wanted to finish reading the soul book for you."

It felt like there was an entire ocean between us, one that I didn't like, but I also didn't know how to bring us back together. I didn't think I needed to apologize, but I also wasn't ready to forgive. I wished I was, but I was holding myself back. I trusted Bridgette wholeheartedly and learning that she possibly didn't feel the same about me hurt.

"Are you sure you're not up for an outing?" I tried to sound lighthearted, but it came out forced.

"I'm sure. I'm about halfway through the book, and I want to see if it has any answers to go with the other book we read." Bridgette looked away from me and began creating a new x in her cross stitch pattern.

If that was how she was going to be, I could be that way too. I said nothing else and went over to my trunk to start selecting weapons for the night's hunt.

CHAPTER TWELVE

Tristan's car lights shone through the front window exactly at one am. Bridgette had already gone to bed, carrying the book with her and shutting the door for the night. I, on the other hand, spent my time after having a light dinner, preparing weapons. On the coffee table laid a collection of fire bombs made with fresh spices from the herb store, a few blessed water vials for Tristan, and a quiver full of blessed water crossbow bolts.

The final piece to my arsenal was the copper retractable spear Bridgette gave to me after the swamp hunt. She kept it in her own personal stash as a way to feel more in control if she began turning into a Venefica. I never asked if she planned to kill herself with it, but it was the assumption that filled the air anytime I looked at it. The spear itself remained compact unless you pressed a button. Then, it became a full sized spear that was lethal. I only saw a copper spear used twice, but it turned both Veneficas straight to dust. It seemed like a solid choice for Tristan to carry tonight to protect himself with.

I let Tristan in the front door, and we silently carried all of the arsenal out to the trunk of the car. I placed my crossbow and quiver gently in the backseat to be removed later. The black leather huntress outfit I wore for these hunts tugged, and I leaned up, readjusting the corset. I placed my mixed metal dagger in the holster on my leg and went to open the passenger side door. It felt familiar, like old times, and I looked forward to sitting in my passenger seat after being regulated to the back last time.

When the door opened, Sarah sat in the seat and gave me a happy wave. She wore a black turtleneck and dark jeans complete with a beanie covering her head. If I hadn't known better, I would have thought she was a ginger cat burglar. My eyes widened, and I turned back to Tristan, who was still situating things in the trunk.

"One second." I closed the door, careful to avoid pinching her in the jam and marched to the back of the car.

"What's up?" asked Tristan, as he slammed the trunk closed.

"What's up?" I tilted my head at him and blinked. "Your girlfriend is sitting in the front seat of the car."

"Do you want me to ask her to sit in the back?" Tristan's brows wove themselves together in confusion.

"No, I want to know why she's here. We're going on a hunt!" I balled my hands into fists, trying to control my annoyance.

"She wanted to come." Tristan shrugged, adding to the desire to punch him in the face.

"We're going on a hunt to kill witch creatures. A Venefica,

one of the most dangerous ones that already has a four person body count, and you're saying she wanted to come?" I groaned.

"I figured you would be fine with it."

"You figured I would be fine with you bringing your inexperienced girlfriend that only knows enough about the witch creature world to fill a brief pamphlet?" I stretched my hands. "We have to take her back."

"We're not taking her back. She'll be fine."

"I can't deal with protecting other people right now." It was enough trying to make sure Tristan was safe, even though he had experience. Sarah would add a level of difficulty I didn't want to deal with.

"I'll cover her. Please?" Tristan gave me a puppy dog stare that I wanted to slap off his face.

I rolled my eyes. I didn't want to go alone, and I didn't want to take Bridgette's car, so I had no choice but to give in to his demands. I couldn't believe he was doing this me. If Sarah got hurt, it would add to the long list of people I let down. I walked to the rear passenger door, entered, and slammed it as hard as possible. Tristan got in the front seat as I crossed my arms.

"Is something wrong?" Sarah looked over at Tristan before checking me out in the back seat.

"Nah. Everything's fine," said Tristan, as he began backing up.

Sarah raised her eyebrows at me, and I shook my head, choosing to look out the window instead. She paused, waiting for me to respond, but eventually gave up. After a while, she messed with the radio until it played a song I never heard of.

I continued to stare down the window as the car passed

through the outskirts of New Meadows. Trees rushed by as we made our way on county maintained paved roads until the entrance of the local recreation park. The recreation park sat halfway between New Meadows and Parksdale and was utilized by both areas. On a normal day, the park was full of children doing team sports or walking the track around the park. However, at this time of night, it was empty unless there were teenagers smoking weed along the fence line that backed up to a subdivision. A strange place for a witch to hunt since there weren't a lot of people around, but this was where Rose indicated the only New Meadows body was found.

Tristan turned in and parked us in the empty lot next to the main building. I took a glance around the park to see if anyone was around, but we were supposedly alone. It was good to be alone, but I felt exposed being the only car around in case a cop came by to do a wellness check for the grounds. My only saving grace was that I believed sometimes people would use the parking lot as a rideshare location. Hopefully, if someone passed by, that's what they would assume for why the vehicle was there.

The car shut off, and we all began unbuckling our seat belts to get the gear out of the trunk. I handed Tristan the copper spear before deciding on something to give Sarah. Picking up a spare fire bomb, I handed it to Sarah, along with a vial of blessed water. At a minimum, she would at least have something to throw. She held them in her hands, not quite sure where to put them, but Tristan pulled a tote bag out of the trunk and handed it to her. Sarah placed the objects in there and strung the bag over her shoulder. I put the crossbow and quiver over my shoulder, allowing my back to get used to the weight. The final touch was a few firebombs and blessed water vials on my belt.

"Where was the body found," asked Sarah, taking her own look around the park.

"Over there in the far right corner behind the playground." I pointed to the small playground situated near the fence.

Behind the playground there was a group of trees before the park area ended with a chain link fence. A perfect place for a secluded walk or to suck out someone's soul under the cover of trees. It made sense to begin our hunt there to see if there was any witch creature evidence left behind the cops may not have noticed.

Tristan locked up the car, and we all began walking to the corner of the park, using the paved walking track. I took the lead, so I wouldn't have to watch Tristan and Sarah hold hands as they walked. Keeping my eyes on the ground, I looked for anything strange, but nothing stood out to me. It was ignorant to think I would find something after a few days passed, but I still wanted to try. However, all I found on the walk was undisturbed brown leaves from the park trees and various places where pet owners didn't clean up after their dogs.

I heard giggling behind me and snapped my head around to see Sarah and Tristan steal a kiss. I rolled my eyes, appalled that they weren't taking this seriously.

"Can we remember we're on a hunt and not a date?" I turned my head back to the front.

"You don't have to be so hostile," said Sarah, as I heard another peck.

I stopped not being able to control the annoyance that plagued me since I saw her in the car. Sarah was sweet, nice, and honestly, everything I wasn't. She had been nothing but kind to me, but tonight wasn't the night I needed this. I could have said something mean like, "No one wanted you here," but I decided to tone it down since she has been nice to me before. Clearly, Tristan wanted her to be here, even if I didn't understand why.

"We're hunting a Venefica, who has already killed four people. Excuse me for taking it seriously." I stopped in the track and turned around.

Tristan looked clammy like he didn't know what side he was going to have to take on this argument.

"I didn't mean it like that." Sarah dropped Tristan's hand and straightened into a power pose. If she thought she could pull that move on me who grew up dealing with Artemis Capp, she was mistaken.

"No, I know exactly how you meant it." I put my hands up to make air quotes. "Chill out, Atalanta. We're not even going to find anything."

Sarah's mouth thinned as her anger grew.

"This isn't a fun outing with friends. We've done that. This is a serious search for a deadly creature that rips your soul out of your body."

Sarah rolled her eyes, so I got closer in her face.

"Do you want to know what it feels like to have your soul devoured? It hurts. You feel your heart shatter inside your body and then spend the rest of your life, if you're lucky enough to live, feeling empty. Those people this Venefica killed spent their last moments in unimaginable agony so intense it froze their mouth open." I got so close to Sarah I could feel her breath on my skin. "So, excuse me if I don't treat this like a playdate."

"You're just jealous I'm having fun with Tristan when you were supposed to have him all to yourself."

I reared my hand back and slapped her without thinking. This had nothing to do with Tristan. I didn't care if they were having fun. I cared about if they got hurt for acting like horny teenagers when a witch was around. Sarah lunged at me, ready to make her own hit, but Tristan stepped in between us.

"Stop it!" He extended his arms out, pushing us both back.

The sting in my hand tingled from the force, so I shook it out and took a few steps back.

"She hit me!" The mark on Sarah's face from my slap blossomed into a beautiful pink. "You're going to let her hit me like that?"

Tristan inspected her face, gently tilting it to check the slap mark. He gave her a soft kiss on the check, and Sarah visibly relaxed. Then, he turned toward me.

"Can you apologize?" asked Tristan in his calm, peacemaker tone.

I licked my lips and sighed. I didn't feel bad for what I did given the way Sarah called me out, but in order to keep the peace, I needed to say something.

"I'm sorry for slapping you. I let myself get out of control." Sarah's face broke into a smile, and I controlled the urge to roll my eyes again. "But I'm not sorry for what I said. We need to take this seriously."

Tristan nodded, satisfied with my apology, and turned to Sarah who frowned at the end of my statement. He raised his eyebrows, and Sarah huffed.

"I'm sorry for being nasty. I will be more respectful about

the hunt." Sarah put back on her smile, but I could tell the edges of it were fake.

"We're almost at the playground. Can we make it without any more arguments?" Tristan looked between us both, and I was pretty sure Sarah and I both wanted to slap him.

Instead, we both nodded and continued on our path. I caught Sarah out of the corner of my eye, rubbing at the slap mark until it finally returned her correct color of pale skin. Tristan and Sarah held hands again by the time we reached the playground, but I chose to focus on the scene at hand. I clicked on my phone flashlight and walked further back, past the slide and swing set to the thicket of trees they found the body in. Tristan and Sarah hung back at the playground, looking for anything strange and to make sure no one was watching us.

My phone light shone onto a fragment of possible yellow crime scene tape remaining stuck in the pine tree's bark. I walked closer to it and touched it, pulling the tape out of the tree to examine it. Holding the light over it, there was no mistaking the yellow plastic tape, which meant I was in the right area. I stuffed the tape fragment into my pocket, rather than littering trash on the ground and moved deeper into the trees.

I squatted on the ground, trying to study the grass and discover where the dead body may have fallen, but I barely saw even a blade of grass out of place. There was nothing here but an empty park with no witch creatures in sight. I leaned my head back to look at the stars in frustration. How did Captrix even do this hunting part if the witches didn't come to you? All I felt was dead ends piling up along with possible dead bodies. I stood back up straight and felt Tristan join me.

"Where's Sarah?" I shone the phone light around the area some more, hoping to see something else.

"She decided to wait on the swing set after what happened."

I tried to read how he felt about the altercation, but Tristan came across as deadpan. I wasn't sure if that was how he really felt or if he was determined to be Switzerland in this situation. Only one thing would make him feel better.

"I really am sorry for hitting her." I turned my phone light off, giving up on that. "She hit too close to the core, and I reacted poorly."

"I know." Tristan was quiet like he was being extra careful to make sure Sarah didn't hear. "Thanks for apologizing, though. I really don't think she meant to aim so low."

He was probably right, so I left the statement hanging in the air. Tristan did his own quick walkaround, coming back with nothing as well.

"So, what are you thinking?" he asked.

I closed my eyes, trying to enter into my intuition mindset to see if there was any information it could give me.

No witch. Only death.

I opened my eyes back up.

"I think the woman was dumped here. I don't know why, but I don't think the Venefica we are looking for has ever been to this park."

"What do you mean?"

"The human or whoever is doing the dumping for the Venefica brought the body here. There's no sign of any witch creatures, and I don't feel anything in this area." I checked in with my intuition again, but gathered the same answer.

"So, we really believe a person is carrying out witch creature trash?"

"I don't have any other explanation, so yeah."

Tristan rubbed his chin, pondering the idea I gave him. I walked down making sure to walk all the way to the fence. I turned my phone light back on, and that's when I saw it. Halfway up the chain link fence was a cut area, long enough for a person to get through and possibly bring a body. Also, this particular fence butted up against a side street that ran down the backside of the park.

"Whoever dumped this Venefica's kill parked on the street and carried them through the fence and left." I squatted down, inspecting the fence closer.

I looked for a spare piece of fabric on the fence or evidence the cut area had been used lately, but found nothing remarkable. Tristan leaned down as well, inspecting the area. He pointed to a dip before the fence solidified in the damp ground. The indentation was covered by a few leaves, meaning it wasn't super recent.

"See that dip? It's probably a shoe print taken by the cops. But look at the size." Tristan crept close to the fence until his hands used the chain link to grip.

"It looks kind of big." I considered walking around the hole to get a better look.

"It's probably washed out a bit, but a larger shoe size normally means a guy." Tristan stood up.

"So, you think we're looking for a male body dumper?" I leaned in closer, pressing my face against the chain link to examine the supposed footprint.

"Maybe? There's no way for us to know if that is our dumper's footprint since it's been a few days."

"Could be a solid guess, though. Take it into consideration, but don't consider it a fact." I stood up and wiped the dew on my hands onto my pants. "This hunt keeps getting stranger."

The odds of a witch creature working with a human to begin with was dismal unless they were a Domum. We already proved we were dealing with a Venefica, so it was an even lower chance of a human helper. But then to consider the Venefica had enough control to choose a man to help her and not eat him?

My brain hurt from all the questions with no true answers.

"I mean, I don't want to be the devil's advocate, but we're assuming the Venefica is controlling things. What if the human is controlling her?"

I tilted my head at him, letting the thought sink in, but dismissing it.

"That would be us assuming a random man has enough witch creature knowledge to contain a Venefica. She can shout spells into air, so containing that would be impossible." I walked from the fence back to the body's approximate location. "Of all the witch creatures to try to control, an elemental one would be easier to manage."

"So, we're dismissing that idea all together?" Tristan followed me.

"All we have are theories. There's nothing solid until we find the witch or the helper." I rubbed my temples, trying to relax.

I felt a tingle under my skin as all of my hairs stood up throughout my body, coupled with an overwhelming feeling something was off.

"Something's not right," I said, pulling my crossbow off my shoulder into my shooting hand.

Before Tristan responded, Sarah's high pitched scream covered the entire area. We broke out into a run, heading back to the playground as fast as possible. I pulled a bolt from my quiver, cursing myself for not loading it earlier. As I clicked it into place, the smell of smoke and burnt flesh attacked my nose.

The woods area opened back up to the playground where we could see little fires in various patches of grass surrounding the place. Sarah's back was pinned near the play structure that led down to the slide. The red hair sticking out from under her beanie looked singed in some places. Tristan's and my eyes darted to the left of the playground, where a figure of fire stood, conjuring another fireball to throw at Sarah.

The Ignis, who I immediately knew was from the swamp, looked stronger than any of the other witches we saw so far. She seemed more complete, like the magic brought her back correctly.

She engulfed herself in flames, but there was one spot, the size of an orange, where I killed her before with the blessed water bolt that remained unlit. Instead, I saw grey, partially decayed skin. There was also a spot on her damp foot doused by a vial of blessed water that crashed on it. Sarah had tried to fight back, but her throw hadn't been good enough. The Ignis's fireball became complete in her hand, and she threw it.

Tristan uncorked a vial of blessed water and tossed it ahead of the fireball. Some of the water landed on it, reducing the size of the ball, but it still landed on Sarah's shirt.

Flames crept up the top, singing fabric and hair as it moved across the body. Sarah screamed again, and Tristan ran for her.

"Tristan!" He turned around for a split second, and I tossed him the blessed water vial I had.

He caught it and continued running. The Ignis, upon hearing my voice, turned and focused on me. I felt the hatred pouring out of her as she conjured another fireball, aiming it toward me. I raised my crossbow, waiting for the sign but heard nothing. I squeezed the trigger, ready to release the bolt into her chest as she released the fireball.

Duck!

I listened to my intuition and hit the ground, accidentally finishing my trigger squeeze. The bolt flew into the air, hitting the Ignis's knee. She screamed as her fireball zoomed over my head. I stood back up and turned around to face the fireball, ready for it to turn around like a boomerang given that the Ignis threw tracker fireballs that followed you until it landed and burned you alive. However, the fireball landed into the grass and began burning, instead of turning around.

Even though she was more complete than the others, the Ignis still wasn't perfect. She could use her original flame powers, but her tracker fireballs weren't working like they should have been. A small favor in the sea of flames and smoke that I was sure would attract the fire department and police soon. I looked over to check on Tristan and Sarah, to see him pushing her up the steps of the jungle gym to the top. Her shirt was no longer on fire, so the vial I handed him worked.

The Ignis yelled louder as she pulled the bolt out of her knee, tossing it to the side. Where the bolt pierced, the flames had died out to reveal more undead skin. With a scream of rage, her flames grew bigger and brighter, allowing me to feel the growing heat. The small fires around the playground also grew and began moving as if she was commanding the fires to burn closer. The Ignis released another fireball from her hand, but she aimed it again at Sarah, lobbing it over the play structure's plastic wall.

The plastic shouldn't have burned like it did, but with the increased heat, it began melting the floor, compromising the old structure even more than it already was. Tristan climbed up to protect Sarah, and I knew I had to deal with this Ignis faster. I reloaded another bolt into my crossbow as I could feel her walking closer toward me, but she stopped to conjure fireballs in both hands. One went back up to Tristan and Sarah, and from the sound of Sarah's scream, the fireball hit its target. The other fireball launched toward me, and I darted to the side to avoid it.

I held up the crossbow, taking careful aim at the Ignis's heart.

Head.

I shook my head at it, believing it could be wrong. I squeezed the trigger, almost launching the bolt.

HEAD!

My mind screamed, and I jerked my hand as the bolt released. It flew in the air until it landed in the middle of the Ignis's forehead. Her eyes widened as she felt the impact pierce her skin and spread the blessed water. Then, her body extinguished itself as she fell back into a spray of dust.

Sirens wailed in the distance, and I knew we overstayed our welcome. I ran to the area where the Ignis perished and grabbed my two bolts, settling them back into my quiver. I looked around the area, figuring the broken glass of the vials wasn't so bad given the time we had left to clean up.

"Atalanta! Help me!" Tristan yelled from the top of the slide.

I ran over, stopping at the end of the slide. I heard Tristan whisper to Sarah who looked like she was laying on the bottom, barely moving.

"Send her down to me. We have to get out of here!"

I noticed motion, and a whimpering Sarah slid down the slide on her back. I shuddered looking at all of the burned fabric and red burns on her body. Her eyes were closed, and she barely moved, apart from flinching if something touched her burns. Tristan jumped down next to me, cringing at the impact of the solid ground on his joints.

"We've got to get her back to Bridgette, but there's no way we can get to the car and leave before the police are here." I looked around as the sirens grew louder.

"I'll go get the car. Can you take her through that hole in the fence we found," asked Tristan.

"Yeah, but what if you get caught?"

"They are going to be running this way. As long as I wait to sneak out the car after they are over here, I'll be fine."

I didn't have time to argue, so I pulled Sarah down off the slide and carried her in my arms. Tristan ran, keeping himself hidden in the shadows back toward the car as I saw the blinking lights of the emergency services entering the park. I ran as fast as I could with Sarah, feeling guilty that I had to toss her up on my body as I moved due to my lack of arm strength. She groaned every time I moved her up until we reached the cut opening in the fence. Since the dumper cut it big enough to bring a body through, I leaned down on my knees with Sarah still on my arms, crawling my way through the fence. The sharp metal tugged on some of my clothes, but I took extra care to keep Sarah's skin safe.

When we made it through the fence, I crept over to a large bush where I sat Sarah down to wait for Tristan.

"You were right," said Sarah in a low whisper. "I shouldn't have come."

I shushed her, trying to not let my guilt well up in me. I heard the fire department arrive at the playground as we continued to wait for Tristan. Time moved by so slowly, but eventually, the car snuck around to where we were. Tristan flashed the lights at me, and I carried Sarah out of the bush to lay her in the backseat of the car, finally taking the passenger seat I wished for earlier under better circumstances.

CHAPTER THIRTEEN

I TOSSED ALL THE books off of the kitchen table to the floor as Tristan laid Sarah down on it. Bridgette ran to the salve shelf, grabbing various creams as adrenaline pumped through her senses. When we arrived at the house, she was still asleep, but after screaming for her a few times and barely being able to to tell her the problem, she was ready to help.

Sarah groaned on the table. She was awake now but spent most of the car ride dozing off and waking up when she rolled on a nasty burn. Tristan stood off to the side in the kitchen, visibly worried.

"Tristan, go into the living room." Bridgette laid the salves she selected next to Sarah, along with a pair of scissors.

We were going to have to cut her clothes off her body. I cringed, already imagining the melted fabric being peeled out of the wounds.

"I've already seen her—" said Tristan.

"I don't care what you've seen. Get out!" Bridgette cut him off and pointed out the kitchen opening.

Tristan opened his mouth to argue, but she continued pointing at the opening and gave him a death stare. He begrudgingly left and only went a few steps down the hallway before stopping.

"Grab the scissors and start cutting her top off!" Bridgette returned to the shelf to grab some other items I didn't pay attention to.

I grabbed the scissors, unable to hold them still as my hand trembled. Squeezing the scissor handles harder, I tried to steady my hands as I placed the blades at the bottom of the singed turtle neck. I made my first snip and worked my scissors up all the way of the shirt, taking extra care to not touch skin. Sarah didn't react, but the cut shirt still stuck to her.

"Pull it off." Bridgette unscrewed the lid of a purple burn salve.

"I don't know if I can." My hands shuddered at the thought of causing her more pain.

"We don't have a choice. I've got to get these salves on her, or we're going to have to go to the hospital."

I forced both of my hands to the bottom of her shirt and began peeling up. At first, the shirt moved away with no issue, but the higher I got, the more the fabric clung so I had to pull it harder. Sarah screamed as the fabric pulled at her damaged skin, so I closed my eyes and continued peeling, eventually reaching the collar. Sarah's skin was completely exposed, and all I saw were blotches of damaged, burned skin. I didn't know what degree burns these were, but they looked like they were going to ruin her complexion forever.

Bridgette laid globs of salve on the wounds, and I held Sarah down so she couldn't leave. The pins and needles feeling of the burn salve must have been working overtime because Sarah thrashed to where I had to figure out a way to hold her legs down too. As Bridgette continued to work, mixing different concoctions of the salves she brought over, I tried to not focus on Sarah's injuries. But they haunted me anyway.

Sarah laid on this table, another person I couldn't protect. I left her all alone on the playground, wanting to focus more on the dead ends rather than protecting her. All Tristan and I had done was leave her there as easy pickings for anyone to hurt. The trashing body under me was the direct consequence of my own mistakes and inadequacy. The same inadequacy that got people in my life killed.

She calmed, finally getting used to the unfamiliar sensations the salves produced. I assisted Bridgette by lifting Sarah's body so she could wrap the wounds in gauze and bandages. I removed Sarah's pants, and we repeated the process with her legs, covering the few burns there until she looked like a mummy. Bridgette went to the bedroom to get one of her house dresses without sleeves and we dressed Sarah's petite body in the extra long fabric, making her almost swim in it. Tristan entered the kitchen, and I helped him move Sarah to the living room couch, where she fell asleep.

"What happened?" asked Bridgette, as Tristan and I returned to the kitchen.

She was gathering up her salves, resealing them and

putting them back onto her shelves. I leaned down and picked up the books I slung off the table, organizing them back into a stack where they belonged.

"We were checking where the body was found, and we left Sarah at the playground because I just had a fight with her. We heard screaming and ran back, and the Ignis was attacking her." Even more guilt washed over me as I imagined the fireball hitting Sarah's shirt again.

I stopped for a second to catch my breath, so I could finish the story without getting too emotional. Tristan looked like he felt just as guilty as I did, probably wondering why he left her at the playground by herself.

"It took me too long to kill her. The fires got out of control, and she kept throwing fireballs at—" I choked on Sarah's name.

Bridgette looked between Tristan and me, still assessing the situation. "Was it a new Ignis or the one from the swamp?"

"Swamp. She looked half dead." Tristan sat down in a chair and put his face in his hands.

"But she was better than the others, stronger. She had full control of her magic except the tracking fireballs." I remained standing, still pumped on too much adrenaline to sit.

"So, the necromancer is getting better." Bridgette sighed. "Did you find anything useful at the park?"

"We think the body dumper is a man based on possible footprints, and they cut the fence open to bring the body in, so it didn't kill her there." Tristan rubbed his eyes, leaning up, but still rested his chin in his hands.

Bridgette didn't hide the look of surprise on her face at that statement, but she didn't speak immediately, taking a moment to ponder the idea in her head.

"Do y'all have any theories?"

"Tristan threw one out earlier." I turned toward him, cueing him to explain.

"I just said what if we were looking at this wrong? What if the Venefica isn't running the show, but instead, the body dumper is using her?"

"Like he has her trapped?" Bridgette looked at me, trying to read my face about this.

"Yes. I didn't say it was right, but it would explain why there is never any sign of her at the scene or any other evidence of a Venefica moving around. The victims are always the same age, like they are being selected." Tristan shrugged.

"It's almost impossible to keep a Venefica contained like that, and I don't understand the possible motive," said Bridgette.

"What do you mean?" I asked.

"Trapped elemental witches can provide fire, water, earth, something of use. Even Mortias can be used like a leashed assassin. Veneficas only consume souls for power to perform spells. And most of the spells aren't something helpful, like cleaning, etcetera." Bridgette paused for a moment, weighing the pros and cons. "Veneficas are incredibly dangerous and hard to contain for everyday power."

A lightbulb clicked in my head. What if somehow my mysteries were connected?

"What if the Venefica is the power source for the necromancer?" I asked.

"What?" Bridgette's face contorted in confusion.

"What if the Venefica was being held, fed, and used as a

power source to bring the dead witches back to life?"

"You're assuming our mysteries are related." Tristan looked as confused as Bridgette.

"Why couldn't they be? Everywhere we see a body dumped, one of the dead witches pops up. What are the odds?" I was trying to remain strong in my assertion, but the more I explained it out loud, the more far-fetched it sounded.

"Yes, but there were no bodies around when the Radix attacked. I think it's more of a witches tracking you thing rather than related to the Venefica issue," said Bridgette.

"You're probably right, but something about these two things happening at the same time makes me feel like they are connected somehow."

"It's an interesting theory," said Tristan. "But I don't know."

I felt defeated, so I didn't want to push the theory more.

"Is Sarah going to be alright?" I asked, deciding to change the subject.

Tristan sat straight up in the chair, perfecting his posture as we waited for Bridgette's response. Bridgette pressed her lips together hard, organizing her thoughts before telling us.

"She suffered some really terrible burns, but the salves I coated her in should help." Bridgette turned toward Tristan. "She'll have to reapply them and wrap herself every day for at least a week."

Tristan nodded, soaking the information in. I remained still, trying to build a wall up around my emotions so the guilt wouldn't consume me.

"The only thing I don't know about is the scarring. I'm afraid some spots on her torso are going to look rough. She may eventually have to go to a doctor." Bridgette seemed disappointed in herself, like she was embarrassed her magic couldn't heal everything for her.

"I'm really sorry, Tristan. About everything that happened." My walls I tried to build were failing.

"It's not just your fault. We both left her there." Tristan took a deep breath. "I should have protected her."

"It's no one's fault. You two saved her as quickly as you could," said Bridgette. "Witch hunting is dangerous. As long as you explained to her the danger, then everything past that was her decision."

"I didn't." Tristan slumped in the chair. "She was treating it as a fun date since we hadn't been able to spend much time together alone. I almost got her killed."

Bridgette and I didn't have the words to give him, so the silence in the air remained thick. I opened my mouth a few times, but the words didn't form the way I wanted them to.

"You were right. Bringing her on that hunt was a stupid idea, and we didn't take it serious." Tristan rose with tears pooling in his eyes. "Just please don't say I told you so."

He walked out of the kitchen before I had a chance to respond. I sat there dumbfounded, not knowing how to make this situation better. I took a seat in the chair next to Bridgette, since my adrenaline finally wore off. My body slumped in exhaustion.

"You never wanted her to come?" asked Bridgette.

It was an innocent enough question, but it reminded me how hostile I had been the entire night.

"No. I didn't think it was a good idea, and I knew I couldn't protect her."

"Is that it?"

"And I was jealous of them acting all lovey dovey in the middle of the hunt. That's what caused the fight. But I would never tell him I told you so."

"I know."

Bridgette leaned over and pulled me in a hug. I hugged her back, almost forgetting our own fight earlier.

I held her close until I finally broke the hug, not realizing it was something I needed after a long night.

"I really am sorry," said Bridgette. "I should have believed you."

"It's okay. I forgive you." I gave her a half smile.

"No, wait." She grabbed my hand before I could stand up to leave the kitchen. "I have been blinded so much with how my own grief has been making me feel that I projected that onto you. I shouldn't have. Now that Artemis is gone, I am supposed to be your biggest supporter. And I failed."

"You didn't fail. You stumbled." I laughed, giving her hand a squeeze. "I'm going to go check on Tristan and Sarah. Then probably go to bed."

"I'm right behind you."

Bridgette followed me out of the kitchen to the living room. It was dark in the room apart from the lamp Tristan and I left on when we placed Sarah on the couch. Bridgette went ahead and walked into her bedroom to wind back down. Tristan sat on the floor by the couch, holding Sarah's hand as she remained asleep. His face glistened in the lamplight, but a quick wipe of his shirt sleeve took away all the evidence of tears. I sat down in Bridgette's recliner, grabbing myself a blanket out of the basket she kept next to it. Setting the blanket on the chair arm, I leaned down to remove my boots.

Tristan remained still next to Sarah, even taking a moment to close his eyes while she took deep breaths. It was nice to see her calm and not in so much pain. The loop of her various screams had plagued the atmosphere all night, so the sound of calm breath was welcome. I pushed my boots to the side and unlaced my huntress corset, adding it to the pile. All that was left was my white undershirt and pants, but I decided to deal with those in the morning.

"You know I would have never said I told you so to you, right?" I stretched the blanket over my legs and leaned back in the recliner.

He met me with only silence.

§

Sarah stayed at the cottage with me while Bridgette and Tristan ran out to do errands the next day. I helped her lean up and down as she adjusted to the fast healing of her skin and mummy wraps. When needed, I would help her reapply the salve as Bridgette instructed, but we spent the rest of the time in silence as we didn't know what to say to each other. I knew I needed to apologize, but I wasn't sure how without coming off like I was giving a lecture about witch creature hunting safety.

So, we found ourselves sitting in forced silence. Sarah remained on the couch, scrolling through things on her phone while I sat in Bridgette's recliner reading *Amissa Anima Mea*. I had made it past the introduction chapters and had been skimming the chapter on soul loss side effects. There was no use reading that closely since I already knew what it felt like to have a fractured soul, but what interested me was a passage talking about what happens to the fractured piece of the soul.

When a soul is fractured, the fractured piece continues living on as long as the entire soul isn't destroyed. It lives in the atmosphere like ether as an unexplainable phenomenon. When the missing piece is meant to be active to process the emotions or spirit of the human, it participates, even though the person can't feel it. The soul piece still remembers its duty and will keep performing it as long as the other pieces of the soul remain intact. This is why the pain of soul pieces missing can be so painful. The rest of the soul is trying hard to communicate with the missing piece, leading to the side effects down below.

I glanced down the page to the side effects recognizing the list that included emptiness, depression, hallucinations, and physical pain. This made me almost feel more sorry for myself, but I latched onto the idea that if I was in so much pain, that meant my soul was somewhere out in the world, waiting to come home. There was still a small possibility that if my soul piece still existed, then I could be put back together. It was the hope that I needed to keep on trying to figure out a way to fix myself.

In these high spirits, I confirmed my coffee friend date with Austin via text message before Tristan and Bridgette returned carrying supplies to make more healing salves and potions for Sarah. I walked toward the kitchen to help Bridgette unpack everything and to see if there was something I could help with when I heard Tristan and Sarah talking in the hall bathroom. I moved a few steps past the bathroom and eavesdropped.

"I'm ready to go home. I have classes and friends that I need to see," said Sarah.

"You were really badly hurt. Bridgette's taking care of you," said Tristan. He was closer to the bathroom door, so I could hear his voice clearer than Sarah's.

"Yeah, she's making the stuff, but Atalanta is the one taking care of me. It's awkward, and she won't apologize."

"What?"

"She looks at me like a dead puppy, and I don't want that kind of sympathy from someone who won't even apologize for me getting hurt."

The door slammed closed, ending my eavesdropping session, so I continued on my path to the kitchen to help Bridgette, trying to ignore the fact that Sarah thought I was looking at her funny. A few minutes later, after I emptied some shopping bags and put the items in their correct place, Tristan and Sarah came into the kitchen. They seemed standoffish toward each other, like the small conversation I heard had turned into an even bigger fight.

"Bridgette, thank you so much for your help, but Tristan's going to take me home so I can rest up some more." Sarah beamed with a grateful smile, but her eyes still shone with anger.

"But I was making you some special soup. It should help with the scarring if I got the recipe right." Bridgette frowned as she stirred the large soup pot on the stove with a wooden spoon.

"I'm sure it's delicious, but I really need to get back home. I'm going to be super behind in all my classes if I don't get some work done."

Bridgette added another spice into the soup, taking a

moment to hold it in her hand to set her intention and then dropped it in the bubbling liquid.

"Don't worry. I can bring by the soup later," I said before Bridgette got her feelings hurt worse.

"I would appreciate that." Sarah gave me the same smile, but mine had more fakeness wafting off the expression.

Tristan remained silent, probably not believing this was a great idea. When Sarah turned to leave, he stayed in the same position, refusing to move.

"I'll walk Sarah out then?" I gave him a quizzical look that he didn't notice because he fixated his eyes on Bridgette's storage rack.

I followed behind Sarah, deciding not to deal with weird Tristan. Passing by the living room, I expected her to be there, but she had already made it out into the front yard. She leaned on the hood of Tristan's car with her mask of happiness and gratitude fading into annoyance.

"He's still in the kitchen, isn't he?" Sarah rolled her eyes.

"I think he's making some sort of stand, but he'll come around."

Sarah laughed a bitter laugh and shook her head. "You know so much about him. I wish I did sometimes."

"It comes with the territory, I guess."

She laughed again, and I felt her pain in my core, even though I wasn't sure where it was coming from.

"I wanted to tell you I'm sorry about everything. I shouldn't have hit you or left you alone. And I'm sorry I didn't kill the Ignis fast enough." I hoped it came across as genuine because I really meant it this time.

She nodded, not confirming forgiveness, but more like

she understood what I said.

"You did your best. Trying to kill the Ignis anyway."

Did I do my best, though? Was my best still not good enough to keep people from getting hurt? Her statement was meant to make me feel better, but it only reaffirmed what I knew about myself.

"I know that you're jealous of what Tristan and I have, but I'm jealous of the relationship you had, even when you couldn't be in love with him."

My mouth went dry, not sure how to respond.

"He cares about you so much. I know how he comforts you and carries you. I'm not stupid." Sarah sucked in a sharp breath. "I just wish I knew he had the same love for me."

"I saw the way he looked when you got hurt. He does care about you."

"Not the way he loves you."

All the air left my body. "I don't know what you want me to do about that. I'm not leading him on," I said.

The front door opened with a thud as Tristan stalked out carrying a paper sack. Bridgette had made him a doggy bag of various medicines, I was sure, but he held it with so much tension in his arms I thought a vein was going to pop out. Sarah stared at me, knowing our awkward conversation was over with Tristan's poor timing.

"I'll catch you guys later then." I gave them a light wave.

Tristan huffed a goodbye, and they were off, leaving me standing there alone once again.

I spent the rest of the day curling up with *Amissa Anima Mea* on the couch, trying to distract myself from what happened to Sarah while Bridgette focused on researching methods on how a witch creature could perform death magic alone. She still wasn't sold on my Venefica theory, so she had to pursue all the possible avenues so we could try to come up with another working idea. After a few hours working on the couch through the rest of the side effects, I moseyed my way to the kitchen where Bridgette was preparing her chamomile tea again.

"Would you like some tea?" she asked, even though she knew what my answer was going to be.

"Of course." I needed a calming drink after the conversation I had with Sarah.

I flipped to the place in the book where I left off, just past the side effects. A few minutes later, the kettle whistled on the stove as I continued reading a little deeper into the side effects chapter about personality changes. Bridgette clicked off the burner and poured the boiling water into mugs with the tea bags already dangling in. She added a bit of sugar to mine and brought it to the table, so it could finish steeping.

Pulling the mug closer to me, I admired the herbal aroma that wafted out. Bridgette held her mug close to her, using it as a hand warmer for the chilly night. When the tea finished steeping, I took a sip, letting the sweetened drink warm my throat. The beverage calmed me, so I could focus on the reading at hand. Bridgette grabbed a book she left on the table too, and I noticed it was the same book about souls she let me read a few days ago. She was studying the same passage, hoping it would speak to her. After reading it a couple of times again, she grabbed her notepad and pen she kept on the table with the books. Furiously, she scribbled down something and went back to the book.

"Did you find anything?" I flipped my page.

"No. I'm brainstorming ideas about what it could mean to see if I can think about it in a different way. These books are old. You never know what they were meaning to get across."

"Want to share?"

"I'll tell you when I think I've got something worth mentioning."

I sighed and read the title of the chapter I was on, "How to Regain a Lost Soul." I scanned the pages, realizing it was the shortest chapter in the book. That didn't bode well for my reading. Sipping tea, I focused on the introduction that murmured about gaining a soul back was difficult and worked my way down the page until I saw what I wanted to see.

When a soul is devoured, it exists in the ether to power the witch until another soul is taken. At that point, the soul will expel itself because another soul has taken its place, but it will still exist in the atmosphere (see chapter on side effects for more information). The only way to put a soul back together is to call it back home. A certain action causes the soul to react and find its way back. However, if someone else apart from the broken soul sufferer performs the action, the soul remains lost forever.

I read the passage again to make sure I understood it and felt sick to my stomach.

"Can I see that book again?" I asked Bridgette.

She took a sip of tea and slid it across the table and made more notes on her notepad. I scanned my way down to the passage that plagued our thoughts since we read it a few days earlier.

If you manage to kill the Venefica before it attacks someone else, the piece of the soul will return to your body and realign itself with the other pieces of your soul.

My Venefica was dead, but my soul wasn't aligned. I turned back to the other book.

If someone else apart from the broken soul sufferer performs the action, the soul remains lost forever.

I read the sentences over and over, hoping different words would show up and prove to me it was wrong. But the words stayed in place, not moving or changing. Tears streamed down my face as I yearned for the piece of my soul floating around in the air. I felt the emptiness fill me up with more despair as my tears turned into a full sob.

"What's wrong?" Bridgette lurched from her chair, running over to see what I read.

I tried to make words to tell her, but my body wrecked itself with sobs as I ached with waves of despair. Snot dripped out of my nose, and I wiped it on my arm. I couldn't force myself to move from the chair to stop crying or clean up.

"Tell me what you think is wrong." Bridgette grabbed my shoulders, steadying me.

Swallowing as hard as I could manage, I tried to make words again. "My soul," I snorted, trying to keep the snot in my nose, "is lost because I didn't kill her."

Recognition flashed across Bridgette's face, and she looked down at my book, reading the paragraph I found about actions.

Then, she read hers again before turning back to the other book and reading slower this time.

"Oh my god." Tears fell from her own eyes as she took the same information in. "Artemis killed the Venefica."

I continued sobbing while Bridgette cried as well, causing what felt like a dark cloud to cover the entire cottage.

"I didn't perform the act."

CHAPTER FOURTEEN

The rest of the evening became a blur as I eventually made my way to the living room couch. I fell into myself under a blanket, reaching a catatonic state where I would lie there with my eyes open, then fall asleep. When I wasn't asleep, sometimes I would burst out into tears, crying until my exhaustion put me back to bed.

Bridgette tried to make me feel better at first, sitting by my side and bringing me mugs of liquids I refused to touch. She read the books over again, trying to come up with a better answer than we realized, but came up with nothing new. Eventually, my state continued for a few days where I ate scraps of food Bridgette forced upon me and forgot what day it was. I lived on the couch only moving to use the bathroom, and after a few days, Bridgette became quiet, not having anything left to say to make me feel better. I mourned my soul, finally giving up hope I would ever get it back. It was too much for me to bear.

Two or maybe three days later, I heard Bridgette open the door to familiar footsteps. I buried my face deeper into the couch, under a blanket to block the sunshine coming in through the window. Muffled voices of Bridgette and Tristan rang through the hall, but I forced myself to doze off again so I wouldn't have to listen to them talk.

The one small favor of losing all hope was my dreams no longer revolved around my mother's death. Instead, if I did dream, I imagined my body floating in the air above everyone. With no true agency, I floated around looking for something, but never being able to find it. A lost soul, looking for something else.

The movement of the couch disturbed my cycle of sleep as I noticed someone sitting down next to me. I should have rolled over and acknowledged their presence, but I didn't want to do anything. The only thing I really wanted was to be left alone or for my soul piece to somehow find its way back home. Neither seemed to happen.

A warm hand laid itself on my calf and began shaking, trying to disturb me from my sleep. I shifted my leg, trying to kick it away, but the hand held firm.

"I know you're not asleep," said Tristan, as he squeezed my calf.

I ignored him, choosing to stare into the back of my eyelids instead.

"Come on, Bridgette says you haven't moved from this couch in days."

He pulled at the quilt that kept the sunlight away, exposing me to the harsh reality of daytime. I squeezed my eyes shut harder, but it was no match for mother nature.

"Talk to me. Please." A pleading note in Tristan's voice caused me to open my eyes.

He sighed and released my calf, realizing I had finally opened my eyes. My stomach gurgled, and I saw the plain waffle Bridgette left on a saucer for me to eat in the middle of the coffee table.

"What time is it?" I leaned up enough to reach for the waffle. It was stone cold, so I left it on the plate.

"Just past noon."

I shuffled my way back down in the covers, considering rolling back over.

"Bridgette said you're not eating, either." He touched the waffle to check the temperature. "Do you want me to warm this up for you?"

"No. I'm fine."

"Clearly, you're not fine."

I ignored that comment and chose to stare at the ceiling rather than look at him.

"Can you just talk to me? We're all worried about you."

"How's Sarah?" The best course of action was to get the subject off me so he would leave faster and I could return to sleep.

"She's healing up fine and feeling better. Looks like there isn't going to be any scarring." Tristan scooted back further into the couch, determined to make himself a spot, so I moved my feet out of his way.

"That's good." My wallowing subsided a bit, knowing Sarah wasn't completely ruined for life like I was.

"You want to tell me what this is about?"

It was about everything, but I didn't know how to say that to him. It was about me not being able to protect Sarah. Not knowing what would happen to me the longer my soul was away from my body. Me finally losing the last bit of hope I had that I could fix myself and be with him. The fact that no matter how hard I tried, I could never bring my mother or my soul back.

I was still that heap of a girl on the warehouse floor begging my ancestors for forgiveness.

I leaned up and shifted my body around until I sat next to him. Tristan opened his arms to pull me in, and I crashed into his shoulder, staring out the window behind Bridgette's chair. His warmth hit me first, followed by the familiar scent of pine trees and soap. The scent still smelled like home, but now it swirled a feeling of emptiness inside. I flinched, but refused to give this up, yet. Tristan rubbed my arm, allowing us to sit in the most comfortable silence we had since the party.

"Sarah doesn't blame you for the playground. I know y'all talked, but she really doesn't," said Tristan.

"It was still my responsibility to keep her safe."

"No, it was mine. I brought her. You told me from the get-go you weren't comfortable with her going. I should have listened to you, but I was being stupid."

"If it isn't my fault, then why do I feel so guilty?"

"Because there's something else fueling that." Tristan reached his hand into my hair, combing a tangle out with his finger.

"Did Bridgette tell you about what we found?" I choked on the word, feeling the tightness in my throat that always came before I cried.

"She mentioned it when she called. She's worried about you."

"I know." I felt bad for making her worry.

"If you don't get up for anyone, you have to get up for her." Tristan let me go and pushed me up to look me in the eye. "She needs you as much as you need her."

"I don't know how to be anything for anyone right now."

"You don't have to be something. You just have to get off this couch." Tristan looked me up and down. "Atalanta, you're dying this way."

"Does it even matter if I pick myself back up?"

"It matters to me."

I squashed the urge to tell him it shouldn't. That he should be more worried about Sarah than me, but I didn't have the heart. Instead, I thought back to when I was at the herb shop and Sarah told me Tristan had read everything in Morgana's collection about souls.

"Did you know?" I peered into his dark eyes, bracing myself for the response.

"Did I know what?" Tristan kept his face blank.

"About my soul? Sarah said you read all of the books in the shop on souls, so you had to have read the one I did."

His lack of response told me everything I needed to know. The betrayal of him not telling me should have hit me harder than it did, but I didn't have the emotional capacity to process anything else.

"So, did you know? Be honest." My stomach gurgled, but I refused to eat the cold waffle.

"I read the book you're talking about, but I didn't put it in the same context as you." He pushed some of the shaggy hair that had fallen in his face away.

"But you had your suspicions. I can tell." Another beat of silence passed, telling me I was onto the truth. "Is that why you started to push yourself harder on me?"

"I didn't mean it that way. I was just hoping if I could make you feel something, it would pull your soul piece from the ether into the right spot."

"So, you've known for months and didn't tell me?" I pushed the quilt off me as anger warmed my body.

"I read it a few nights before we broke up. I didn't want to tell you and you lose hope like you have now."

"What is the point of having false hope? I'm never getting my soul back." I sniffled, trying to choke back the combination of angry and sad tears. "You need to leave."

"I never meant to hurt you by not saying anything."

"Every time you leave something out, I or someone gets hurt." It was a low blow, but the truth at this moment.

Tristan's lips thinned, understanding what I meant. I wasn't prepared for the look of hurt on his face that I was sure felt similar to the betrayal I felt right now.

"Fair enough. I'll let Bridgette know I'm gone."

He got up off the couch, and later, I heard the door slam. I leaned back down and rolled back over on my side, catching another wave of sleep.

When I woke up again, darkness covered the living room. Bridgette left the lamp off, but I saw a glow coming from the hallway, meaning she was in the kitchen. I grabbed my phone from the coffee table and looked at it for the first time in days. A ton of missed questions about dinner from Austin, a few from Tristan asking how I was before his visit, and even a text from

Sarah. I ignored them all, clearing the notifications as I leaned up on the couch. The waffle that was left on the coffee table earlier had disappeared. I stood up, hearing my stomach gurgle, knowing I couldn't put off eating anymore. My legs staggered at the sudden usage, and it took me a few steps to get them working in proper order to make it to the kitchen.

Bridgette sat drinking a cup of tea when I laid my phone on the table before sauntering to the refrigerator. She barely looked at me as I opened the fridge and searched for something to eat. I noticed a PB&J made that was sitting on the top shelf and pulled it out, assuming it was one of the meals Bridgette was planning on trying to get me to eat later. I made myself a cup of water and sat down at the table with my sandwich. Biting into it, I found myself astonished at how good it tasted and wondered how long it had really been since I had eaten a full meal if a sandwich tasted this good.

"Are you feeling better?" asked Bridgette, taking a cautious sip out of her cup.

"I guess so." I wolfed down another bite, finishing the sandwich in record time.

"I'm glad you're eating again."

"My stomach found it necessary." I drank a long sip of water, realizing how dehydrated I was as well.

Bridgette said nothing, and I observed how tired she looked. Dark circles with all of the color drained from her skin. Her usual glitter from within was dulled enough she could have passed for entirely human in the sunshine. No matter how angry I was with him, Tristan had been right about one thing. Bridgette needed me as much as I needed her.

"I'm really sorry," I whispered, unable to conjure the correct words for what I needed to say.

Bridgette took another long sip from her mug, and the worry lines on her face deepened.

"You have every right to be upset. I just wish you wouldn't shut me out."

She rose from the table, placed her cup in the sink, and retreated to her bedroom, causing a new guilt to stir inside me. I sat at the table alone with my thoughts and a cell phone full of unread text messages and missed calls. Starting with Sarah, I braved opening them.

Sarah's text said, *I'm sorry if what I said was too much. I didn't mean to dump on you.* I thought about sending her a reply, but I noticed the message came in two days before. Too late to give a thoughtful reply.

I moved away from Sarah's text to read through Austin's messages. All of them consisted of questions about dinner plans and then evolved to ask if I was ghosting him. It seemed the relationship had set sail while I was asleep. I wasn't sad about losing him as a potential partner. I didn't want or need that. But it disappointed me to lose a chance at being friends with someone whose life didn't revolve around witch creatures.

Tristan's texts were a collection of ignored messages asking how I was and giving updates on Sarah until they abruptly stopped after his visit. Before I moved on to missed calls, a fresh text from Tristan came, to my surprise. The message had a link to a newspaper article discussing a new murder victim in Parksdale. The article provided little information except a new body had been dumped and was a victim of a possible serial killer. I glanced at the picture of the crime scene provided where a bystander barely obscured the photo of the dead college aged girl. I didn't need to see her face to know a Venefica froze her mouth open. A person I didn't save because I was too busy being asleep to do so. Tristan really knew how to make a point.

It seemed like my only choice now was to make peace with a new kind of forever soulless normal or go back to being a corpse on the couch. I clicked off the phone screen to settle with the idea. If I didn't pick myself up, someone else would die.

I thought about visiting my mother's grave to tell her about what happened like I had done in weeks before. Visiting this time seemed wrong, though. Even though she couldn't hear me or talk back, I could still hear her reactions to what happened.

I can't believe you let another girl die.

If she was still alive, this never would have happened. Facing her grave now would only allow me to crumble back onto the couch again. If I went to the couch again, I didn't know if I could pick myself up a second time. I tried to think of what my mother would do in a time like this and quickly found the answer by trotting down the door to Bridgette's bedroom. A light knock separated me from her.

"Come in," said Bridgette through the door frame.

The door creaked when I pushed it open to reveal Bridgette lying in bed under the covers. She pulled her hair up into a messy top bun with random curls falling down that couldn't make it in. She cradled a book in her lap, using the glow from her side lamp to read it.

"I'm going to try and go out for a bit of patrolling. See if it will help me feel better," I said, taking a step into the room.

"I don't really think that's a good idea since you just got off the couch." Bridgette's concern became evident on her face as she straightened up in the bed. "I'll come with you."

"No, I want to go alone. I need some space to think."

"That's not a good idea."

"Maybe not. But if I don't, I'm going to end up on the couch again."

"You're not even in fighting condition. Look at yourself!" She tossed the book to the side.

I hadn't really taken the time to look, but I felt weaker from being a couch vegetable for the past few days. However, something told me deep down that if I didn't do something or channel myself into a purpose that I was going to die. The only purpose I could think of now that I wasn't on speaking terms with anyone was hunting witches. I didn't have anything else. No hobbies, no boyfriend, no friends.

"I have to go out there. It's my duty," I said. "It's what she would do."

"The same duty that got Artemis killed?" Bridgette's concern was turning into a roaring fire of anger.

It was a low blow, hitting me deep in a place I was trying to push away. I physically flinched and swallowed hard.

"You are the only part of her I have left, and I refuse to lose you like that too." Bridgette's jaw quivered.

She was trying to tell me something, but I wasn't great at reading between the lines.

"Can I go for a drive then?" I had to figure out a reason to get away from that couch somehow.

"You'll stay in the car? Won't get out?"

"I'll stay in the car." I didn't want to make a promise I couldn't keep, but a sentence could be disregarded if needed.

Bridgette nodded as her jaw still shook. I decided to take my chance before she changed her mind and went to change into a black long sleeve shirt and jeans. No huntress outfit tonight since I was going to stay in the car, but I took a moment to grab my dagger and the copper spear just in case I needed to step out of the car for a moment.

Before I made it to the door, Bridgette stood in the hallway with her car keys dangling in her hand. They were slightly out of my reach, like she didn't know if she should give them to me. As if giving them to me would change the balance of life itself. She didn't want to make a wrong decision.

"Please." Bridgette held the word out extra for emphasis. "Please be careful. I'm begging you."

The keys shook in her hand, clanging together as they touched. I grabbed them to stop the noise, but she continued to hold them firm in her hand, not letting them go.

"Please." Bridgette stared at me with a fear and intensity in her eyes that made me want to squirm.

"I'll be careful. I'll be back in a little bit. I don't plan on being out too long."

She released the keys, and regret covered her face. She wanted to do everything in her power to stop me from going. I gave her a quick hug where she held me longer than I thought was necessary, and I was off to the car.

CHAPTER FIFTEEN

I ENTERED THE CAR and adjusted the seat forward a smidge so I could reach the pedals better before pulling down the visor to check my face in the car mirror. It has been a few days since I actively checked my cheek spot, and I wanted to know if it still looked awful. I took a deep breath, tilted the visor to the correct angle, and glanced in the mirror. Reflecting back at me was a healed cheek with no black spots to see. A small divot, like an acne scar, remained. I assumed that would heal with time and flipped the visor back up before pulling out of the driveway.

Music sang through the car speakers as I listened to the radio louder than Bridgette normally liked. The music encompassed me, providing a wall against all of the thoughts scratching at the chance to be at the forefront of my brain. Riding to the sounds of the music, I drove, not having a care in the world, and hummed along with someone else's heartbreak. Lights blurred past the car as I made my way into town. A chill ran across my body, so I turned up the heat higher as I passed the New Meadows welcome sign and continued driving down the familiar streets. I didn't pay attention to the road signs until I went through a four-way stop into an area covered with matching houses.

My heart sank as I passed recognizable neighbor residences, realizing I accidentally ended up in my old neighborhood. I considered turning back around, not wanting to go down memory lane, but my body guided me to my childhood home. I guess my psyche decided if I refused to visit my mother's grave, why not torture me in a different way by making me remember what my normal used to be.

I pulled the car over to park on the street, taking in what was left of my old home. The city cleaned up the ash and debris pile that had once been there, leaving a barren landscape. A realtor sign hung by my old mailbox, announcing the lot was for sale. Bridgette made me promise to stay in the car, but I couldn't bear looking at the area through glass. I stepped out of the car, making sure to tuck my dagger and spear into my back and pocket, and slammed the car door behind me. Then, I walked across the street to get a better look at the realtor sign.

The woman on the sign was white and had long blonde hair. She wore a black suit along with a plastered on fake smile. I wanted to knock the sign over and stomp it into the ground, wondering how they could ever put a price on this land. The realtor looked so happy as she got rid of the one thing of my childhood I had left. I kicked at the sign once, making it cock-eyed, and walked further into the lot.

The grass was greener and more lush in most places now than what I remembered. I attributed it to the lack of consistent lawn maintenance until I reached closer to where the house used to sit, where the grass was shorter, peeking its way into fresh growth after the fire. The grass had been ash once, ruined beyond repair, but still managed to find a new life. It reminded me of my own situation, even though I wasn't sure how to grow back after being burnt to a crisp.

I squatted down, feeling the smooth blades of a lusher area in my hands, trying to remember what home felt like. I plucked a blade and observed it, visualizing the backyard that had grass like this once. That backyard had been filled with my grandparents' laughter as we drank sweet tea during the hot summers. Mom would peek her head out of the back door to tell them she was going out. Sometimes my grandma would tag along, but most of the time, we spent the afternoons with her telling me stories of my ancestors. Not the parts where they died, but the fun parts where they saved entire cities. I wish she had told me how they handled the hard stuff and kept going no matter what.

A terrible smell hit me, knocking me out of my reverie and forced me to cover my nose. Standing back up, I dropped the grass and kept my hand glued to my face as I looked around for the odor. My eyes settled on something, laying where the corner of the house used to be. I walked closer to it but stopped when the smell got too strong. My body stiffened as my eyes understood what they were seeing. A dead body, way past its best by date, was dumped on the lawn. A nauseating coincidence that made me spin around in panic, looking for a person watching me.

Taking steps back away from the body, I considered my

options. Call the police again and risk a New Meadows officer realizing I was the daughter who used to live here that left under mysterious circumstances. Or I could rush back to the car and hope no one saw me here tonight and would report the body soon. The stench was getting uncontrollable, so I was sure a neighbor would have to smell it any minute now. Before I could make the right decision, a sense of dread covered me, and a buzz in my head came as my intuition detected something in my surroundings. I scanned the area close to the body again, continuing to move backwards to the car.

I blinked, not believing what I was seeing. A scraggly looking woman, wearing a white flour sack dress with a sick brown tie dye from blood, stalked her way toward me. Her neck laid to the side as if it was broken, but she placed her hands on each side and tilted it, cracking it back into place. Her knotted black hair was coated in a gray dust that reminded me of the last time I saw her in a small pile in the warehouse six months ago. She smiled at me, revealing the nasty yellow teeth that haunted me in my dreams for so long. Pure terror encompassed me as the Venefica who stole my soul lifted her hand and flicked it, tossing me a few feet to my left. I rolled, trying to catch my footing as I pulled the copper spear out of my back pocket. She opened her mouth, trying to taunt me, but only squeaking noises came out. The necromancer managed to bring her back powers and all from dust but didn't take the time to repair her vocal cords.

My intuition livened up as I understood what this meant. No working vocal cords meant she couldn't chant Latin spells. The only thing she was working with was her telekinesis powers. It didn't give me a huge advantage, but it was still better than having to deal with nasty spells. I jumped to my feet as the Venefica tried to speak more. The fury evident on her face when she lifted both hands and pushed them forward with force. This time, I flew in the air backwards, not knowing the best way to brace for impact. I tucked my limbs in before my back hit the ground with a thud, knocking the air out of me. Coughing, I tried to refill my lungs with air as the Venefica came closer.

I leaned forward, scrambling to my feet once again as the Venefica sniffed the air and smiled through her anger as she caught the scent of my broken soul. She licked her lips and cracked her knuckles, preparing for another throw. I pressed the button on the collapsed spear, and it shot out to its full length as I began running toward her. She moved her hands again, sending me back, but this time I used the spear to catch me, so I wouldn't fall down all the way.

Let her get closer, said my intuition.

The idea of letting her even this close to me filled me with fear, and I couldn't believe my intuition thought that was the right thing to do. But I knew it was never wrong, yet this was the hardest thing it had ever asked me to do. I let her advance on me more, deciding not to move this time. As she got closer, strings of salvia started showing in the grin she wore. The Venefica threw me down again onto my back, and this time I let her, while keeping a firm grip on the spear. Before I could react, she was on top of me, straddling me, opening her mouth wide as she sucked in a huge gulp of air. I felt my soul break apart again, but I pushed through the pain and flipped over so she was on the bottom. She didn't have the ability to chant a spell to hold me down this time, so there was no way I was going down that easily.

The Venefica thrashed under me, but I shoved my left elbow into her throat as I got the spear ready in my right hand. Before she could flick her hand to send me off, I plunged the spear into her undead heart. She erupted in a muffled scream and poofed into dust, making me fall onto my elbow and roll onto my back. I took a deep breath, trying to calm my adrenaline, and looked in the air to see a wispy bunny hopping around with joy. My mouth opened, and the bunny hopped in, squirming its way down to nestle itself with my soul. I gasped as my fractured pieces reconnected together and felt an overwhelming warmth coming from my chest. My eyesight vanished, replaced with blinding light.

I felt everything.

And then the vomit came.

I forced myself to roll onto my knees as I threw up what I assumed black tar tasted like. It was thick and gooey and so wrong as it coated my mouth and poured out. I closed my eyes as my body lurched more.

In the blinding light, I saw Tristan on the night of our first kiss, falling into the memory. He looked so ashamed as his shaggy hair fell into his eyes, but I looked into them, feeling the love potion buzz drag us closer together like magnets. He tried to stop me, but I refused to give up this perfect moment. I needed to know what his lips felt like and leaned in. Our lips touched, and unlike the first time, in this corrected memory, I felt the sparks that were meant to happen. The warm and fuzzy feeling of new love heated my belly. Little butterflies danced in my stomach as blossoming love tingled its way through my limbs. I never needed to kiss anyone else ever again.

I vomited again, thicker black liquid as I expelled more

of what I thought was the negative feelings I felt because of not having a complete soul. Or my body was rejecting the reconnection since I had lost my soul too long. I had no idea what to think as I plunged into another memory.

Tristan held out his hand, visibly shaken by the dust pile settling into the ground. He held the copper spear, since Morgana had forced him to plunge it into her when she attacked me. I took his hand, overcome with gratitude and pain. I didn't think I could love him more in this moment, knowing how much he sacrificed to save me. No matter what he had done before to get us to this place was erased by him saving my life.

I freefell in my head at a rapid speed as I jumped in and out of memories corrected by the piece of my soul that had been watching since it had been lost. It was a rollercoaster I thought would never end.

I laid on the bed with Tristan the night I broke up with him, but this time we were giggling as he played with strands of my hair. I still felt the grief of losing my mother swallowing me whole, but with Tristan, this time, I didn't feel so empty. The witches had been quiet, so it was a chance to relax and build our relationship more. This time, when he stroked my face and leaned in for a kiss, I was warm and safe. When he deepened the kiss, I didn't want him to stop, and I wrapped my arms around his neck the way I should have the first time. Our bodies pressed closer, and the heat in the room rose.

I fell onto the ground, unable to keep my balance anymore from heaving. I rolled onto my side, so I wouldn't choke as more black liquid came out of my mouth, dribbling onto my chin. A bit of pain surged through my body as my soul continued to strengthen the reconnection.

My mind flashed again, and I was on the porch with Tristan, leaning my head on his shoulder after having another terrible nightmare. He held his arms around me, and when I fell asleep, he took the time to carry me back to the couch. He cared so deeply for me and made me feel so safe before laying back down next to Sarah.

Sarah. I forced myself back up onto my hands before crumbling again with the next wave of vomit.

As I entered the living room of the party, I saw Sarah in the corner with her vibrant red hair, looking at Tristan with sparkling green eyes as she waited for him to come back to her. Tristan left me, and I turned to see him kiss her for the first time. I felt my heart shatter into a million pieces. That was my boyfriend, my soulmate, and seeing him kiss her didn't make me jealous. It made me want to curl into a ball and mourn losing a true love.

My body shook on the ground, devoid of any strength I had left as I prepared myself for another wave. But a few minutes passed, and my stomach and body settled. My soul finally forced itself back together, and it exhausted me from feeling six months' worth of emotions. Even though I didn't want to move, a smile mixed with heartbreak came across my face.

I was in love with Tristan, and I knew it now. I had to tell him.

CHAPTER SIXTEEN

I PUSHED MYSELF UP from the ground with the strength I had left and began staggering over the piles of vomit and the dead body. Stumbling my way over the curb, past the realtor sign, I made my way to the car, eventually making it into the front seat. I cranked it and pulled away, taking a moment to make sure no one saw me. Tristan's apartment was only five minutes away via car, and the realization settled in that I would be telling him I loved him in mere seconds. Panicked breath mixed with excitement filled my lungs as I raced to the apartment, turning four way stops into rolling sideways glances.

I tried to imagine how he would react. Would he feel conflicted because he was dating Sarah now, or would he pull me in for a kiss? I tried to think of the look of relief on his face after finding out I was whole again. Warmth flowed over me, fueling me to make it faster to the apartment before I bubbled over with anticipation.

In a few minutes, I parked the car in front of the herb shop and glanced at the time. It was around midnight, so it was almost a guarantee that Tristan would be awake. I pulled the mirror down to check my appearance and realized my hair had bits of the black vomit at the ends. I spun it into a bun at the back of my head and secured it with a hair tie found in the cup holder. After pulling a few non vomited strands down to create some wisps around my face, I checked the rest of my appearance.

Dark circles crowded under my eyes per usual, and I was paler than normal from living on the couch, so I squeezed my cheeks to make more red come to the surface in an effort to appear more alive. I noticed a small dribble of vomit next to my lips, so I wiped it away, feeling more prepared. This was the first time I was really going to see him for what he was meant to be—my boyfriend and my soulmate. I took the metal stairs up to Tristan's apartment two at a time and stopped to control my breath before reaching up to knock.

I hesitated, getting nervous at the thought of telling him what happened and how I felt. I knew it would come with complications because of Sarah, but he needed to know. A moment passed, and my body found the nerve to knock. I pounded on the door a few times and waited outside as a cool breeze brushed by. Shifting my weight back and forth, I moved to keep warm, but no one came to the door. I reached up and knocked again, hoping this time Tristan would arrive. Behind the door, I heard the sound of shuffling feet that paused to check the peephole before opening the door.

Tristan opened the door, shaggy hair tousled around his face, and he wore low strung blue plaid pajama pants with no shirt, showing off his lean muscles. My eyes widened as I really saw him, and it felt like little sparkles were almost falling off him. He was the handsomest man I'd ever seen. Nothing I ever saw online that I cut into my scrapbooks before the fire compared to who was standing in front of me.

"Hey." Tristan yawned. "Is everything okay?"

I noticed the sleep crust pooled in the corner of his eyes. "Were you asleep?" I asked, feeling my heart sink a little. He stopped staying up for me.

"For a few minutes. I haven't been staying up as late."

"Oh, I'm sorry. I didn't mean to wake you up." My palms grew sweaty as the nerves settled in. This wasn't how I imagined this moment going.

Tristan's mouth opened to say something, but we both remained silent as footsteps came from the back of the apartment.

"Is everything okay?" asked Sarah in a sleepy voice, as she stifled a yawn.

She wore an oversized gray t-shirt that I had seen before on Tristan and nothing else. She was sleeping here with him. My heart sank all the way to my toes, and the new feeling of heartbreak I was experiencing magnified.

"Everything's fine. Atalanta came by to..." Tristan looked back at me, expecting me to finish the sentence.

Sarah and my eyes met, and I saw the way she looked at him and how messed up she looked from the park. I could still see the ripple of a wound dressing under the shirt. She looked exhausted, and she stared at me like I was an alien from outer space invading her territory. It reminded me of the conversation we had in the yard a few days ago, when she confessed to me she didn't think Tristan loved her as much as he loved me.

Sarah turned her gaze from me to Tristan and looked at him with such sadness in her eyes, like she knew why I was there. I told her I wasn't leading him on, yet I was here to destroy everything she wanted. I didn't know if she loved him as much as I did, but she saw him in a way I should have been looking at him for months. The guilt washed over me, and I knew I couldn't ruin her relationship this way, even if I was truly in love with Tristan. Not telling him right now could be an act to make up for the hurt I caused her before. Sarah was a good person and didn't deserve to have her heart break like mine was right now, especially after what happened at the playground.

"To tell you I was driving around and saw another dead body where my house used to be." I squeezed my hands, holding back the emotion that threatened to pour from me in retribution for the secret I forced myself to keep inside.

"Aw man. Are you okay?" Tristan opened the door wider and beckoned me inside.

I paused, not sure if I wanted to be trapped inside with him for too long if I was going to hold on to this secret. He motioned again, so I continued into the apartment.

"I'm fine. Luckily, there weren't any witches there." This lie was harder to say than the others I told, but I got it out anyway. "But I haven't reported the body. I'm hoping one of the neighbors will smell it."

"Smell it?" Tristan walked over to Sarah and wrapped an arm around her waist.

"It wasn't fresh and reeked. I couldn't get close enough to look at it."

"That's awful." Sarah frowned, taking in the idea another person had died.

Tristan leaned down and kissed her forehead, a sweet gesture that loosened Sarah's frown. The action made me crumble further in myself and want to die. If I didn't leave soon, I would burst.

"But really, that was it. I would have just sent a text or called tomorrow if I knew you were asleep." I made my way toward the door and opened it. "I'll talk to y'all later."

"Wait." Tristan dropped his arm from Sarah and followed me out the door.

I turned around and met his beautiful brown eyes, and for the first time, I looked deep enough to see the swirls of honey in them. I wanted to reach up, touch his face, and never stop looking at the color.

"Are you feeling better?" Tristan touched my arm, halting my getaway.

"I'm fine." I gave him a big smile and squeezed my hands again.

"How? You just went to your old house and saw a dead body. And found out there's no way to fix your soul."

"I'm fine, really. If anything, fake it till you make it." I saw Sarah through the open doorway, staring at Tristan touching my arm. "I'm sorry for blowing up at you when you came by. I wasn't in a good place and took it out on you."

I had to get out of here.

"It's fine. But are you sure you're okay?" Tristan's hand lingered, heating my skin.

I nodded, making sure to keep a smile before I gave away my true feelings.

"I told Bridgette I wouldn't be out late, so I need to get back." I shrugged off the hand, regretting it as Tristan's warmth left my body. "I'll talk to you soon."

I began my descent down the stairs before Tristan could stop me again and demanded myself to not look back to see him on the stoop. When I reached the bottom stair, the door slammed. I winced at the sound and continued my lonely walk down the alley back to the car. A walk that normally took minutes felt like hours as I dragged my feet. I thought I would be kissing Tristan right now, making up for lost time. But I had been too late and was left with nothing to show.

When I made it to the car, I saw a hooded figure wearing a black cloak walking around the vehicle like they were looking for something. I put my right hand on my back, ready to pull my dagger out if needed. I didn't want to fight any other witches tonight, so I was hoping this was just a curious person who decided to do a once over on the car. A strong breeze flew through, creating a bitter cold that made my teeth want to chatter. My intuition clicked on, and I said a silent prayer, hoping the person wasn't a Mortia like I was beginning to believe.

"Can I help you with something?" I lifted my shirt, taking hold of the dagger's holt.

The cloaked figure stiffened and began to turn around. I straightened up as well, knowing Mortias could appear anywhere they wanted. If she acted like most of the other Mortias I fought before, she would appear behind me to get the jump on. I had to be ready. When she finally faced me, the

Mortia flipped her hood down to reveal her face.

My mother, Artemis, stared back at me with cold, black eyes and pale skin. I shook my head, loosening the grip on the dagger, not believing what was standing in front of me. She was in new clothes now, not the ones we buried her in, and she appeared like a full-fledged Mortia. A small line ran across her throat where Morgana's knife originally cut her, but it was nothing like the gash I remembered.

"Mom?" I stuttered, still not sure if what I was seeing was real.

The Mortia cocked her head to the side as if she was remembering some lost part of herself and disappeared. She reappeared a couple feet away from me, and there was no mistaking it was Mom. Her angular features remained true, even though her face was the wrong shade of pale. Gone was the sun kissed tan look she normally had, now replaced with death. Her pixie cut blonde hair remained short, but I noticed it was longer than what she normally allowed it to get. Mom stared at me, trying to place me before conjuring a small snowflake in her hand and blowing it toward me.

The little snowflake glided in the air, and I reached out my left hand to catch it as she disappeared. The snowflake melted in my hand as I ran to the car. I had to know if it was really her, even if all signs pointed to yes, so I raced back to the cottage, ignoring every speed limit sign that came across my way.

Pulling into the cottage driveway on two wheels, I slammed the car door with the keys inside and ran to the backside where my mother was buried. I pushed myself, gasping on the night air as it pierced my lungs until I saw the wooden cross we made her come into view. I dropped to my knees and turned my phone light on to inspect the ground. The grass was disturbed and parts of the soil were turned over as if someone had crawled their way out. When I saw her that night, she was not a spirit; she was a freshly risen witch creature brought back to life. She had screamed from the pain the resurrection had brought her.

"No, no, no," I said to the ground, as I tried to put it back into place as if that would will my mother back into her grave.

I sat down on the ground, trying to avoid a catatonic state as I accidentally dropped into my intuition mindset and found my mind's eye moving to the cottage, searching for Bridgette. She was lying wide awake on the bed, looking at the ceiling. I pushed myself down, pressing the images of my mom in the alley and then me looking at her disturbed grave. Bridgette flinched, but my mind pushed the image of the tiny snowflake drifting into the air. She snapped up out of bed and threw the covers off.

Opening my eyes, I left my mindset and stared at the disturbed soil again. Not only had I seen her after she rose, but I was almost sure it was my mother watching me in the woods a few nights ago. How could I be so stupid? I ignored all of the signs, not taking time to visit her grave out of shame and since things had gotten so busy. If I only realized sooner, maybe there was something I could have done or made it to where she was resting now. But she was so real when I saw her, not the disturbed ghost I'd seen before. Killing a ghost and laying them to rest would have been a lot easier than murdering a full-fledged being.

I heard Bridgette running from the house, and she dropped to her knees as well when she reached the graveside. She examined the ground, observing the disturbed soil. The grave hump should have been smoothing out now, but it was jagged and concaving in. The idea of the ground trying to suffocate my undead mother sickened me. How could the necromancer be so careless to bring her back like this?

"What's going on?" Bridgette trembled, letting dirt run through her fingers.

"She's risen." I wiped my dirty hands on my pants and sniffled.

The chilly night air passed through again, making my nose run even more.

"But how?" Bridgette dug deeper with her hands like she was hoping to feel a decaying limb.

"I don't know, but I've seen her. She's a Mortia now."

Tears streamed from Bridgette's eyes as she lost her mind. She screamed at the ground and hit it with her fists. Doubling over, she wailed in pain and fury, not exercising the normal control she had over her emotions. I reached over to help her, but her head snapped up, revealing little black tinges on the corner of her eyes. Her jaw twitched as she balled her fists harder, digging nails into her palms.

"I'm going to kill this necromancer." Bridgette stood, barely holding it together.

I'd never seen her with this much rage, and I knew she was on the tipping scale of pushing herself too far.

"We will kill this necromancer." I stood up and touched her arm.

Bridgette softened a bit, releasing her hands. The black on the edges of her eyes remained, but the initial cloudiness cleared. By the time we made it inside the cottage, her eyes had returned to their normal brown with silver flecks in them. We sat down on the couch as a fire crackled in the fireplace. The fire showered me with warmth, allowing my nose to warm up and stop running. Bridgette took deep breaths to finish calming herself, so we could discuss what was happening.

"How many times have you seen her?" Bridgette crossed her hands in her lap and relaxed her shoulders.

I swallowed hard, realizing I had to tell her about the first time where I lied and said I was sleepwalking.

I took a deep breath and sighed. "I saw her the night after I fought the Radix at Tristan's party."

"You mean the night you told me you were sleepwalking?" Bridgette tensed, pressing her lips into a thin line.

"I wasn't sure what exactly I was seeing, so I lied."

"You could have still told me, even if you weren't sure."

"You would have thought I was crazy! That was right after you told me I didn't fight an undead witch. How was I supposed to know you would believe me when I told you the ghost of my mother was floating across the lawn?" My voice rose a few octaves. I meant to keep myself calm and steady, not sound attacked.

"When else have you seen her?" Bridgette's hands tightened in her lap, and she pressed her lips even harder.

"I think she's what was watching me in the woods the other night."

"Someone was watching you in the woods? When you asked me about the protection veil?"

"Umm, yeah." My tangled web of lies was getting revealed now, and I wanted to crawl under a blanket in order to not answer any more questions.

"And you didn't tell me about that, either? You said you thought it was an animal."

"I didn't think it was important once you told me more about the veil. I didn't know it was her then."

Bridgette let go of her hands and rubbed her eyes. "I don't even know you anymore." She stood up and walked to the fireplace. "All you've done recently is lie to me."

Everything was falling apart around me. It seemed like anytime I tried to fix things or solve a problem, it only led me to more lies and hurt the people I loved the most.

Bridgette kept her back to me as she warmed her hands with the fire. She grabbed the fire poker and stoked it before adding another log. I could apologize, but an apology wouldn't put a dent in the betrayal she felt. I would know. However, other things had happened I needed to tell her about.

"I know you're mad at me, but there's something else I have to tell you."

"What is it?" Bridgette stared into the fire.

"I drove by my old house, or what was left of it. There was a dead body dumped there."

"Did you report it?" Bridgette turned around, facing me again.

"No. It was really smelly, so I'm hoping the neighbors will catch a whiff and do it for me. I didn't think it was a good idea for me to report two bodies in a row."

Bridgette nodded. "Were there any witch creatures there?"

I bit my lip, not sure what to say. I wanted to tell Bridgette about the Venefica and that my soul was back, but I pictured sharing that information at a happier time. But I also told her I would stay in the car and not go hunting. No matter what I said, I would unravel another lie. The problem was I didn't know which lie would be worse to keep. I wouldn't be able to hide the fact that I fixed my soul from Bridgette for very long, and I assumed if I didn't tell her, she would be just as hurt as she was now, if not worse. I sighed, knowing what I had to do.

"It was a trap, like usual. I got out of the car to check the body, and she appeared." I pulled down the sleeve of my shirt, covering my hand as a brief distraction.

"She?"

"My Venefica."

Bridgette's eyes widened. "You weren't supposed to get out of the car. I told you to stay safe."

"I know, but I wanted to look around the property. I fought her and won."

"So, your soul is back together?" A peek of excitement shone behind Bridgette's hardened expression.

"Yeah. I puked a ton of black stuff and relieved all of my moments my soul piece had been experiencing in the ether."

Her expression remained torn between celebrating for me and the betrayal she felt from all of my lies.

"I need some space to think." Bridgette marched out of the room and shut the bedroom door behind her.

I grabbed the quilt off the couch and crawled my way to the fireplace. Sitting down in front of it, I stretched the blanket over my legs and curled up into it. I spent all this time trying to get my soul back, believing it would solve all my problems. But as I stared into the fire, I felt almost as empty as I did before without a complete soul.

A log crumbled into embers, feeding itself further into the flames, and I related to it. I had been lying to everyone. Feeding Bridgette white lies so she would trust me, only to have that blow up in my face. Lying to Tristan about being okay and pushing him further away. Even going as far as keeping the secret that I loved him. Worst of all, I lied to myself, thinking I was doing the right thing this whole time.

I didn't even recognize myself anymore. Where was the girl who only wanted to honor her mother's memory? I stopped checking her grave, and if I had been visiting regularly instead of getting caught up in everything else happening, I would have known sooner what was going on. More minute decisions ran through my mind, and I could only see the wrong choices I made every time. All of those choices led me here, curled up in front of a fire alone.

Even with all the sacrifices I made, I was nowhere close to knowing who the necromancer was or why a person was keeping a Venefica as a pet. Better yet, why I was being targeted specifically with all the dead bodies and witch creatures. Having a dead body show up at my childhood home was way past coincidence, but I had no list of people that would want to hurt me beyond the list of random witch creatures.

Dead ends. Exposed lies. And a complete soul that didn't make me feel better. That was where I was, not knowing what to do next with no one to call upon.

CHAPTER SEVENTEEN

WHEN I WOKE UP around noon, I heard no sounds, so I assumed Bridgette was still in her bedroom, keeping her distance from me. I peeked out the front window to make sure the car was still there. It was, so I took it as a confirmation that my original assumption was right. Even though I slept in, I still felt exhausted from all of my tossing and turning on the couch, so I stumbled into the kitchen for something to eat. After devouring a plain bagel and a cup of coffee, I tried to figure out what to do with my day.

Bridgette wasn't talking to me, so there was no reason to believe I would spend the day with her. I didn't want to push my luck talking to Tristan since it was already hard enough for me to keep my secret from him. There was nothing that needed to be done at the cottage, so it left me with dead time.

Sauntering out to the porch with my crossbow, I was

determined to do something productive with my day. If I was being targeted specifically by a necromancer, I needed to make sure my skills were top notch. Not to mention my mother, the Mortia, was on the loose. I shuddered, forcing myself to adjust the crossbow slung on my back. The training balls Bridgette and I normally worked with sat at the end of the porch, abandoned since we weren't using them. I didn't need Bridgette to train, but her being there made it better. The lonely balls stared at me, so I grabbed one, deciding to make it into a target for practice.

I walked to the edge of the tree line until I found a tree with a crook to place the dodgeball in. Loading a fresh bolt, I backed a good distance away to practice my shot. With the sight of my crossbow set on the yellow sphere, I squeezed the trigger, hurling the bolt toward the tree. The bolt thudded to the right, sticking itself into the tree trunk. I rolled my eyes, annoyed with my miss, and loaded another bolt. I set my sight again on the yellow, double checking my aim before letting another arrow go. This time, the bolt remained true, sticking out of the ball. The sense of satisfaction that should have come didn't wash over me. I shot another arrow, and it landed under the second bolt. Again, I felt nothing.

My heart sank as I walked to collect the bolts, knowing what was missing. Bridgette came out with me most of the time when I did target practice like this. She would fill the air with her voice by complimenting my shots. Sometimes she would wave her hand to provide resistance, so I could get used to shooting against witch creatures that manipulated my bolts.

As much as I thought I could pretend Bridgette's absence didn't bother me, I found myself ruminating on the lack of her. I hadn't understood how much I appreciated her until she wasn't here. Sighing, I removed the ball from the tree, noting the fresh puncture wounds. They reminded me of the corpse I witnessed at my old house before the Venefica attacked. If training without Bridgette wasn't working for me, maybe I could try searching for a lead on the necromancer. I knew I left the car keys in the driver's seat of the car, so I wrote Bridgette a note detailing where I was going and left it on the refrigerator.

The drive into town took me longer than last night because I took care to obey the speed limit signs and stopped a block away from my house, deciding to walk the rest rather than do a drive by. Bridgette kept a navy baseball hat in the back of the car, so I put it on, hoping it would help me not be recognized from afar. I wasn't too worried since most of the neighbors never saw me since I spent all my time in the house, so I didn't think they would easily know who I was. I knew if they got too close, though, they may be able to pick out similar facial features to my mother, so I wanted to remain as incognito as possible.

Walking down the sidewalk, I heard the bustle of people moving and muffled conversation as I got closer to my house. I crossed the street, making sure I was on the opposite side, so I could see the land from a distance. When I got a few houses away, I saw the few police cars parked on the street and yellow crime scene tape blocking off the lot. The realtor's sign had disappeared, probably figuring there wouldn't be a sale anytime soon. I squinted my eyes, looking at where the body had been last night and saw nothing. Thankfully, it seemed like a neighbor had reported it and the coroner had already taken it away. My stomach dropped a little when I saw little number markers around where I puked last night. I didn't know what kind of evidence that would give investigators, but I knew I couldn't be caught looking at the scene, so I speed walked back to the car.

There was only one place I could go to talk to someone about a dead body, so I started driving to see Rose at the coroner's office. When I got there it was a little past one, so I hoped it was the beginning of her shift. I parked the car and entered the lobby, mentally preparing myself for the bleach and fake lavender smell. When I walked up to the small window in the lobby, this time a woman a few years older than me sat behind the computer texting. Even though the bell rang when I entered, she remained glued to her phone. I laughed a little to myself as I realized Rose really got rid of the last guy that worked here and replaced him with someone doing less work than he was.

I stood behind the glass for a minute, expecting her to open it and see what I was there for, but the receptionist never looked up. Growing impatient, I tapped on the glass, startling her. She set her phone down on the desk and opened the window, being careful with her long, hot pink acrylic nails.

"Can I help you?"

"I need to speak with Rose."

"She's going to want your name." The receptionist picked up the landline and started pressing the numbers.

"Atalanta Capp."

The receptionist closed the window, but I could hear her speaking to Rose, even though it was muffled by the glass. She sat the phone down with a click and slid open the window.

"She'll be here in a moment. Have a seat." The receptionist closed the window again, picked up her phone, and resumed her texting.

I decided I didn't want to sit in the uncomfortable waiting chairs this time, so I moved to the center of the room and waited for a few minutes until I heard the telltale sound of Rose's shoes on the linoleum. She opened up the wooden door to the lobby and beckoned me to follow her through the door.

"I wasn't expecting to see you back here so soon." Rose walked quickly toward her office, and I struggled to keep up with her. "I'm sorry if I seemed rushed today. I need to submit a report about a new body ASAP."

"That's actually what I'm here to talk to you about, if it's the body I'm thinking of." I followed Rose into her office and took a seat in one of her guest chairs.

"What body are you thinking of?" Rose took a seat in her chair and shook her computer mouse to make her monitor come back to life.

"The one found at 226 Briarwood Street. It would have been a bit smelly."

"That one only came in a few hours ago. I processed it earlier." Rose pushed on her glasses, readjusting them on her nose.

"Did that body seem like the others we talked about before?"

"Yes, the woman's mouth was frozen open like the others, except this body was a few days old. The others were dumped only a few hours after they were killed."

It was the work of the Venefica and body dumper, that was for sure, but another Venefica popping up after another one's kill in the same place was odd. Too many times I had run across bodies and undead witch creatures. Once or twice, an odd coincidence. This many times made Tristan's theory of the necromancer and body dumper seem logical. If I could get Bridgette to talk to me, I would have to get her to think about that theory again.

"Do you know where the victim was from?" I asked.

"Not yet. No one has come in to claim her. That's why I need to finish the report so investigators can start comparing her photos to missing people." Rose clicked her mouse a few times.

"Anything else you could tell me?"

"Actually..." She opened a folder on her desk that had a few papers with notes written down. "I found some possible metal shards in a head wound on the back of her head. It looked to be copper, but the investigators would have to test it to make sure."

"But the head wound didn't kill her?"

"No, it was only some trauma to possibly knock her out." Rose closed the folder. "I really need to write this report. Is there any way you can come back later?"

"You're fine. I think I've got all I need." I thought about asking Rose if she knew anything about my vomit piles I saw marked, but I didn't want her to know I was at the crime scene. The less she knew, the better.

Rose scurried me out of her office and gave me a light wave as I made it out of the building back to the car. I sat down in the driver's seat to check my phone. There was still nothing from Bridgette saying she got my note, or any other messages, so I turned the screen off, trying to think about the copper.

Copper wasn't something normal people kept around. A not normal person keeping a Venefica trapped would need a ton of copper to keep the witch at bay. Maybe somehow that translated into the woman dying? It was a long shot, but I wondered if I could check in with hardware stores in the area to see if they sold large batches of copper to anyone. I shrugged, trying to think of any stores that sold copper locally, and remembered the Lake Hardware store was down the street from the herb shop. I decided to stop in there and see if they sold any copper on my way back to the cottage.

I drove past the herb shop, noticing the open sign and considered going in to talk to Tristan and give him an update, but decided against it. Just past the herb shop, the small Lake Hardware store came into view. I had never been in here before, but it looked harmless enough, so I parked the car and made my way inside. A customer was checking out at a small counter in the front, and I wandered through a few aisles that consisted of a pegboard style organization system. I walked past the various hanging tools until I found a small plumbing section where there were pipes. Squatting down, I noticed there were a few copper looking pipes, so I picked one up and looked at it closer. It was completely copper and not just a coated pipe. Something that could possibly be made into a way to contain a Venefica.

The pipe rattled the display as I put it back on the shelf, causing the cashier, a middle-aged man with a salt and pepper beard, to peek around the corner.

"Is there something I can help you with?" The cashier wore a red polo with the Lake Hardware store logo on it and made his way into the aisle with me.

I stood up knowing I didn't have a good cover story. You would think after all the lying I had been doing, I could have come up with something for this exact scenario.

"I was, uh…" My brain searched for a story to sell, "looking at your copper pipes. I'm thinking about doing a project with them."

"What kind of project?" The man smiled.

"A craft project." I needed to steer the conversation elsewhere. "Do a lot of people buy these?" I motioned at the pipes, hoping this would be enough. "I need a lot of them to make what I'm thinking about."

"I'm really not sure. Most of the time my son does the stocking nowadays, and he tells me what to order. Let me ask him." The man beckoned me to accompany him.

I followed, weaving between the aisles and pegboards until we reached the front counter. The man walked to what I assumed was the back and returned a few minutes later.

"So, this girl wants to know more about our copper pipes, and I figured you would know more about them than me," said the man over his shoulder, as he returned to the front of the store.

The person he was talking to emerged, and I found myself staring at Austin wearing a matching company polo, just like his father. The resemblance was undeniable. My mouth dropped open, but I recovered to put on a smile. Austin raised his eyebrows at me and licked his lips.

"Austin will be able to help you. Let him know if you need anything else." The man gave me a smile and walked away to greet another customer entering the store.

"So, you're looking at copper pipes to do a craft project?" Austin approached the counter and leaned across, looking all too eager to hear my answer.

"Mmhmm." My mind stopped working, and I almost forgot to finish my sentence. "I'm making something that needs a lot of copper pipes, and I noticed you didn't have that much. Do you always almost sell out like that? I don't want to get invested and not be able to finish the project, you know?" This was turning into word vomit.

"Right." Austin twirled his hair with his fingers, not convinced by my crafting tale. "Well, those pipes normally don't sell out, but someone bought a bunch a few weeks ago." He moved to the computer and began typing. "But we should have them back in stock in a few days, you know, for your craft project."

Well, that answered my question about someone buying a ton of copper in New Meadows, meaning the Venefica trapper and body dumper lived in town most likely. However, it didn't get me out of this awkward situation.

"Great, that's what I needed to know, so I appreciate the information." I considered turning on my heels and running out of the store but forced myself to give him another smile.

"Come on, be honest with me." He dropped the helpful employee act and was talking to me like when we had coffee before.

"Be honest?"

"You haven't been returning my texts about dinner, but you take the time to show up to my family's hardware store and make a story up about a craft project?" Austin rolled his eyes. "Why are you really here?"

To get information about a crazy body dumping person with a Venefica as a pet? Definitely couldn't say that, but Austin had finally given me a way to lie to get out of this situation.

"Sarah told me your family owned this store, and I wanted to come in person to tell you I was sorry for ignoring you."

Austin raised his brows and seemed to relax.

"I had a really bad depressive episode and did nothing but sleep the past few days. I'm feeling better now, but I knew if I just texted that, you wouldn't believe me." I added a shrug for emphasis, happy with my lie.

"You're right. I probably wouldn't have." Austin sighed. "I meant it when I said I had a really good time getting coffee the other day."

"I did too, which is why I felt so bad once I was feeling better."

"Did you still want to get dinner? I'd be willing to give you another chance." Austin smirked.

I wasn't really sure that I wanted to go out to dinner with him now that I had true feelings for Tristan, but there didn't seem to be a better way to get out of this situation.

"I would really like that if you still want to go out again." I forced myself to blush to make the comment seem more authentic.

"How about tomorrow? I can pick you up on the side of the road again. Unless you finally want to give me your address?"

"No, side of the road is good. Around seven?"

"Seven works for me. I'll also do an inventory check on your crafting supplies before I come." He laughed, causing a more genuine smile to come out of me.

"Thanks for your due diligence. I really appreciate it." I laughed, stepping a few paces back to get ready to leave out the door. "I'll see you tomorrow then."

"I'll be looking forward to it." Austin gave me a prize winning grin that crinkled his eyes.

I waved and made my escape out of the front door.

§

Driving back to the cottage was quiet. I decided not to turn on the radio, so the only sound I listened to was the rumble of the tires on the pavement. I drove through the veil as the sun was starting to set. A few lights were on in the cottage, so I hoped Bridgette would be out of her room this time and actually talk to me. The silent treatment hurt worse than the time she threw me across a clearing when I had broken ribs.

Following the smell of Bridgette's cooking, I walked to the kitchen to find her over the stove, stirring something in her large soup pot.

"Hey," I said, the word coming out more awkward than I wanted it to.

Silence reigned as Bridgette continued stirring the pot, so I took a seat at the dining table. I didn't expect for her to not even acknowledge my presence, so the diss stung a bit.

"Are we still not talking?"

She clanged the spoon on the pot, making any extra liquid remain in and sat the spoon on the counter. "I was focusing my intention on the soup." Bridgette's words were dead pan as if a robot was speaking them.

Silence entered the room again, and I tried to think of my words carefully, not wanting to upset her. Nothing seemed to want to come out the right way, so I stayed silent as she continued stirring. I looked at my nails, preparing to pick at my cuticles when I heard the stove click off.

"What kind of soup did you make?" I looked over at the steaming pot that was lifting off the burner.

"Creamy chicken and mushroom." She carried the soup to a trivet on the counter next to the coffee pot. "It's supposed to help me relax."

"It sounds delicious." I felt stupid talking around the problems hanging in the air.

Bridgette pulled two bowls from the cabinet and grabbed a ladle to spoon soup into them. After dipping, she brought the steaming bowls to the table and sat one down in front of me. The smell of the soup wafting into my nose caused my mouth to water, so I was even more thankful when she handed me a spoon. I took a spoonful of soup, blowing off some of the heat, and immediately felt more relaxed as the food entered my stomach. Bridgette's magic had crafted the soup perfectly. The more bites I took, the further I sank into relaxation.

"So, what did you do today?" asked Bridgette, also clearly relaxed by the soup.

"Some training. Then, I went to talk with Rose to figure out if the body I saw was the same as the others." I blinked fast, coming out of my relaxed stupor.

"What did she say?"

"Same wounds like the others, but this one had copper in a head wound. Rose thought she hit her head on something."

Bridgette nodded as she ate another spoonful of soup.

"So, I went to the local hardware store to see if they sold something that could work, and they happened to be sold out of almost all their copper pipes."

Bridgette raised her eyebrows. "That's an odd coincidence." She pushed her empty bowl toward the center of the table.

"I really don't think it is. I'm almost starting to think Tristan is right. The necromancer and the person with the pet Venefica are the same."

"I don't know. It seems too far-fetched. I mean, what are the odds?"

"Every time a dead body killed by the Venefica shows

up, an undead witch is there. These witches clearly don't have much going on because they aren't brought back correctly, so there's no reason, unless it's intentional that they would always be there. We've got copper head wounds made possibly out of pipe, which could also cage a Venefica."

"Okay, if we follow this line of thinking, did you figure out who bought all the copper? If they were buying at the hardware store in town, they have to be local."

"No, I didn't get a chance to dig that far because apparently Austin's family owns the store."

Bridgette made an 'oh' face, pressing her lips together and feeling the awkwardness I endured.

"But we know they have to live somewhere between New Meadows and Parksdale to be buying the pipe from there. If they wanted to buy a bunch in bulk, they could have just driven to multiple stores in Parksdale," I said.

"True. But they are using Parksdale as a dumping area, so they go there a lot."

All signs pointed to the fact that our necromancer was local. It was just figuring out who.

"I think I may have a way to figure out who brought the pipe if I ask right. I have a date with Austin tomorrow, so I may be able to squeeze some information out."

"A date? What about Tristan?" Bridgette looked at me with confusion.

The relaxation brought on by the soup dissipated. I forgot I hadn't told her yet. I really didn't want her to be angry with me again. Things had seemed normal for a few minutes, and I enjoyed sinking back into old times.

"Please don't be mad," I said, putting on my best pleading look.

The confusion wiped away from Bridgette's face, and she put on a deadpan mask.

"I haven't told Tristan about my soul yet. I tried, but I chickened out." Shame forced my cheeks to redden.

"Why?"

"Because Sarah was there, and they looked happy, and I couldn't hurt her after what happened at the park. If I told Tristan, he would be faced with a weird choice that would hurt someone. I would rather be the one who's hurt. It's what I deserve."

Compassion flickered in Bridgette's eyes, and she softened. "But you love him, don't you?"

"Yes. I really do, but I'm too late. And it's not fair for me to mess everything up because I got my soul back."

"Don't you think he has the right to know, though?"

Yes, he did. I knew he would want to know, but I didn't want to make things more challenging between us. If he hadn't moved on, things would have been different, but he had Sarah, who was a good person.

"He deserves a chance to be happy with someone who's normal. Someone that can make him forget about this world I'm stuck in. If I don't tell him, he has a chance." I swallowed, feeling the lump form in my throat.

"He deserves to know. How long do you really think you can keep this from him?" She pierced me with a look of disappointment at my continued lying game I was playing with everyone.

"I don't know. I haven't figured that out yet."

We were both silent, and I swallowed another throat

lump, trying to keep myself together. I made my choice to not tell him, and it was something I needed to stick by. I was sure he would find out eventually, but by then, he would be in love with Sarah and it wouldn't cause him as much distress. Then, it would just be missed timing.

"So, I'm going to go on the date with Austin to see if I can figure out who bought all of the pipe. Then, we can pay them a visit and make sure they aren't hiding a Venefica in their spare bedroom." I tried to make it lighthearted, but it came out sad and flat.

"Atalanta." Bridgette reached across the table and grabbed my hand. "You deserve a chance at a happy ending and love. I don't know why you sell yourself so short." She gave it a squeeze and let my hand go before standing up to gather our soup bowls.

I settled with her statement, not entirely sure if I believed her before swallowing a final lump in my throat.

CHAPTER EIGHTEEN

THE ICY WIND WHIPPED around me and made the trees sway in the breeze as I stood on the side of the road, waiting for Austin to pick me up. The wind was blowing in a fall storm that I knew was going to be cold and messy, so I hoped Austin would be here before the rain hit. I had no idea where he planned on taking me for dinner. For some reason, I didn't think to ask when we were talking yesterday, so I hoped my jeans and a blue long sleeve shirt from Bridgette's closet would be fancy enough. I bundled my black fleece jacket around me, hoping to shield my body from the wind chill as Austin's car came into view. He slowed down as he got closer, not wanting to kick up dust in my face, and stopped in front of me. I raced into the car, thankful to be out of the chilly air. Austin put on his famous grin as he turned the heat up a little more for me.

"I really could have picked you up from your house. It would have been no problem." He pulled away from the curb and started driving in the opposite direction from town.

"It's fine. I would hate for you to mess up your car driving down that road." I held my hands over the air vent, letting the heat defrost them. "Where are we going tonight?"

"I was actually thinking about driving to an Italian restaurant in Parksdale. Is that okay with you?"

I swallowed before coming up with a response. I hadn't planned on going that far. Instead, I was hoping for a quick sit down dinner where I could ask Austin about the copper and be back in a few hours. Going all the way to Parksdale meant I was going to be stuck with an extended drive and have to sit through dinner.

"It sounds fun! I've never been to an Italian restaurant before." I grinned to sell the line.

"Really?" Austin raised his eyebrows before refocusing on the road.

I forgot how sheltered I was again. My upbringing was strange, but I hadn't thought twice about exposing myself with Austin because when I said things like that to Tristan, he never reacted to my strangeness.

"Yeah. My mom was more of a meat and potatoes kind of person." Not entirely true, but she didn't make spaghetti often when I lived at home.

Austin nodded, accepting my response before putting us on the main road to Parksdale.

"Does your family have Italian a lot?" It sounded dumb once I asked it, but I didn't have a better question.

Austin laughed, diffusing the awkwardness as rain began falling on the windshield.

"We actually used to go to the restaurant I'm taking you to all the time. We have another store in Parksdale, so the family is always around." He turned on the windshield wipers, clearing the glass.

"Oh, cool. I never realized you had multiple stores."

"Only the two. I float between both since my dad is stepping back. I think he's planning for me to manage the business so he can retire."

"Is that what you want?"

"I don't know. I always thought I wouldn't have to decide because Lorelei was planning on becoming a publicist, so I knew we would move away. I wasn't going to have to make an active decision."

I nodded, understanding all too well the issues that came with familial duty and legacy.

"But now?" I asked, as I watched a raindrop rush down the car window.

"Now, I'm single and expected to be the man that runs the family business." Austin sighed.

"You know, you never mentioned the business when we were having coffee before. Why?"

"It's not as important to me as you think. Plus, I was trying to learn more about you."

I gave a weak smile, trying to lighten the mood, but we ended up riding a bit in silence until the Parksdale city limits sign came into view. The city lights were shining bright as the sun set, looking like a kaleidoscope through the raindrops that continued to fall. Austin drove us into the downtown area close to the club, but parked closer to where I had my encounter with the Ventus. Sharing one umbrella, we walked to a back alley one over from where I found the body until Austin showed me into a hole in the wall restaurant.

Bella Mia was the cutest Italian restaurant I had been in, not that I had much to compare it to. White and red cliche tablecloths covered the circle tables scattered throughout the place. Dimmed overhead lights allowed the lit pillar candles at the center of the tables to bathe patrons in a warm glow. Paintings that I assumed were meant to represent the Italian countryside lined the walls, making a quintessential Italian place for a Southern audience. I knew this probably wasn't what a restaurant in Italy truly looked like, but at least it felt homey.

Austin spoke with the hostess like they were old friends, and a server gave him a light wave as we were seated at the most secluded table. A vase held a few red roses at the end of the table closest to the wall. Instead of the pillar candles on the other tables, our table had a few tea lights in the center. The attempted romantic atmosphere wafted off the table, but all I could focus on was the lack of light. The darkest corner for privacy made reading the menu hard. I wondered how embarrassing it would be for me to use my phone flashlight.

"What should I get?" I asked, choosing to not rely on the flashlight.

"You would probably like the chicken alfredo. It's a classic, and they make the sauce from scratch." He laid his menu down on the table as a warm basket of breadsticks appeared.

A thin brunette server, not much older than us, wearing all

black appeared with a ticket pad in hand. The server took our order, leaving me and Austin alone until the food was ready. I took a sip of water out of a fancy goblet glass, needing the spare moment to process what was happening. The coffee shop had been easy. I didn't have my soul back and had no genuine feelings for anyone. I knew I could date if I wanted to, even if it didn't become anything. However, this encounter felt high risk because of all the things I knew I felt. It was harder to play with someone's heart when you knew what it felt like for yours to break.

"So, how long has your family owned the hardware stores?" I set my glass back on the table.

"Uh, my dad bought them when he was in his late twenties, so a little while. We've had them my whole life I think." Austin took a breadstick from the basket and broke a small piece off.

I nodded, floundering at the conversation.

"What do you like to do for fun, you know when you're not cataloging creatures?" Austin ate another piece of breadstick.

"I really don't know. I don't have a lot of time outside of that." I stopped, trying to think of what I used to enjoy before becoming a Captrix consumed my life. "I used to enjoy making scrapbooks. Artsy kinda stuff."

I smiled, remembering my old get out of town scrapbook lost in the fire. I hadn't thought about creating another one lately, but I missed sourcing the pictures to make a new world.

"I'm into artsy kinda stuff too. But I like building things with stuff around the hardware store." Austin finished devouring the breadstick. "That's why I was extra curious about your art project."

He gazed at me, piercing my entire body with eyes. I shifted in my seat as if it would help me escape his intense stare.

"Oh, right. Yeah, just trying to branch out." I sounded ridiculous, but it was a good segue into me asking more about the pipes. "Did you look into the inventory for that?"

"I did. It looks like we will have another shipment at the end of the week. Should be more than enough for your art project." Austin made air quotes on art project.

I choked out a laugh that must have sounded awkward based on Austin's quizzical expression. But this was my chance, so I pushed onward, trying to forget my weirdness.

"Did you ever see who bought it all?"

"Not really." He moved to the edge of his seat. "Some guy around town, I think. Probably a tradesman."

I deflated, knowing this was the best answer to my question I was going to get. The date being for information was a complete bust. I grabbed one of the straws left by the server for our drinks and added it to my drink so I could fidget with the straw wrapper. Ripping up the white paper soothed me and helped me forget I was stuck in another awkward silence.

Austin reached his hand across the table, holding the hand doing most of the tearing. I stopped and looked up at his face of concern.

"Are you sure you're having a good time? I'm getting a vibe." He held my hand too tight until I pulled it away.

"I'm not sure if you want me to be honest." I placed both of my hands in my lap to protect them from being grabbed again. "I thought I could do this, and I wanted to try, but I'm still in love with Tristan. And I don't know if I'm capable of moving on right now."

It felt good to be honest, something I hadn't done much

of lately. My body seemed more relaxed, relieved to push off something holding me down. Austin tightened his jaw and pulled his hand back to him, scrunching it into a fist.

"I've already hurt someone before by not being honest and–" The server brought out steaming bowls of pasta, forcing me to stop my thought.

She added a bit of cheese on top of our two orders of chicken alfredo before setting the food in front of us. My stomach rumbled, happy to see fresh food, but I felt dirty eating it now. Austin lifted his fork and started chowing down, so I followed suit, slower, still trying to gauge his reaction. When we were halfway through our meal, and after the server stopped by to refill our drinks, I tried finishing my sentence.

"Austin, I just don't want to make the same mistake again. And I don't want to lead you on or give you false hope." I sat my fork down with a little over half of my pasta left, not able to stomach another bite.

He looked annoyed but unclenched his jaw. A few more bites went into his mouth while he contemplated my confession.

"I'm glad you were honest with me. Maybe I was trying to move on too fast." He smiled, but it appeared forced at the edges.

My phone vibrated in my pocket, and I pulled it out to look at the screen. Sarah's name splashed across with a call. I declined it and sat my phone face up on the table.

"What was that?" asked Austin, sliding his empty plate to the table edge.

"Sarah. I'm not sure what she wants, so I'll call her back later."

The server stopped by at the table again, laying down the check and taking our plates away. Austin snatched the receipt before I had the chance to and laid down cash on top. My phone lit up with a text from Sarah showing SOS and police siren emojis. I tilted my head, wondering what her problem could be as my phone vibrated again with a call from her. I sighed and answered the call.

"Atalanta! We have a problem," said Sarah, panicking on the other end of the line. "I need you." She gasped as she lost her breath from speaking too fast.

"Slow down." I straightened in my chair. "What's going on?"

"I can't find Tristan. He's not answering my calls or texts. Has he talked to you?"

"Not since the night I came by." I met Austin's eyes as he studied me. "Are you sure you can't get a hold of him?"

"I've been trying for hours." Sarah's voice cracked as she choked back a sob. "I swear I'm not overreacting. He's never dropped off like this."

"What's going on?" Austin handed the check to the server as he waited for me to fill him in.

I covered the phone speaker with my hand. "Sarah says Tristan's missing. Have you heard from him?"

"Are you with Austin? Has he heard from him?"

I removed my hand from the phone since it wasn't stopping Sarah from hearing me.

"Not since yesterday, I think." Austin shrugged. "Are you sure she's not overreacting?

I returned the shrug to him.

"He hasn't talked to him, either," I said into the phone.

"He really is missing then. I don't know what I'm going to do." Sarah sniffled as her pitch got higher.

"How about I stop by the apartment, and we can check

in on him?" I looked at Austin with pleading eyes, hoping he wouldn't mind a detour home for his friend.

He nodded back at me and rose from the table. I followed behind him out of the restaurant with my cell phone stuck to my ear, grateful the rain had stopped for now.

"That would make me feel better. I feel crazy right now." Sarah composed herself and let out a deep breath. "I'll see you there in a bit?"

"Yeah, I'll get Austin to drop me off, and you can take me home."

We said our goodbyes, and I hopped in Austin's car.

"Thanks for doing this. I know it hasn't been the most ideal date." I cringed at my own words.

"Nah, it's fine. It's strange for him to not answer, but I doubt he's missing." Austin backed out of the parking lot and put us on the road to New Meadows.

I swiped at my phone and hit the number to call Tristan, leaving the audio on speaker phone. Sarah could have been worrying for no reason, so I had to check for myself to make sure Tristan wasn't ignoring her. He never missed a call from me if he could avoid it, so I hoped our special relationship would come in clutch this time as well to solve this issue.

The call rang twice before heading to voicemail, causing my heart to sink as I ended the call. Maybe Sarah was right.

CHAPTER NINETEEN

The ride to Tristan's apartment was awkward, but somewhat bearable. Austin understood the sense of urgency in the car, so he took turns running twenty over the speed limit and slowing down when he thought a cop would be nearby.

I was proud of myself for admitting the truth rather than playing out the charade of a romantic relationship. I knew who my heart wanted, even if I was determined to not tell Tristan the truth about my soul for now. Even though I did the right thing in this incident, I couldn't shake off the sense that Austin felt different.

As he drove, he held his hands hard on the steering wheel, turning his knuckles white. A complete 180 from the cool, collected driver he was before. He also seemed to be calculating something as his eyes remained glued to the road. I was an invisible being in the car to him for now.

After a long drive of radio music being the only thing heard in the car, he made the turn into the back alley leading up to Tristan's apartment. Sarah stood at the bottom of the stairs, pacing in an oversized black hoodie I recognized as Tristan's over dark jeans. I mentally shrugged off the pain I felt seeing her wearing something of his again. Austin put the car in park and left the engine running.

"Do you want to come inside and help?" I unbuckled my seatbelt.

"No, I think I'll drive around for a bit. See if I spot his car or something." He pressed the unlock button. "Can Sarah take you home?"

"I'm sure." I opened the car door, taking my cue and exiting, but stopped to lean my head back in. "Thanks for dinner. I'll let you know if we have any updates."

"Don't mention it." Austin gripped the steering wheel harder as I closed the car door.

He backed out of the alley while I approached Sarah, who stopped pacing long enough to look at me and follow me up the stairs to the apartment door. When we reached the top, I stood off to the side, waiting for Sarah to open the door, but she didn't move.

"You don't have a key?" I watched her, expecting her to rummage through the purse hanging on her left shoulder.

"No, I thought you did." Sarah looked down at her shoes.

"Oh." She was right. I did have a key, but I hadn't brought it with me on my date.

I looked around the door until I spotted a loose brick, barely sticking out an inch. Grabbing it with the tips of my fingers and nails, I pulled the brick out a smidge until I got a better grip.

Sarah watched with interest as I shimmied the brick all the way out, revealing a key duct-taped to the brick behind the loose one. I reached my hand in the hole and unlocked the door with the spare key, before replacing it behind the loose brick.

Sarah followed me inside, stunned at the secret hiding spot. Her not knowing there was a spare key intrigued me, and I wondered why Tristan hadn't shared that with her when she seemed to be over here all the time.

"Tristan? Are you here?" I yelled, closing the door behind me.

We waited at the door for a beat, but no response came. Sarah ran to Tristan's bedroom while I walked toward the kitchen. Nothing was disturbed, and it looked as normal as I had ever seen it. A pizza box sat next to the trash can and a few dishes remained in the sink. I took a look at them, deciding they were from eating dinner the night before. Walking through the rest of the kitchen, I tried to look for any signs of breakfast or lunch but found none. The fridge was almost empty, but Tristan could have gone out, so it wasn't much of a clue.

"His bed doesn't even look like he slept in it last night." Sarah returned from the bedroom, panting from her run.

"When's the last time you heard from him?" I closed the fridge door and spun around to face her.

"Last night." Sarah pulled out her phone, scrolling through text messages. "Around eight."

I listened to my intuition as I gazed around the kitchen and living room. Everything was perfectly in place with no signs of any fight. If something happened to Tristan, it wasn't inside this apartment.

"I'm not saying you're wrong, but nothing seems off. Just like he hasn't been here all day." I shrugged.

In my gut, I knew something was amiss since he didn't answer my call, but there wasn't anything here to justify that feeling.

"He wouldn't disappear and not talk to anyone like this." Sarah picked at her cuticles and stared at the ground. "At least, I didn't think so."

"Did anything happen when you talked to him last?"

"We had a fight." Sarah let go of her cuticles and huffed in frustration.

"A fight? About what?"

"You."

It felt like a ton of bricks fell onto my body as I found myself at a loss for words. How was I supposed to ask about a fight they had about me? Sarah rolled her eyes at my lack of speech.

"I got mad after you visited. I accused him of putting you over our relationship, and he didn't like it. So, we've been distant." Sarah's face contorted in a mix of sadness and anger. "But I never thought he would ghost me."

My heart sank. The whole reason I avoided telling Tristan about my soul was because I thought I was doing him a favor, but again, I found myself ruining his life and a new relationship. I assumed I was giving Sarah a fair shot at happiness with him after almost getting her killed, but my efforts were futile. What more could I give up to make amends for the things I caused?

"I'm sorry. I didn't mean to get in the way if I have been," I said.

"It's not that. It's fine." Sarah ran her fingers through her hair. "I'm probably being clingy."

"No, you're right. Tristan isn't the kind to ghost. We'll figure out what's up, and when we do–" My heart cringed at what I decided to say. "I will give him some more space, so I'm not in the way."

I couldn't look at her out of fear I would give myself away. I didn't know how well she could read me, but something had changed that caused her to see me as more of a threat. There was no way Sarah could know I had my soul back when Bridgette was the only one I told.

"You don't have to do that. I know you have a close relationship."

"No, I can. Don't worry about it." I kept my voice so cool and nonchalant I almost believed myself. "Why don't we go talk to Bridgette and see what she thinks?"

I took one last look around to make sure I hadn't missed anything. Sarah nodded, and we left the apartment, taking extra care to lock the door behind us.

$

One cup of tea later, since Bridgette denied us coffee, Sarah, Bridgette, and I gathered around the kitchen table. Sarah had filled Bridgette in on her story, glazing over the details of her and Tristan's argument. I added in the idea that he hadn't been in the apartment since last night. Bridgette took a long sip of her tea, pondering our story.

"I agree with you. It's strange behavior based on what I know, but you did have a fight. Emotions run high and can make people weird." Bridgette sat her empty cup down, allowing her adult wisdom time to penetrate.

Sarah looked annoyed by Bridgette's idea, but I understood

where she was coming from. However, things seemed to be a bit more than a lover's quarrel.

"He's not responding to me, either," I said. "I've tried calling him a few times."

Bridgette stood up, grabbed her cellphone off the kitchen counter, and made a call on speaker phone. The call rang twice before Tristan's voicemail came on, and she ended the call.

"Okay, so he isn't responding to anyone, including me." Concern washed over Bridgette's face.

"It's weird whether we had a fight or not," said Sarah.

"You're right, but we still don't know if something happened or if he's just pissed off." Bridgette sat back down, this time sitting her phone on the table.

"And we have no leads to what happened," I said.

"What if witches took him?" Sarah crossed her arms.

Bridgette looked at me, trying to read my face to see if I believed that was an option.

"I didn't feel anything or notice any witch creature signs. It only looked like he left."

"Outside?"

"Nothing there, either."

"This is insane. Something is off here, and you know it." Sarah stood, pacing the kitchen.

I couldn't decide if she really thought something fishy was going on or if she still felt guilty about their argument. Either way, she felt so passionate about Tristan being gone in a way that I wondered if I should be as worried too.

"Austin didn't seem super concerned when I told him. Strange, but not panicked." I watched Sarah stop pacing and turn to look at me with disgust.

"And why would he know anything about this?"

"I thought they were friends? You even asked me to ask him?"

Sarah ran her tongue over her teeth and sighed before responding. "Yeah, they were best friends before Austin started dating Lorelei and became obsessed with her and dropped everyone. They were just reconnecting. The first time they've really hung out lately was at the party. You know, the one where Tristan caught you kissing him?"

My eyes widened at the new realization. It explained a bit more about Tristan's reaction, but this whole time Austin had acted like they had been close. My face flushed as I gave Sarah a small nod while Bridgette looked back and forth between us, watching the verbal match.

"Austin used their friendship so he could hang out with Morgana. To be honest, at some point, I figured they were banging behind Tristan's back." Sarah looked nauseous.

Who had I been hanging out with? I felt so stupid.

"Why didn't you tell me this before? You said he was fine!" A bit of fury rose in my chest.

"Of course I did! I wanted you to be busy!" Sarah's anger faltered a bit. "I needed you to have someone other than Tristan."

Understanding didn't dampen the rage brewing inside, so I closed my eyes to give myself a moment before responding.

"I'm sorry you're so insecure with your relationship that you decided to set me up with a problematic dude. And then lied to me about it."

Sarah's cheeks flared, and her normally pale skin turned tomato red.

"How do you expect me to be secure when I see the way you look at each other?" This time she didn't falter. Only the pain of feeling like the wrong girl screeched out.

"Enough! This isn't helping." Bridgette held her hands up in the air, signaling us both to stop.

Sarah and I peeled our eyes away from each other to look at Bridgette. She lowered her hands to the table.

"Tell me what else we know about Austin." Bridgette's voice was calm, causing a dramatic break compared to the screaming match before.

"His family owns two hardware shops. One sold the copper pipe." I took a moment to think. "He and his girlfriend broke up a little bit ago because they couldn't handle long distance."

"Anything else?"

"His ex, Lorelei, was kinda strange. We used to be friends when we first started high school, but she changed. She started mumbling to herself and became jumpy." Sarah shrugged. "It's hard to explain."

"Did she also visit Morgana?" said Bridgette. She seemed far off as if she was pondering an idea that she wasn't ready to say.

"Maybe? A lot before we graduated. She liked the products and wanted to help her with advertising, I think." Sarah returned to pacing with frustration clear on her face. "What does Lorelei have to do with anything?"

I perked up at that question, ready to hear Bridgette's response. I hadn't been following her line of questioning. With this question, though, she would be forced to reveal what she had been contemplating.

"Is it possible she could have been a witch?" Bridgette

stared at Sarah, searching for her initial reaction.

Sarah and I both looked at Bridgette with shock. The inquiry was enough to make Sarah freeze her pacing again.

"I don't know. I never really thought about it." Sarah rubbed her forehead.

"Did her skin shimmer or glow?" I asked.

"Maybe? She always wore a cardigan, but her face was just radiant, like a good skincare routine. You know?"

I didn't know since my skincare routine has been nonexistent the past few months, but I understood what she meant.

"What if she was a Domum?" I looked at Bridgette.

"Then, it's possible Morgana was helping her stay in control. The mumbling could have been her talking to her power if she was using too much."

"Which means Austin knows a lot more about witches than he's letting on." I thought back to when I told him about my family cataloging creatures for science and how he didn't flinch. "He knows what I am."

This realization made me stand up from the table to breathe. I refused to get nauseous or let this impact me in any way. Yet, I could feel the droplets of sweat forming on my forehead as my hair stood up on my arms. The feeling of someone knowing more about you than you thought was overwhelming and intrusive. I hoped I kept all my cards close to my chest with Austin, but I was merely standing there naked as he already knew what he wanted.

"Atalanta?" Sarah reached out to touch me but stopped and drew her hand back in.

I blinked a few times, trying to get Austin's face out of my head. His smile at the coffee shop, the genuine interest he had in my life. The claims of wanting to be more than friends. I wanted to laugh at the idea that a guy had once again played me, but instead, I felt disgusted. I couldn't even blame my stupidity on a love potion this time. Pathetic.

"Something feels off about Austin. I don't know if he's our necromancer or what, but I feel like he's connected somehow." I took a glance at the cooling kettle on the stove, considering if another cup of tea would calm my nerves.

"What does this have to do with Tristan missing? I'm sure he would know if Austin was a witch or—" Sarah searched Bridgette for the correct term. "Warlock creature?"

"Men rarely have powers, and if they do, it's very basic Domum stuff. Like how Tristan has a talent for potion making. There's no way he could raise witches from the dead."

"I don't know if Austin has to do with Tristan missing or not, but he's now a person of interest in what's been going on. Whether he has the power or not," I said. "For all, we know he could have sold the copper pipe to the person doing all this."

"Fine, but Tristan is what I'm worried about right now," said Sarah.

"Bridgette, is there any way we can track him?" I returned to the table to sit down next to her.

"I could try something. Not for too long, though, because it takes a lot of power." Bridgette stood up and left the kitchen, returning with a book in hand. "I tried it once for myself, but I couldn't get it to work because a witch blocked me."

She flipped to the right page and sat it in front of me. Sarah walked over, stopping behind me to peek over my shoulder.

I skimmed the title and contents of the spell, realizing it was a spell to find a lost lover. It required a couple with a strong connection to allow love to seek them out for you, revealing their location in a bowl of water.

Sarah's eyes widened, and she took the seat next to me to read the spell requirements again. Bridgette rummaged through her cabinets to grab a large bowl and filled up the warm tea kettle with cold water from the sink. She sat them both on her end of the table before acquiring the correct herbs from her shelves. With a handful of glass jars with masking tape labels, Bridgette sat back down, pulling the book away from Sarah and me to read the spell again for herself.

"So, who wants to do the chanting?" Bridgette unscrewed the lid off a jar of dried rose petals, stealing a glance at me before looking at Sarah.

"What are the requirements?" Sarah fidgeted with her hands, trying hard to not pick at them.

"You need a strong mutual love connection and a need to find them." Bridgette unscrewed the rest of the lids off her herbs and took a deep breath to center herself.

"I mean, I can try. We've been dating for a few weeks." Sarah looked over at me. "It wouldn't work for Atlanta since she can't love, right?"

Bridgette's face tightened as she chose not to reveal my truth. I nodded, hoping the spell would work for Sarah, so I wouldn't have to be in the equation.

"Let's try it then, shall we?" Bridgette stared at me, wanting me to volunteer for the spell.

I remained silent, content with letting Sarah try. Bridgette grabbed her kettle, pouring the water in the bowl. She mumbled gratitude for the ingredient as she set her intentions. Then, one by one, she sprinkled in fuzzy weed, rosemary, and caraway before finishing with some rose petals. The herbs made a dirty pinkish water in the bowl, but Bridgette nodded at it, content with her spellwork.

"You're going to put both hands on the side of the bowl and think about all the positive memories you have with Tristan and how you feel about him. Then, I will tell you the chant to repeat. Okay?"

Sarah nodded, scooting closer and reaching her arms across me to touch the bowl. She closed her eyes, concentrating, before a smile spread across her face.

"Now think about how much you need to find him. When you have the intention in your head, repeat after me."

Sarah nodded again, losing her loving smile. She circled her fingers around the smooth edge of the bowl as she waited for her line.

"I need you to complete me," said Bridgette.

Sarah hesitated, but eventually repeated the line back. "I need you to complete me."

"Please show me where you are."

Sarah repeated Bridgette again, and I watched the water turn pinker and make small bubbles.

"Again, until you feel like you should stop." Bridgette watched the bowl, waiting for something else to happen.

She squirmed in her seat, but Sarah repeated the chant over and over. Bridgette shook her head as the bubbles in the bowl dissipated and the water turned from rose pink to black.

Sarah's eyes snapped open, and she pulled her hands back as if the bowl bit her. She flipped her palms up, and I noticed they were red as if she was holding a hot bowl of water, not whatever room temperature the bowl was supposed to be.

"I messed it up, didn't I?" Sarah looked up from her hands, disappointment painted across her face.

"No, you did your best." Bridgette stood, taking the bowl from her to the sink to throw away the spoiled spell.

"Can I try it?" I asked, wishing I could disappear from the room altogether.

Sarah's eyes darted from me to Bridgette, trying to figure out what was going on.

"I don't know if I can do it again." Bridgette rinsed out the bowl and rubbed her arms to calm the chill bumps that had formed during the spellwork.

"Please," said Sarah quietly, swallowing a lump in her throat. "We have to make sure he's okay."

Bridgette stared at her with a pained expression before bringing the clean bowl back and refilling the kettle. She didn't even ask if I could do this, probably because she already knew it was possible. Herbs dropped into a fresh bowl of water, followed by rose petals that returned the water to a light pink.

"Same method and chant." Bridgette slid the bowl to my hands. "Let me know if you need to be guided through."

I nodded, wrapping my hands around the bowl, taking the smooth surface in with my fingertips. Closing my eyes, I tried to focus on the good memories I had with Tristan. I sifted through them all, trying to find one that encapsulated our love for one another, but found myself stuck on our encounter the other night on the porch.

The blanket draped over our legs and how I could feel the warmth radiating off Tristan as I leaned in closer. Then, it was a friendly gesture, but in my returned soul, I felt the urge to snuggle closer and to become a part of him. He projected the safety I needed when I remained lost in the world. Tristan rubbed his hand along my spine, trying to soothe my bad dream as I laid my head on his shoulder, caving into the need to feel okay. Even though it didn't happen this way last time, in my memory, I imagined him giving me a soft kiss on the forehead as I fell asleep in his arms. Encompassed by this feeling of love and security, I knew I meant the chant I needed to say.

"I need you to complete me." The bowl warmed beneath my palms.

I needed to find Tristan. I needed him to feel not so broken. My soul needed him to complete me.

"Please show me where you are." Emotion bubbled up in my body as I desired Tristan like a drink of water on a hot, muggy day. "I need you to complete me. Show me where you are."

I dropped the please, not wishing to be polite anymore. I needed him to tell me where he was. Sarah gasped, but I refused to open my eyes and lose my focus.

"I need you to complete me. Please show me where you are, Tristan." This time on the chant, I felt my need to conjure tears. I was distraught that he was gone and I couldn't find him. I wasn't complete. I was broken without him.

My body lurched over the bowl and a few of my tears fell in. I opened my eyes without thinking about it and saw a pink and lavender gradient coloring the water in the bowl. Little bubbles scattered themself around, but they popped, rippling into an image of a paved road.

"Say the chant again." Bridgette leaned over to look at the contents.

"I need you to complete me. Please show me where you are," I repeated, feeling the bowl get dangerously hot on my palms.

The water rippled again, showing a white colonial style house with a red door. Sarah leaned in closer to see the images appearing in the water. My phone vibrated in my pocket, breaking my concentration. The image began breaking apart as Bridgette grabbed the bowl with her hands, trying to use her own power to stabilize the spell. The water rippled again, trying to show another image, but Bridgette jumped back, falling out of her chair onto the floor. I removed my hands and reached to grab her, causing the contents to turn black as the spell fizzled out.

"Are you okay?" I got out of my chair, followed by Sarah, and we both went to the floor for Bridgette.

Bridgette curled into a ball as I noticed all the hair on her arms standing up. I heard her mumbling to a voice I couldn't hear as she tried to get a hold of her body. I placed a protective hand over Sarah, forcing her to scoot backwards on the floor.

"Bridgette?" I scooted myself back a bit, knowing what she was trying to keep at bay.

She rolled herself onto her back and looked up at the ceiling. I saw the little tinges of black crowding her eyes, but they dissipated as Bridgette got more under control.

"I shouldn't have tried to contain the spell. I'm okay." Bridgette drew in a deep breath before scratching at her arms. "At least, I think I am."

The same feeling of guilt I seemed to always carry with me these days moved over me again. If I had done the spell first instead of playing a charade with Sarah, Bridgette wouldn't have had to push herself so far. If I told Bridgette I was sorry now, then I would have no choice but to tell Sarah the truth if she didn't already realize.

I turned to look at Sarah, studying her face. She was trying to keep it serene, but something in her eyes told me she knew she was the other girl now. If I was her, I knew this would hurt me more than what transpired in the park, but she was so resilient to continue to push forward no matter what, because she needed Tristan to be safe. If I told her I was sorry now, it would confirm the truth she was processing in her mind.

So, I remained frozen, unsure of what to do as Bridgette leaned up enough to sit on the floor. She scooted herself backwards to lean up on the fridge as she heaved breaths like she just finished a marathon. My phone vibrated in my back pocket again, forcing me to pull it out to check the caller. Austin's name glowed on the screen.

"It's Austin. Should I answer it?"

"Might as well," said Sarah, keeping an eye roll at bay.

Pausing, I weighed my options. I really didn't want to deal with Austin right now, especially at this moment, but what if he had information about Tristan? I didn't think he would call this soon otherwise. Closing my eyes, I swiped the screen to answer the call and lifted the phone to my ear.

"Hey. I wanted to let you know Tristan just showed up at my house in case you were still out looking for him."

"Oh, thank God." Immediate relief washed over me. "Is

he okay?"

Sarah slid closer to listen to Austin's response. I pulled the phone down and put it on speaker phone, so she could hear better.

"A little roughed up like he got in a fight, but I think he's alright."

My stomach clenched. What if Tristan had gotten in a fight with witch creatures and I wasn't there to help him? Sarah tensed next to me, and I knew she had to be thinking the same thing.

"I'm here with Sarah. We can come check on him if you don't mind," I said, trying to keep the fear overwhelming me out of my voice.

"Can you come alone? Apparently, him and Sarah had a fight?"

Sarah's face grimaced as her tiny argument came back to bite her in the butt once again.

"He can't still be mad about that, right?" It was a weak line, but also my last ditch effort to mend that argument.

"I don't know what he's mad about. He's just been going on about boundaries and stuff. He's not making sense. Maybe he hit his head?"

I listened closely for Tristan's voice in the background, hoping I could discern something apart from what Austin was saying.

"Even better of a reason for me to let Sarah know, so we can both come over. It sounds like something's off."

"He's only asking for you," said Austin in a harsh tone.

Sarah flinched, backing away from me as if I been the one to slap her across the face.

"I still have to let her know what is going on. She's his girlfriend, not me."

I added the last part as an olive branch, but instead of taking it, Sarah gave me a look so fierce that I knew she was burning the peace offering in her mind.

"Do what you gotta do, but don't bring her here." The irritation rose in Austin's voice.

"Can I just talk to Tristan? I want to make sure he doesn't want her to come."

"He's unavailable right now. Are you coming or what? I need to know how long to keep him here."

I heard a groan on the line, but I couldn't make out if it was Tristan or not. The groan got louder as the sounds of Austin shifting items infiltrated the call. Everyone in the kitchen sat up straight, knowing the sounds we were hearing were suspicious, including Bridgette, who was still using the fridge for help. Sarah waved her hand in front of my face and mouthed "just go." I pleaded with her using my eyes. I really didn't want to go in there alone or further complicate the number of delicate situations I was in. Sarah looked at me again with the same fire from before, so I decided to do what she wanted.

"I'll be there in a few. Text me your address." I hung up the phone before Austin could make any more requests.

CHAPTER TWENTY

We all sat there in silence as the phone became a brick in my hand. The weight of the situation wasn't lost on me. Tristan was injured and probably with an accomplice of the necromancer we've been looking for the whole time. I also possibly single-handedly crushed his current relationship by proving I loved him with a spell.

I stood up, breaking the frozen state everyone sat in, and walked over to Bridgette to help her off the floor. She took my hands, relying on my strength to stand up. For a brief time, I thought maybe she could be my backup to Austin's house, but her weakened state proved she didn't need to push herself any further. A transforming Domum was the last thing I needed on my plate with all the things I was already juggling.

Sarah stood up as well while I gathered Bridgette, and they

followed me to the living room, where I needed to rifle through my chest. I leaned down to open the chest, deciding this was a case for the full huntress outfit, but with minimal weaponry. Maybe a leather corset would come off as a sexy come on rather than alert Austin. But I also had no idea how much he knew about me.

"You're not really going to go alone, right?" asked Bridgette, taking a seat in her recliner.

"I'm not sure what other choice I have." I piled my huntress clothes next to the chest before taking out my lucky penny and mixed metal dagger.

"We'll ignore his request and all go together." Sarah huffed and crossed her arms, remaining in the living room opening.

"Because that's a good idea." I slammed the chest lid before wincing at the fact that what I said came out too sharp.

I passed Sarah in the door jamb, moving to the bathroom to change into my huntress outfit. When I returned, they were discussing our situation next to the recliner in hushed whispers.

"Would y'all like to share?" I tucked my dagger into the pancake holster in the small of my back.

They turned to look at my entrance and quieted their side conversation. Bridgette wore a look of concern, while Sarah appeared annoyed.

"I don't think it's a good idea for you to go alone," said Bridgette.

"What other choice do I have?" It sounded harsh, but I was at a loss for anything nicer to say. "You can't fight right now, and I'm not risking a transformation."

"I can go with you. We can tell Austin I wouldn't let you go without me," said Sarah.

"We don't know what kind of condition Tristan is in or what sort of trap this is. You could get hurt again." I didn't add the fact I didn't want to see that happen again or be responsible. Seeing Sarah almost die once was enough for me.

"Exactly, this is a trap. You shouldn't go," said Bridgette, infusing her tone with authority.

"But it's Tristan. I can't not go try and save him." I thought about all the times Tristan had been there for me on the phone and how he killed his own mother to save my life. "If it was me, he wouldn't hesitate."

Sarah turned her head like I slapped her, and I regretted not filtering the words before I said them.

"He still wouldn't expect you to go on a suicide mission. You can't do this alone," said Sarah through gritted teeth.

"What would you have me do? Austin can't see you. He's too volatile to test his boundaries right now."

"She is right about that," said Bridgette.

Sarah pondered her idea until she settled on the one she thought was the best.

"You can go in the house alone, but Bridgette and I will wait in the wings in case you need backup. If you do, we'll storm in and try to distract Austin while you get Tristan out. Then, we can come up with another plan once he's safe."

"There's still a chance you both could get hurt. I can't be worried about that and Tristan."

Sarah's face reddened as her anger boiled to the surface. "You can't protect everyone! It's not your responsibility!"

I stood there dumfounded at her outburst. She repeated something to me I had been trying to tell myself all along.

"Just because I got hurt doesn't mean you can treat me like a baby. I'm not as helpless as I seem."

"I didn't mean to make you feel like that," I said, barely squeaking it out. Before when we were fighting, it wasn't hard to go toe to toe with her, but now I felt blindsided.

"It's my choice," said Sarah, calming her voice a bit. "I'm coming whether you like it or not. It's better for my and your health if you focus on keeping yourself safe."

Her expression told me this was a battle I wasn't going to win. I considered fighting against her one more time but decided there wasn't enough time to continue going rounds until I won.

"How will you know if I need backup? It's not like I can signal you inside a house?" I sighed.

"We need a safe word you can tell us if things go sideways," said Sarah.

Bridgette nodded, leaving me with the task of coming up with this safe word. I pondered trying to pick out something that would be easy to type or say, but rare enough that I wouldn't use it by accident.

"Bold." I wasn't one hundred percent confident, but it was the first thing that came to mind.

Sarah and Bridgette looked confused but let it go, accepting the word without arguing.

"If you go dressed like that, Austin will know you're on to him," said Sarah.

I glanced down at my full huntress outfit, taking in the leather and extra pockets. This outfit was functional and made for dealing with witchy surprises. Not wearing it would be like storming a hornet nest with no bug spray.

"She's right. You can't go wearing that." Bridgette rose from her recliner to go to her bedroom.

She returned a few moments later with an oversized baby blue t-shirt and handed it to me. I held the plain cotton shirt in my hand, imagining how easy it could catch fire or tear from a fight. They were right, I knew that, but putting this on felt like it would cause a crack in the courage I dug up to walk into this scenario. I walked back to the bathroom, defeated, and took off the leather pants, replacing them with the stretchy jeans I had on earlier. I threw on the t-shirt over my corset and holster and tucked in the front to give myself some shape and help the flowy shirt from getting in the way if I had to fight. As I returned to the living room, I tucked my lucky penny in my pocket.

Bridgette and Sarah stood ready with supplies of their own. Sarah dangled the potion belt in her hand with a few spare fire bombs attached to it. My crossbow was slung on Bridgette's back with a full quiver of different types of bolts. I gave her a quizzical look, but she shrugged.

"You never know when you need it." Bridgette readjusted the heavy straps on her shoulder.

I shrugged in agreement and walked to my chest, grabbing the special obsidian necklace and a lighter to complete my ensemble.

"Do you have any more spice we can put in this necklace?" I cracked open the fake obsidian, seeing the empty reservoir from the last time I used it.

"I should have a little bit. I made some more," Bridgette said, taking the crystal from me to the kitchen, along with the crossbow.

The crystal returned full, and I clipped it back on the necklace. It was a subtle way to bring in another weapon, even though it wouldn't get me too far. But it saved my life once, so the necklace had proven its helpfulness. My phone buzzed in my back pocket, so I took it out, seeing a text message from Austin with his address. I texted back that I was on the way and put the phone back in my pocket.

"Are you sure you want to go inside alone?" asked Bridgette.

"He's just a man, and we already know Tristan is at his house from the spell. I think I can handle Austin if I fight witch creatures on a regular basis."

Sarah rolled her eyes, but said nothing as Bridgette handed me her car keys.

"Sarah and I will be close by in case something goes wrong. If you really need me, I'll be there." Bridgette held my car key free hand, giving it a small squeeze and dropped it.

Sarah, Bridgette, and I walked out to our respective cars, loaded the gear, and began our drive. I watched the rearview mirror as we passed through the protection veil to see the glitter rain down. My heart lurched a little, knowing we had left our last ring of safety. From this point on, everything was unknown, and I didn't like that.

We turned on the dirt road and made our way toward New Meadows to Austin's house. As I drove, I thought about turning on the radio, but it seemed wrong to listen to music in this situation. So, the drive was quiet except for the sound of the wheels rolling along the pavement, making a humming ring in my ear. The hum droned on, causing me to lose my focus into my thoughts.

I lost myself to the memory of sitting on the sofa in Tristan's apartment a few months after our mothers died. A greasy, opened pizza box wafted the smell of a cheese pizza with peppers into my nose. Tristan and I had already dug in, starving after an evening of walking the streets of New Meadows. A movie droned on the TV that I wasn't paying attention to, even though we took the time to turn down the lights to focus on the film.

Tristan sank deeper into the old couch, his eyes flickering between me and an action sequence of the movie. I savored one last piece of pizza, almost moaning over how delicious the cheese tasted after a long night before closing the box. After wiping my hands on a spare pizza joint napkin, I buried myself deeper in the couch, pulling my knees into a cross-legged sit. An explosion boomed on the TV, and I tried hard to focus on the action hero, saving a small child from the wreckage, but my brain wandered.

"Why do you keep doing this with me?" I felt Tristan's hand shift closer to mine, and the heat from his fingers made my hairs stand.

"It's something to do." His eyes looked away from the movie, and he fumbled with the remote to turn the volume down. "Plus, it keeps my mind off things."

"Aren't you afraid of getting hurt?" A loaded question because it could refer to this facade of a relationship we had or hunting witches.

"Sometimes, but I made a promise to you." A beat passed, and Tristan pressed his lips together before sighing. "Do you want me to be honest?"

I nodded my head.

"Witches don't scare me because I know you would do anything to save me if I got in trouble."

I nodded again, noticing myself leaning closer to hear the rest of what he had to say.

"I'm more afraid of getting hurt by you," said Tristan softly.

Sarah's lights flashed behind me, bringing me back to driving. I tightened my grip on the wheel as I noticed the sign for Austin's subdivision and braked hard enough to make the turn. Sarah followed behind for the first couple of houses, but when I made a turn to go down a cul-de-sac, Sarah's car kept going straight. They finally left me on my own in this collection of houses that looked exactly the same except for a different window placement here or there. One thing I noticed about the houses as I passed through was that they all had different color doors.

A way for the homeowners to have a sense of self expression, I guessed, but it made my job easier. If Tristan was really with Austin, then I would roll up on a white house with a red door like the spell indicated. But all of these houses were white and even with my slowing down to a snail's pace, they all blurred into a cloud outside of the car window with different flecks of color from the doors. I thought I turned into the wrong neighborhood until I finally came to the end of the road where a giant white colonial house sat with a red door marking the front. The house had to be one of the biggest in the neighborhood, but it looked innocent, as if nothing bad could happen here. It was the picture of suburbia with its manicured hedges and a lawn so green it represented a color from a crayon box. I knew Austin's family owned two hardware stores, but the stores clearly were doing well based on this.

I stopped the car on the curb just before the long driveway and shut the engine off. The driveway was large enough that I could have driven up the entire way and parked right next to the front door, but I wanted more time to walk up and take in the surroundings before interacting with Austin. Stuffing the car keys in my back pocket with the lighter, I slammed the car door, cursing the fact women's jeans never had front pockets. I longed for my huntress pants now more than ever, with all of its amazing pockets to store all the things I needed. But I didn't have them, so I had to make do as I walked up the driveway.

The lush green lawn seemed harmless enough, and there wasn't any shrubbery a necromancer could hide behind, so I felt a little bit safer than I had when I first drove up. I noticed a fence set further back behind the house and what I thought could be a pool. My intuition didn't react, remaining calm, even though I was listening to it more than usual for a sign of something being wrong.

Before I knew it, I found myself on the porch, staring at the red door. I wasn't sure if I should knock, ring the bell, or send a text, so I froze, trying to decide what to do with my hands. Ringing the bell made the most sense, or at least it did in my mind, so I walked closer to the door and pressed the button, praying Tristan was behind it.

CHAPTER TWENTY ONE

The bell ding donged, breaking the silence of the night, and I took a step back from the coarse welcome mat under my feet. Goosebumps scattered themselves around my arms out of nervousness, even though I wished it was because they sensed something. Turning my head, I checked over my shoulder, refusing to turn my back from the door. This porch felt too open. There was nothing for my back to rest upon to make me feel secure, so I could feel every time a night breeze blew past.

Footsteps stomped their way to the front door, so I took a deep breath and tried to fix my face into more of a deadpan instead of the look of fear plastered across my face. I placed my hand on my back, fingering the holt of the dagger hidden there as the lock clicked. The door swung open, revealing Austin standing behind it in the same outfit as dinner, except his hair was more disheveled and pulled back into a bun. Sweat beaded off his forehead, and I hoped he was nervous about the encounter too.

"Hey, glad you could make it." Austin peeped over my shoulder to peer down the driveway. "Did Sarah come with you?"

I released my grip on my knife and put my hand at my side.

"No, I managed to get her to stay back."

"Good, good." He opened the door wider, allowing me to see into the home.

The foyer was a two story opening accented by white shiplap walls, black stairs, and dark hardwood. Even without entering this house, I knew it was going to be a perfect rendition of a southern farmhouse decor style.

"Is Tristan okay?" I tried to spy him behind Austin, but all I could see was a long hallway leading further into the house.

"He's a bit upset, but I think he's fine." Austin waved me in over the threshold.

He shut the door behind us, clicked the lock back into place, and began strolling through the house. I swallowed the bile that jumped into my throat and followed him. I wasn't trapped. There was no reason to feel anxious. I was in a quiet suburban home where I was sure Austin's parents were just upstairs.

"You said he was roughed up on the phone?"

"Kind of? He looks like he got in a fight but won't tell me anything about it."

I followed Austin through the house, mulling this over in my mind. There was probably only one reason Tristan would keep a fight a secret. But what witch creature could he have fought on his own? Another one raised from the dead?

We entered an open living room and kitchen that was empty

apart from furniture and decor. A gather sign hung on the wall over the couch, but there seemed to be no one in this house to gather.

"Where is everyone?" I asked, trying not to gawk at all the various farm animal art that lined the kitchen.

"Tristan is out in the pool house, and my parents are on a mini vacation trip. Their anniversary was this week."

I controlled the expletive that wanted to escape. The last thing I needed was no one else to keep Austin in check in case he was a crazy necromancer servant.

"Pool house?"

"Yeah. It's our hangout spot. We have a TV and stuff back there."

It seemed normal enough for Tristan to be out there, but I couldn't shake the ominous feeling hanging over me that something was off. My intuition pulsed with warning, and I knew whatever was going on in the pool house wasn't good. I considered reaching out to Sarah now, but I needed to confirm if Tristan was really out there first.

Austin opened a pair of French doors between the living room and kitchen to reveal an amazing patio and pool area. Concrete stretched through the backyard, leaving small spots for ornamental grass to give it an earthy feel. The fence I spotted earlier encased the entire area, going behind what looked like a mini house. The pool house had the same white siding as the main house and even two windows framing a small red door.

I squinted, trying to see in through the windows, but only saw the back of light blocking curtains. I turned my attention to the rectangular pool to my right, noticing they winterized it with a cover on top. The rest of the pool area was bare apart from a rogue pool chair still left out to face winter. Everything seemed so normal and not sinister at all, but my intuition refused to let me shake the feeling that something was off.

Austin tolerated my following him up to this point, but he slowed his gait the closer we got to the pool house. I tried to slow down too, but it appeared unnatural. However, the idea of having him behind me wasn't smart, and I knew that. I continued walking, permitting him to move behind me, but not allowing him so much distance that I couldn't feel his presence. I stopped when we reached the door of the pool house to let him pass and open the door.

"It should be unlocked," said Austin.

I reached my hand up to the doorknob and gave it a turn before pushing the door. My chest was tight, anxious about what could be on the other side. When the door finished swinging open, it opened to a large room with cream colored walls and light reddish colored vinyl plank flooring. Pool noodles and floats spread throughout the room among various buckets of pool chemicals for easy access. The faint sound of a TV floated through the entry from further down a hallway, and I could see flashing lights coming from another room.

I stepped into the space, dodging a box of pool tester strips left too close to the threshold. Austin followed, shutting the door behind him, so I stepped in further to give him some room. Out of the corner of my eye, I saw him lean down to move the tester strips box, so I walked a little further in to see if I could get a better look at the TV area. My skin prickled and all the hairs stood on end, leaving me more alert than I had been all night.

I dropped into my intuition, listening for any nuance it

would give me, until faint instructions from the voice in my head became clear.

Duck.

Diving forward, I bent my body in half as I felt a whoosh of air sail over my head.

Turn around and grab.

A simple instruction, so I lifted my body back up, turning to the left. A glint of metal swung back toward me, so I grabbed at it. Stings of pain rushed through my hand, and I thought I felt my wrist bones rattle. I kept my grip firm and snatched back a copper pipe from Austin. His face contorted with surprise and anger as he reached back for his weapon.

Hit.

I swung the pipe, leaving it at the same height until it made contact with Austin's face. An audible crack rang through the room as blood sprayed out of his nose. He turned his face back to me, showing the blood flowing from his crooked nose. It was a once in a lifetime shot guided by my intuition.

"Where's Tristan?" I yelled, as I swung the pipe into Austin's stomach.

He folded over with a cough and reached to his back, standing up with a gun pointed at me.

"Drop the pipe." He clicked the safety off the gun.

My fingers tightened their grip as I hesitated to drop it. Austin spat blood onto the floor with the rest of his nose spray.

"I won't ask you again." He moved the barrel of the gun to my left shoulder, aiming a little lower on my chest than I liked.

My reflexes were fast when I was in tune with my intuition, but I didn't know if I could dodge a bullet. It was a risk to try. Austin's finger squeezed at the trigger of the gun, making the decision for me. As the loud bang erupted, my intuition jumped in.

Move right.

I shifted my body to the right in a fluid movement, making the bullet land in the wall behind me. Austin groaned in frustration, and I swore I saw his eyes flare.

"I knew fighting you was going to be frustrating, but I didn't know it was going to be this bad."

The gun aimed at my feet, and I felt my intuition rise up more. It wasn't a quiet voice anymore, knowing the danger I was in.

Run backwards.

I didn't have time to ponder the strange request, so I moved backwards on my feet. Another bullet rang out, landing close to my foot, so I quickened the pace, rushing down the hallway toward the sound of the TV. Austin kept firing at my feet, corralling me to the location he wanted me to be in. I felt the room open up behind me as the sound of the TV became louder. Defense had been the main objective so far, but I needed to do something before I kept backing myself into a corner. The pipe remained firm in my hand, but I didn't think I could swing it without taking a bullet.

"Drop the pipe, Atalanta."

I backed up another step, bumping into something hard. The room had a large sectional, a TV, a popcorn machine, and a foosball table I was currently about to sit on. There was no room in here to move, let alone do a full blown fight, which was why Austin forced me in here in the first place. He huffed, wiping some blood from his nose onto his shirt, and opened a door behind him. The door opened up into a dark room, so Austin reached behind the doorjamb and flipped on a switch while keeping the gun pointed at me.

The light shone on a foot I knew was Tristan's. The rest of his body was sprawled out on the floor, but I could only see his lower half. Austin took the gun off me, turned, and aimed it at Tristan.

"Drop the pipe." Austin looked back over his shoulder, and I understood what he was insinuating.

While I was able to dodge bullets with intuition, Tristan didn't have that skill. There was no choice. The pipe clanged on the ground as I dropped it from my hand. Austin nodded, and if I hadn't fractured his nose, he probably would have smiled.

"Put your other weapons on the table." Austin stepped forward, still making sure the gun pointed at Tristan.

I thought about claiming I didn't bring anything else, but I figured Austin wouldn't fall for that. The dagger was an easy give, but I hoped he wouldn't recognize jewelry as a weapon. I reached to my back, pulled out the holster, and laid my dagger between blue foosball men before putting my hands up.

"I have nothing else."

Austin's eyes shifted up and down my body.

"And your phone."

"I can't do that." A lie formed in my head. I needed to get the safe word out there, so Sarah and Bridgette would know something was wrong.

"Why?"

"I told Sarah I would text her to let her know everything was okay once I saw Tristan."

"So?"

"If I don't text her, she will come storming in here. Is that what you want?"

"Let her." Austin shrugged. "Phone."

I pulled my phone out of my back pocket along with my keys and set it on the table with the dagger. The lighter lingered in my pocket, and I hoped it was slim enough to go unnoticed.

"Now, walk into the room with Tristan." Austin motioned with the gun, and I thought about snatching it from his hand to put a bullet in his head.

When I passed him, I considered fighting him, but the need to keep Tristan safe outweighed the urge. Austin moved the gun from Tristan and pressed it to my temple. The cooling metal was as foreign to my skin as the pressure pushing deeper into my temple was.

Can I reach the gun in time? I asked my intuition.

No.

A response I didn't want, but it forced me to keep my arms pinned to my side. Austin's hand moved down to the small of my back, pressing into where my dagger should have been. He curled his fingers, digging into my corset through my shirt, as he pushed me further into the room.

No matter what I did at this point, I knew this wasn't going to end well. I still wasn't sure of Austin's condition, but it was time to send the code word to Sarah and Bridgette. I dropped into my mindset, choosing to send a message to Bridgette since our bond was stronger. My consciousness drifted, searching for Sarah's car until I found it down the road from mine. I observed them chatting in the car. Sarah was sitting on her hands, trying to control nervous energy. Bridgette stiffened, feeling my presence.

Bold. I pushed the word to her, trying to be gentle. Her hands shot to her temple, but she didn't bend over in agony, so I knew I was getting better at not being too harsh. I tried pushing the image of the pool house, but the butt of the pistol collided with my temple, pulling me out of my mindset.

My head throbbed as my brain fought the urge to close my eyes.

"I still can't believe catching a Captrix was this easy." Austin chuckled and moved me further into the room.

I forced my knees to stay straight and not buckle. He lifted the gun again to give me a knockout blow, but stopped halfway when a beeping sound emerged from his pocket. Austin groaned, lowering the gun as he pulled out his phone. He glanced at the screen before slipping the phone back in his pocket.

"Freaking Sarah."

My eyebrows perked up, knowing I got my message through.

"I'll be back in a few," he whispered in my ear. His hot breath made my stomach turn.

Then, he pushed me hard, launching me to the ground. As I crashed into the floor and Tristan's feet, the light flicked off, and the door slammed behind me. I heard the lock turn, knowing he had trapped me in this room for now. My heart raced as the pain stopped pulsing in my knees. A shoe dug into my ribcage, so I tried to reach forward to push myself up. Cool, smooth concrete reached my palms once I passed what I assumed were Tristan's legs. I felt around on the floor, frustrated with my lack of sight, until I tumbled off him.

I felt trapped in an endless void of darkness, waiting for my eyes to adjust. Even under the door where I came from didn't have a bit of light slithering in. I sat upright, feeling around with the span of my arms, but felt nothing but air. If I didn't know better, I would have just assumed this was an open room with nothing in it. However, the odds of that being true was low. My only hope right now was Sarah providing enough of a distraction so I could find a way out of here before Austin came back.

"Tristan?" I reached down, feeling for the foot I knew I was close to. "Tristan?"

I shook his foot and waited for a response. Nothing came, so I shook it harder. A groan came from further in the room where I assumed his head laid. My eyes adjusted to the darkness more, and I made out his body shape that began to move.

"Atalanta?"

I listened closely for the shifting of his body as he pushed himself up.

"We've gotta get out of here," whispered Tristan.

"Obviously," I said, not changing the volume of my voice. It seemed unnecessary to whisper when our captor wasn't here.

Tristan shushed me, and hands felt around my legs until they traveled up my arms, content with finding me in the darkness. The heat from Tristan's skin warmed mine as he leaned his face in closer, almost touching my nose with his.

"You don't understand." His voice barely made a whisper now, and it took my brain a moment to process what he said.

"What is it?" I lowered my voice more this time, still refusing to match his whisper.

He tightened his grip on my arms in fear, or possibly protection. It was hard to tell without me being able to get a read on his face. I slipped my right arm out of his grasp and reached for the lighter in my back pocket. My arm shook a bit from the slow, controlled movement as I tried to control the unease I felt in the room. My fingertips brushed the cool metal of the lighter, and I held it out to the right, trying to avoid anything that I couldn't see.

I pulled my thumb back on the lighter wheel, causing a spark to flick into the air. Tristan's grip remained firm on my arm, but he didn't try to stop me. Pulling harder and faster, another spark left the lighter before a flame finally erupted. A glow shone around the room, faintly illuminating Tristan's face and cast a shadow off his body. I peered at him closer, able to get a real look at him now. His lip had a cut against it, clotted with blood, along with a forming bruise on his jaw from a fist fight. The normal clear blown eyes I was used to looking into seemed foggy from disturbed sleep. I wanted to reach up and touch his face to try to soothe his wounds that I understood didn't come from a witch creature fight. However, my attention turned to the other objects becoming visible in the flame's light.

The left side revealed the purpose of the room where a collection of beach towels laid folded on a built-in shelf along with spare sheets and blankets, ready for a pool day or movie night. I moved the lighter back toward Tristan's face to scan the other side of the room, but the metal started to burn my thumb. I breathed in, trying to ignore the flame singeing my skin. The flame illuminated the right side of the room, showing plastic storage bins and what I thought was a working table. The heat of the lighter became too much, so I cursed and released the wheel.

"Everything is fine. It's just a storage room." I shook out my hand to cool my thumb.

Tristan's grip didn't loosen. My reassurance fell on deaf ears.

"You don't know." He felt for my hand and took the lighter.

"What is it?" I didn't want to sound so irritated because

I had no idea how long he had been in this dark closet, but his lack of telling me what was going on was becoming annoying.

"Me." A voice cracked through the air to the right.

My body perked up involuntarily at the new sound as my intuition tried to get a sense of the room. I tightly closed my eyes to listen to whatever information my intuition could discern.

Witch.

The flicking sound of the lighter forced me to open my eyes as Tristan lit up the room. He moved the lighter in one smooth motion, pointing the flame at the area I couldn't get to before. A large pot rested over a propane cooker hooked to gas, but behind it, I noticed the shine of copper metal. Crawling forward, I avoided the flame by keeping my head low. Tristan moved his hand to my ankle, determined to not let me venture far. I peered around the pot and gasped.

CHAPTER TWENTY TWO

Long, bony fingers pulled a body closer to the metal, and I crawled closer to get a better look. Tristan's grip tightened on my ankle, a physical cue that I wasn't allowed to go any further. I huffed in frustration and stared harder as thin arms came into view, covered with stringy black hair from a head I couldn't see. The figure snorted and picked up her speed, propelling herself into bars of copper I understood to be a makeshift cage. A wisp of smoke sizzled into the air as she touched the metal, leaving the room with an overpowering smell of burnt skin and hair.

She yelped, leaping back, and curled into a tiny ball of bones. My intuition told me I was looking at a witch, but to me, she looked more like a corpse. The flame went out, and I listened to Tristan suck his thumb where the metal wheel of the lighter had been burning it. I reached back and took the lighter from him, striking it back up again. When the flame lit this time, she was back at the bars with only inches separating her from the copper. Tristan, being distracted with caring for his thumb, loosened his grip on my ankle, so I took the chance to get closer. The witch creature gave me a painful smile, and I glanced at her eyes, seeing nothing but black.

Venefica.

She muttered some lines I couldn't discern. My body fell forward, extinguishing the flame as Tristan snatched me back to him by pulling my ankle. My stomach slid across the floor, and I planted my hands to stop the forced movement.

"Is that—"

"Lorelei."

"—a Venefica?" I pushed myself up to an upright sitting position. "What?"

Silence invaded the room as Tristan and I both tried to wrap our heads around what we just said. I pressed my lips together hard until my thoughts centered.

"You're telling me that Venefica corpse over there is Lorelei? Austin's ex-girlfriend Lorelei?"

"I'm sure it's her."

"Then, why does she look like that? I mean Veneficas aren't beautiful, but she's—"

"Starving. I don't know what he's doing to her."

"Hungry," moaned Lorelei. "Souls so close."

The smell of burnt skin penetrated the air as she cried out from touching the copper again. My brain swam in theories, not sure which one to pursue. Bridgette, Sarah, and I had thought Austin could have been keeping Lorelei caged to help her after her transition based on the soulless bodies we found, but starving her didn't make any sense.

"We thought he might have been taking care of her. The way she looks she should be dead."

I lit the lighter again, this time immediately shining it toward Lorelei. She turned her head to flame and muttered words of Latin, but the spell she tried to cast never materialized or she was too weak to make it work. Her body looked so thin as a pair of dirty jeans hung off her hips, the gap between the band and her stomach proving she had been here for a while. A college t-shirt covered in holes engulfed what Austin's actions left of her frame as matted, greasy black hair circled her pale face. Starvation sank the rest of her features in, destroying what was once beautiful.

Searching her face and body, I tried to determine if she really was alive or another necromancer byproduct until I decided no one raised her from the dead.

"Lorelei?"

She ignored me, muttering more words of Latin and comments about hunger.

"Can you talk to her?" I turned to look at Tristan, the flame light dancing across his face.

"I've tried a few times, but it's hard. She's so different."

"Try again?"

"Lorelei." Tristan scooted next to me, venturing closer to the cage.

Lorelei tilted her head at the sound of a familiar voice. She grunted and moved herself back toward the bars.

"What happened? What did Austin do to you?"

"Need souls to make power." Lorelei whimpered, and her

head fell forward, almost hitting the bars.

Tristan went to ask her another question, but the sound of the pool house door slamming stopped him. I let go of the lighter, putting us back into darkness as I slipped it back into my pocket.

"Lay back down," I said.

Tristan obeyed, and I shuffled myself to lie down next to him. Footsteps grew closer, and I mentally prepared myself for whatever came through that door. The lock clicked, and the door burst open. A hand banged against the wall, searching for the light switch until it was found. Light poured into the room from an overhead fixture as the door slammed closed. I squeezed my eyes shut, getting used to not being in darkness and flame light.

"Sorry that took so long." Austin moved into the room and went toward the cage side. "Getting rid of Sarah is virtually impossible."

I bit the inside of my cheek to not give a verbal response. Sarah had done the job I asked, and for what? Tristan and I were still stuck in here with her possibly being injured on the outside. My stomach flipped. What about Bridgette?

"Luckily, she believed me when I told her y'all had run off. After I let her check the entire house."

I struggled to keep the sigh of relief in. Even if I was still stuck in here, Sarah and Bridgette were still safe. And they both had an idea where we were.

"Did you meet my love?"

On that remark, my eyes flew open as I held in a retort about the meaning of love.

"You mean the witch creature in the cage?" I cursed myself for not keeping that comment in, but I could only filter so much.

"It's always bothered me how you refer to them as creatures, like they are less than you." Austin slung a bag onto a table next to the cooker pot. "Baby? You okay in there?"

Lorelei whispered some words, her mind clearly in a different place than her cage.

"She gets a little spacey when she's hungry." Austin shrugged.

He spread some ingredients out on the table and a book, taking time to flip to his desired page. Tristan leaned up beside me and touched my hand. I took solace in the touch, realizing I wasn't alone, but also realized that whatever I decided to do could kill him if I made the wrong choice. But I didn't have a plan. The necromancer wasn't here. All I had was a starving Venefica and a servant to deal with.

"So, how long has Lorelei been in a cage?" Tristan squeezed my hand, hinting that my question may have been the wrong choice.

"For about six months." Austin looked over his shoulder, and I saw his eyes flash with anger.

My heart dropped into my stomach. She had been starving for six months in a cage that hurt her every time she touched it. How long had it taken for her mind to go? A fate worse than death, if you asked me. Something too cruel even for a soul-devouring monster.

I took another glance around the room as Austin laid the pistol on the table with the rest of his ingredients. The chain of my necklace weighed on my neck, reminding me I did have one weapon left. I could set off a diversion fire bomb, and Tristan and I could make a run for it. My main problem was the unaccounted for necromancer.

"When is your necromancer friend going to show up?" I asked, as I fiddled with my necklace to make sure it would open and shut with ease.

Austin laughed so hard I thought he would double over with tears in his eyes.

"You really haven't figured it out, have you? I thought Captrixes were supposed to be amazing and smart." He sucked in a breath between laughing fits.

His laughter struck a chord in me and the fact he called me stupid. I shook off Tristan's hand and stood up, ready to punch him straight into the cage with Lorelei. Austin stopped laughing and looked at my newfound posture.

"I'm the necromancer, you idiot." Austin lifted the lid of the pot. "If you don't sit back down. I will shoot him. Lorelei won't care if he's dying when she eats his soul."

The word soul woke Lorelei from her distant thoughts. "So hungry."

"I know, baby. I know." Austin grabbed the gun and pointed it at Tristan. "Sit."

I begrudgingly sat back down on the ground. How could I fight magic wielding witches, but be stopped by a simple handgun?

Tristan scooted back to the wall near the shelves of sheets. I stayed in the center of the room, trying to come up with a new plan as my head reeled with the new information.

We never clocked Austin being the actual necromancer. Sure, I thought he was helping them and possibly taking care of a Venefica, but not bringing witch creatures back from the dead. Bridgette herself said that he didn't have magical power, so Austin's admission was mindboggling.

"But how?" I still couldn't wrap my brain around the idea.

Austin sat the pistol back on the table and turned back around to face me before resting on the table.

"Lorelei."

Tristan and I both looked at each other, confused. Then, my original theory donned on me.

"You're siphoning power from her?" No wonder Lorelei looked like a shell. Everything she did eat got pulled from her for Austin's witch raising.

"I don't like that word. I would say she's helping me."

"She doesn't look like she's being helped," whispered Tristan.

Austin's eyes darted to him.

"At first, she was in perfect condition, but she had to give me more power to perfect the spells." Austin looked back to Lorelei, and his body softened at her appearance. "She just needs to eat something, and she'll look good as new."

My brain spun in the new information until it settled on one thought.

"You brought my mother back from the dead."

Tristan's eyes widened, not knowing my mother was back. I didn't have time to explain now, so he forced himself to return to a deadpan glare at Austin.

"Correct. She was one of my first ones, so I don't know how she survived."

"But how did you find her? She's on property that's protected." My mind reeled, wondering what I could have possibly done wrong.

"You."

"Me?"

"I took a strand of your hair at the party during our little kiss." Austin darted his eyes at Tristan, looking for him to have a visceral reaction.

Tristan remained calm, keeping his face blank. I knew me kissing Austin bothered him a bit, but I didn't know that it should have a reaction. He was with Sarah, after all. But that didn't stop me from feeling dirty, like my one kiss tainted me with a giant mark reserved for people who made out with random guys at parties.

"That's why I didn't think it would work since I raised her based on your DNA," said Austin, continuing his monologue. "She must have found a Mortia clan able to help her. The rest of the witches were more difficult, and I had to find pieces of them at the swamp or in your house's ash."

It made sense now why she was so ghost-like and in pain that night. She was an incomplete resurrection. His admission also made me understand how he kept bringing witches back from my past, even if him searching for my jeans with Venefica vomit made me even more uncomfortable.

"But why?"

"Because I wanted you to know what it's like seeing a ghost of someone you once loved." Austin moved to the cage, reaching his hand through the bars.

Lorelei moved closer, even though she bent down like she was expecting to get hit. Austin gently caressed her face.

I wanted to scream at him that I already knew what it was like to see the ghost of my mother. To have her haunting my dreams and know that one wrong decision I made got her killed. The pain he wanted to put me in already surrounded me like a plastic bag and I could barely get air.

"How did you even know where to find all of those things?" It was one thing for Austin to have raised the witches, but the amount of information he knew was astounding.

"A knowledge spell here and there with the help of Lorelei. It wasn't too difficult once I knew where to look."

"Why Atalanta, Austin?" asked Tristan. He straightened his body as it rested on the wall.

"Don't you mean why both of you? It's not a mistake you're here too." Austin went back to his working table and measured ingredients into his pot, taking a moment to hold them in his hand like I had seen Bridgette do before.

"Okay, why us?"

"Because you're the reason she's like this." Anger strained his voice as Austin fought not to yell.

"We didn't do anything to her," I said.

"You took away the only person who could help her."

"Who? My mother?" asked Tristan.

"Exactly. She was helping Lorelei control her powers, and you two had to go kill her."

"She tried to kill us first!" I wanted to punch him now more than ever. How could Austin make this about Morgana? She did everything to herself.

"I don't care. What I cared about was Lorelei! After Morgana died, she turned without guidance. You think I wanted to keep her in a cage?"

"Did you plan on starving her too, or was that an afterthought?" I asked.

Stop, my intuition warned, but this had gone too far.

"You blame us for her turning, but who do you blame for that state she's in? She's barely alive!" My jaw quivered. "If anyone here should be punished for something, it's you."

Lorelei cried softly in the background as if she was agreeing with my statement, causing Austin to ball his fists. He grabbed the gun and shot a bullet into the wall right above Tristan's head. Drywall dust rained down, giving a white coating on the top of his hair. I gasped as Tristan shook, trying to contain the adrenaline from almost being shot.

"Here we go. All high and mighty Atalanta. A Captrix savior of humans with a pristine moral compass. Tell me, how do you get that when you're the reason everyone around you dies?" Austin lifted the back of his shirt and placed the pistol in the waistband of his jeans.

The low blow settled into my stomach, but I tried to not let him see he got to me. Anger still stirred inside, but the fear of Tristan dying, becoming another one of my casualties, reigned supreme. Austin walked closer to me and kneeled down, putting his face inches away from mine. Fingers entwined into my hair, snatching my head back as his warm breath covered my face. I refused to turn away.

"You killed your mother, got Sarah almost killed—" he leaned in closer to whisper in my ear, "and you're going to be the reason Tristan dies too."

Austin let go of my hair and stomped over to Tristan not giving me a second glance. When he reached Tristan, he put his hands in his hair, pulling out strands. "Now you're going to help me bring Morgana back to fix Lorelei."

"She turned to dust. She's not coming back," said Tristan

through gritted teeth.

"Your soul plus Atalanta's fancy one should be enough to fix that." Austin inspected the hairs and nodded his head before dropping them on the floor. "Plus, it's not the first witch I've risen from dust." He took a special look at me, and I knew what he meant.

"She's not going to be able to help you anyway," I said. "She turned into a Venefica before she died."

"You're lying!" Austin reared back and punched Tristan in the jaw.

Tristan blinked rapidly, trying to recover from the hit. Austin grabbed his shirt collar and shook Tristan backwards, making his head connect with the wall. Then, he dragged the dazed Tristan across the room, settling him in front of Lorelei's cage.

"Here you go, baby." Austin grabbed a zip tie off of the work table and pinned Tristan's hands to the cage.

Lorelei creeped closer, sniffing the air for the scent of the soul close by. I flinched, knowing what was going to happen next if I didn't do something about this. Austin ignored my movement, pulling the pistol from the place he had it tucked on his back, and laid it on the table with the other ingredients. He leaned down and turned the cooker on under the pot. The scent of gas permeated the air, choking me a smidge as a blue flame began boiling the ingredients. My eyes focused on the gun left unattended on the table.

Lorelei's face appeared next to Tristan, and I noticed the ends of her hair turning white as she mumbled a Latin incantation. Tristan arched his back and groaned in pain. His mouth opened, and a small wisp began moving in the back of his throat.

Do I have enough time, I asked my intuition. Panic consumed me, but my mind went silent as my intuition weighed the question.

Yes.

It was the only answer I needed.

I rose from my feet in a leap and darted to the worktable. Austin reached for the gun, but I grabbed it first, snatching it just out of his grasp. The safety remained clicked off, so I pointed the gun at his shoulder. My ears rang with a loud bang as Austin screamed, stumbling backwards. I raced to Tristan with the weapon still in my hand as his soul exited his mouth. His soul took on the form of a translucent fox, whose eyes darted around the room in confusion. Lorelei sucked in a deep breath, opening her mouth to devour the creature. I needed my dagger to stab her with, but it still sat on the foosball table.

I pushed my hand into my back pocket, searching for my lucky penny next to the lighter. The penny tumbled in my fingers, and in a weird déjà vu moment, I shoved the penny into Lorelei's mouth. She bit down on my arm, sinking her teeth in. I screeched as I ripped my arm from her mouth with new half moon teeth marks laying against my other scars.

She coughed as the copper penny burned her windpipe, falling back further into the cage. Tristan's fox ran back into his mouth, and he gasped when his soul piece nestled back where it belonged. I yanked at his arms, trying to break the zip tie. His arms snapped, staying pinned to the bars. Lorelei vomited in the cage, sending the penny onto the floor. Austin stood with blood running out of his shoulder wound. I aimed the gun at his other shoulder and pulled the trigger.

Click.

I pulled the trigger again. No bullet came out. If he didn't have a pulsating shoulder wound, I was sure Austin would laugh. This wasn't the time to give him the upper hand, so I threw the gun at Austin's head. The gun connected with his forehead, and he stumbled backwards again.

Returning my focus to the cage, I watched Lorelei crawl forward on all fours, recovered from the penny. She began her spell, stalking up to Tristan. Turning back to the worktable, I grabbed a knife and used it to cut the zip tie holding Tristan's wrists. His hand fell down in his lap as he shuffled away from the cage.

Lorelei wailed, upset at losing her easy prey. I ignored her and grabbed a zip tie from the table, putting it between my teeth. I approached Austin, who was rising from the surprise gun throw, and punched him in his fractured nose. He screamed, and his hands flew up to his face to cover his nose from more blows. I grabbed his shoulders, taking extra care to tighten my grip on his gunshot wound, and kneed him in the groin. Austin crumbled onto the ground, powerless without Lorelei's power or his leverage of killing Tristan. Grabbing his shoulders again, I dragged him to the same spot he secured Tristan and zip tied his wrists over his head to the bar.

"Don't do this," said Austin through gritted teeth. He turned around and saw Lorelei crawling closer.

I ignored him and turned around to help Tristan off the floor. He stood up slowly, watching the events unfold by the cage. Lorelei spoke her incantation with more force, finding her spirit now that she had the chance to seek revenge on her captor.

"What are you doing?" Tristan's eyes searched mine for an answer.

"I need you to grab my dagger and phone from the table,"

I said, looking away from him.

Tristan opened the unlocked door and stepped out into the entertainment area, finding my stuff where I had been forced to put it. I looked at Austin as his mouth opened and his soul slithered out of his mouth in the shape of a snake. The wisp didn't look confused. It struck forward, trying to escape the magic that pulled it to Lorelei's starving mouth. Tristan returned behind me and handed me my dagger and phone.

"We can't do this." Tristan stared at the cage, watching Austin's soul snake float closer to Lorelei's mouth.

She chomped at it, narrowly missing the cage bars. I stayed quiet. Tristan placed his hand on my shoulder.

"We can't kill him." Tristan turned me away to face him.

"You know what he did." I choked on the words, not realizing I was becoming emotional.

Tristan pulled me in close, but even the warmth of skin, this feeling of being home in his arms that I needed, couldn't make me forget Austin brought my mother back from the dead. It couldn't make me forget the cruel person who sat beside the cage that starved someone he loved for months. To me, letting him die in this way would be justice for everyone involved.

"If we kill Austin, we are no better than him," whispered Tristan in my ear.

Austin screamed, and I knew Lorelei had finally gotten the first bite of his soul. I looked back to see Austin, who was now dangerously pale from his gunshot wound, let out a second piece of soul. His last piece. Tristan let me go and ran over to him.

"Please Atalanta, for me."

I didn't move from my spot and let my eyes drift to

watching the second snake wisp floating out of Austin's mouth.

"You owe me this." Tristan leaned down and tried to push the soul back toward Austin's mouth, but it drifted through his fingers.

My jaw quivered, and I knew I owed him. If I didn't spare Austin, Tristan would never forgive me, and I couldn't live with that, even if I planned on letting him be with Sarah. I walked over, holding the dagger in my hand, and leaned down in front of the cage. Lorelei ignored my presence, focusing on drawing the rest of Austin's soul to her. I reached in the cage and grabbed her head, pulling her closer to me as the snake wisp almost touched her lips.

She screamed when I plunged the dagger into her stomach. Her mouth shut, and the soul rushed back to Austin to nestle itself into a fractured soul. Tristan cut the zip tie and freed him from the bar. Austin leaned on Tristan to stand as I opened the door to the cage. Lorelei turned to dust, leaving only a grey pile of ash with the mixed metal dagger on top of it.

"Take him out of here into the house. Meet me out front," I said, picking up my dagger.

I walked further into the cage to pick up my penny that had been vomited out earlier as Tristan and Austin shuffled out the door. I let them get further away as I wiped my penny on my pants before putting it back in my pocket. Walking out the door behind them would have been simple, but I didn't believe Austin deserved easy after I spared him his life.

Sarah rushed into the room, heaving, and clutched a fire bomb in her hand.

"Are you okay?" The words tumbled out of her mouth. "I saw Tristan and I—"

"I'm fine." I ignored the goose egg that had risen to the

surface on the side of my head. "We just need to get out of here."

The cooker pot raged on, with most of the ingredients burned on the bottom. Blue flames licked the bottom of the pot and it gave me an idea. I ran my fingers over my necklace, remembering the fire bomb spices I kept inside. A dusting of these mixed with propane would explode the pool house. A fate I found fitting to remove evidence and stick it to Austin one last time.

"We're going to blow up the pool house. Are you up for it?"

Shock covered Sarah's face, but she nodded.

"I need you to leave the fire bomb at the entrance and go out to the pool. I'll be there in a second."

Sarah left without hesitation and I waited until I thought she was a safe distance away. I pulled the necklace off and loosened the crystal lid, so the ingredients would fall on the gas in a few moments. Sauntering over to the cooker, I moved the pot off to the floor. The blue flame glowed brighter now that nothing prevented it from towering high. I turned the propane up before stretching the necklace across the metal pieces.

Then I ran, faster than ever before, as the flame began breaking down the necklace. As I raced out the door of the pool house, Tristan and Austin were making their way through the French doors of the main house. I continued to run, passing the pool as the building imploded with a loud bang. Sarah began running with me as well as we tried to escape the blast. Wood flew past our heads, but I didn't turn around. The smell of smoke permeated the air as the heat of fire warmed my back behind me.

I grinned, knowing it was finished.

CHAPTER TWENTY THREE

I STOOD OUTSIDE OF Austin's front door with Sarah waiting for Tristan. He was getting Austin setup on the couch, helping him call 911 for the explosion and his bullet wound. I didn't care what story he gave as long as it didn't involve me, Tristan, or a witch creature. The door creaked open as I started hearing sirens in the distance. Tristan stepped out and joined us to walk down the driveway to the car.

"Did you warn him?" I picked up my pace. I wanted to be further out of the neighborhood before the emergency services arrived.

"That you'll kill him if he stepped out of line? Yeah, I think he got the message."

I nodded, feeling content. It was one thing for me to show mercy. It was another to have to deal with an ongoing necromancer problem.

"Did you really have to blow up the pool house, though?"

"Did you want to explain about the witch creature stuff?

Tristan shook his head, confirming my point.

"What happened to your car?" I asked, remembering it was missing.

"It's around the block parked in front of another house. Or towed by now."

"I'm leaning toward towed, given that I didn't see it on the drive in, but I could have missed it." I gave him an encouraging smile that was met with an eye roll and a sigh.

As we made our way down the driveway, we met a running Bridgette armed with my crossbow. She was shaking and ready to fight. Sarah had taken too long to report back to her.

"We're okay," I said, stopping her and making her turn back around.

"What happened?" asked Bridgette, as she calmed down.

She looked Tristan and me over, calculating our wounds and what remedies she could make to help them. We reached the end of the driveway to find Sarah's car parked behind Bridgette's blue sedan. Sirens wailed closer, and I knew we were running out of time for a clean escape.

"I can explain, but we really need to get out of here," I said, rushing to get into Bridgette's car.

"I'll ride with Sarah and explain," said Tristan, corralling Sarah to her car.

I wanted to talk to Bridgette and let her know everything, but my heart sank a little as I watched Tristan enter Sarah's car. Instead of sulking in the interest of time, I started the car to begin the drive back to the cottage. We sat in silence as a fire truck, police, and an ambulance passed me when I exited the subdivision. I let out a breath, releasing some of the anxiety I had about being caught, and pressed onward.

"We were wrong, Bridgette. Austin was the necromancer and the keeper of the Venefica." I looked up in the rearview mirror to see Sarah's lights following closely behind.

"How?"

"He was siphoning Lorelei's—the Venefica's—powers. That's why the transformations were wrong."

"I can't believe it." Bridgette tucked her hair behind her ears, processing the thought.

"He was trying to raise Morgana by starving her." I choked on the words, finally feeling the waves of emotion I kept suppressed.

Bridgette tensed her jaw before touching my arm. "That wasn't your fault."

I nodded. I believed her, but it was still hard for me to grasp that I didn't have control of what happened. Every action I did still felt like a never-ending tumbling of dominos. I swallowed the feeling, keeping it to myself for now, and focused on keeping the car on the road.

"Atalanta, something is touching the protection veil." Bridgette dug her fingers into the seat.

"What is it?" I pressed harder on the gas.

"I can't tell. It's something new." Bridgette closed her eyes. "Yet familiar."

She reached for her phone and texted Tristan the news. Bridgette looked uneasy, and her uncertainty affected me as well. After a long night of dealing with Austin, I wanted to crash onto the couch, not deal with whatever was waiting for us at the veil.

"Are they breaking through?" I asked, as the dirt road came into view.

"No. It's like they are just touching it." Confusion painted Bridgette's face.

I made the turn onto the road and slowed down into a crawl. The car lights shone on the dirt and trees, creating a tunnel of open woods. I looked out the window, trying to see or anticipate what was coming, but saw nothing. Sarah turned onto the road behind me, blinding me with her headlights, making it even harder to see. A shimmer cascaded as we approached the opening of the protection veil. But before I could turn the car onto the driveway, I noticed a hooded figure standing off to the side.

The dirt shone red from the brake lights when I stomped the pedal, bringing the car to a halt. Sarah stopped behind me too, but left her car running. I put mine in park and shut off the engine before stepping out.

"Who's there?"

Car doors slammed behind me as Bridgette, Tristan, and Sarah all stepped out after me. The hooded figure kept their back to me but touched the veil. It rained down glitter for a moment before stopping and pushing the hand out. The veil seemed as confused as Bridgette had been in the car about this visitor.

"Hello?" I pulled out my dagger from my back.

I stopped a few feet away from the visitor. The heat from the rest of the group was on my back, so I knew they remained close. I heard Sarah whisper, but I couldn't make out what she said.

"I can see you." I started to get annoyed by the lack of response.

The hooded figure turned around, and I studied their

outfit—a dark black cloak and nondescript black clothes underneath. They tilted back their hood, and I stared at the face of a Mortia. A Mortia that I now recognized as my mother. Bridgette gasped and took a step forward to stand beside me.

"Mom?" My grip on the dagger loosened.

"I guess that's who I used to be." Her voice came out creaky like it was one of the first times being used.

"How are you here?" asked Bridgette, anguish flooding her voice.

"Don't you mean why?" Mom lifted her hand and conjured a little snowflake, making the night air turn freezing.

Our breath began making little clouds in the air every time we exhaled. Sarah's teeth started chattering from the change in temperature. Tristan walked forward to cover my left side, so we built a wall between Sarah and my mother.

"Why are you here?" The dagger remained in my hand, but it almost made more sense to drop it.

I knew I was staring at the face of a Mortia, but she was still my mother in appearance, and somewhat personality. There was no way I could kill her. I wasn't strong enough to fight her and be the reason she died a second time.

"I came to warn you." Mom crushed the snowflake in her hand. The temperature rose a little, but remained frigid.

"About what?"

Bridgette sniffled beside me, and I knew she was doing her best to keep it together. When I told her before, she had a visceral reaction, but she hadn't physically seen the transformation. Now, both of our worst nightmares stood before us.

"I'm not your mother anymore."

She should have just punched me in the stomach. I swallowed hard.

"If I see you again or if you come after me, I will kill you." Her black eyes fixed on all of us before looking dead at Bridgette. "All of you."

Grief welled in my chest as I realized this wouldn't be an easy second chance to save her or repair our relationship to what it was once before. We were now chess pieces on opposite sides of the board. Her, a queen for the witch creatures, and me, a pawn for the Captrixes.

"I love you." I tilted my head back to stop tears from spilling from my eyes.

She said nothing and took a few steps forward. I wiped moisture from the corners of my eyes.

"But if you hurt people, I'll have to kill you." I stared right into her black eyes.

Mom gave me a grin and held back a chuckle.

"I expect nothing less from my old daughter." Mom pulled her hood back over her head. "See you soon."

She disappeared into thin air, leaving no trace. The air around us immediately warmed back to the temperature it had been before. I let out the breath I was holding in before tears began rushing down my face. I sobbed as Bridgette pulled me into a hug. She cried her own softer tears while I ugly cried. Tristan reached forward and rubbed my back. Before I knew it, Sarah approached, and they wrapped me and Bridgette into a group hug. We stood there crying for a long time as I came to an even darker realization. I made a promise to myself to stop lying to everyone, and here, I made a statement into the night

that I knew was a lie.
I would never be able to kill her.

CHAPTER TWENTY FOUR

A FEW WEEKS LATER, I woke to the sound of Bridgette shuffling through the living room. My eyes opened to darkness, not used to not having morning light first thing. I had been sleeping better after the hunt, but every once in a while, I still had the occasional terrible nightmare that woke me up screaming. I used to dream about what happened in the past and tried to fix my mistake to save my mother's life. Now when I dreamed, I was the one holding the knife to slit her throat.

But today, I pushed those thoughts away because I was determined to be okay for Bridgette's birthday. I had been asking her for the past week what she wanted for her gift, but the only thing she requested was for me to watch the sunrise with her on her birthday. It didn't feel like enough after how close we had gotten, but every time I pestered her, she insisted that was all she wanted.

"Are you ready?" whispered Bridgette, grabbing a blanket from the pile by her chair.

I pushed the quilt off and grabbed my pajama pants I left on the floor.

"Ready as I'll ever be." I slid on the pants and followed her out the living room.

We grabbed zip up hoodies from the coat rack by the door to shield us from the cold. Bridgette shrugged hers on and zipped it over her night dress. We took our place on the steps, and she spread the blanket over our legs. I snuggled it up high, watching the first gleam of light spill over the sky. She leaned forward, resting her elbows on her knees. Time passed, and the dark sky brightened into orange and pink. Birds chirped in the woods off the front of the house.

All in all, it was serene, and everything in the world didn't seem so hard or crazy. I understood why Bridgette would want this as a birthday gift.

"Happy birthday." I slid the covers down and gave her a hug.

She smiled and patted my arm.

"Thank you for doing this with me. I thought we could both use some quiet."

"Anything you want today."

Bridgette sighed, staring into the sunrise.

"I love you." I had never said it to her before, but I knew I felt it. "I don't say it enough, but thank you for doing this with me. For being here with me."

"You don't have to thank me."

"No, I mean it. After everything that happened, you could

have kicked me out. You didn't have to keep helping me." I swallowed, feeling the emotions rise in me. "And I haven't been treating you fairly. I was so worried about not being the reason someone else gets hurt that I lied to you and kept you in the dark. It wasn't fair."

"Losing Artemis has been hard on all of us. We all experience grief in a different way. It's okay." Bridgette squeezed my hand. "I love you too. But I've been keeping you in the dark also."

"What do you mean?"

Bridgette looked away and stared at the sky, pondering her next words. Then, she looked back at me. "I haven't been honest about my relationship with Artemis. Yes, we were friends, but we were also more than that."

My mouth formed an 'o,' realizing what she meant. It didn't matter to me that they were a couple, but more puzzle pieces were fitting together. Mom had always seemed happier coming back from some late night hunts that I assumed were with Bridgette. It also explained Bridgette's visceral reaction to losing her and seeing her raised from the dead. She wasn't just watching her best friend change; she had watched her lover become someone she didn't recognize.

"I'm sorry for being so angry with you before or not being there for you when you needed it." Bridgette closed her eyes. "I loved her. Losing her has been one of the hardest things in my life."

"It's okay. We haven't been our best selves lately, huh?"

"But we're getting better."

We both smiled half grins and laughed. I felt the release of tension as mine grew bigger. For the first time in seven months, bliss covered me while I was sitting on a porch watching the sunrise.

Tristan arrived in the afternoon holding a cake, steaks, and salad ingredients, with Sarah in tow. He offered to grill us all some steaks for dinner as his birthday gift to Bridgette, which she happily accepted. It thrilled Bridgette to have the night off from cooking, so I helped set up an outdoor eating area so she could watch Tristan. She may not have wanted to cook, but she couldn't resist observing to make sure the meal was perfect.

I watched Tristan as he grilled, sitting in my own chair next to Sarah and Bridgette. They were lost in a conversation about plants, but I found myself lost in the flex of Tristan's arm muscles when he flipped the steaks. We were communicating more now, but I also kept my promise to Sarah to give them space. He still always found a reason to call or text me every day, and I couldn't resist not talking to him. I didn't want to miss or shut him out again.

My heart swelled as I let my mind have the daydream that he was mine again. This time would be so different since I felt the same love he did. We could be the complete soulmate package. Tristan grinned at me, catching my gaze, and I smiled back as I focused on his lips. This time, if I kissed him, I knew I would feel the fireworks I missed the first time.

He waved me over, and even though I should have said no, given how much I was lusting after him at this moment, I walked over. The smell of steak and burning charcoal hit my nose first before the smell of his pine tree scented shampoo and deodorant wrapped me into the familiar scent of home. Tristan switched the tongs from his right to left hand and extended his arm to give me a side hug. I returned the hug, savoring the feeling of his arms around me, and dreamed of falling asleep in those same arms. I needed to feel that once more before I really let him go.

I also needed to get a grip.

"I'm going to go get you a tray and the rest of the food," I said with probably too large of a grin.

It took all of my will power not to run into the house, but upon entering, I ran to the bathroom and splashed cold water on my face. The cold water knocked me a bit out of my pining, enough so I could function. It was my choice to not tell Tristan about my soul and give him a chance to be happy with someone else. I was now facing the consequences.

I returned to the grill with a tray and helped Sarah get the rest of the food setup. We all ate dinner together, laughing throughout, and had a good time. My favorite part was getting to watch Bridgette blow out the forty-three candles Sarah and I littered her cake with. There wasn't any spot on the round cake that wasn't covered by a candle, so when Tristan lit them, they all combined into one large flame. Bridgette managed to blow one giant gulp of air and secure her wish.

"What did you wish for?" I asked.

Tristan, Sarah, and I all leaned forward for the answer.

Bridgette laughed. "If I tell you, then it won't come true!"

I shook my head and helped Sarah clear the plates. We took them into the kitchen together, and I started washing the dishes in the sink. Sarah put away the leftover salad and cake into the fridge before joining me.

"Atalanta?" Sarah took a bowl from me and started drying it.

"Yeah?"

Sarah and I had been cordial to each other the past few weeks, and we had even been texting each other regularly. I wanted to build a friendship with her, so I was giving it my best shot.

"I need to talk to you."

"I'm here." I scrubbed a plate.

Sarah exhaled loudly, like she had been holding in her breath for hours. I laid the plate in the rinsing water and stopped washing dishes.

"What is it?" My eyebrows peeked in interest.

"I'm going to break up with Tristan tonight." Sarah spit the words out so fast, it took my brain a few moments to process.

"Why?"

"I'm not stupid. I don't know why you haven't told him yet—"

"What?" My voice sounded like a squeak.

"I know you fixed your soul."

"You don't know—"

"Hush!" Sarah raised her voice. "You were the one who found him with the tracking spell. I see the way you look at him."

"Sarah, I—"

She held up her hand to stop me. "I'm not going to be the other woman or force him to make a choice that I know I would lose."

I was speechless. I didn't know how to reassure her that I wasn't trying to get in the way. It was never my intention to make him choose, which was one of the reasons I hadn't told Tristan about my soul.

"It's not fair for you not to tell him. I know he still loves you." Sarah bit her lip. "I'm not going to stand in the way of either of your happiness."

"Sarah, don't."

"I won't tell him your secret because you need to, but I'm

not changing my mind."

I didn't know how to tell him now that it had been a secret for so long. Keeping my soul a secret was one of the last ways I could protect him and give him a chance to not be wrapped up in the Captrix world forever.

Sarah walked out of the room then, leaving me with the rest of the dishes. I rushed to finish them, but by the time I made it back to the yard, Tristan and Sarah were already at the corner of the house having an intense conversation. Bridgette remained in a chair around the table, oblivious to what was happening around her. I considered running over to Tristan and telling him it was all a mistake and he should be with Sarah, but the solemn look on his face told me the deed was already done.

Tristan threw up his hands, and Sarah walked away. He trailed after her, but she sped over to me and Bridgette.

"I have something I need to tell you all." Sarah pulled an envelope out of her back jeans pocket, twirling it in her hand.

Beads of sweat lined her forehead, but I wasn't sure if she was nervous or worked up from breaking up with Tristan.

"None of you are going to like it. But I wanted you to know that the friendships I've made are true, no matter what y'all think." Sarah paused to gain more courage.

Bridgette and I looked at each other with confusion while Tristan shook his head in sadness and anger. Sarah forced the envelope into my hands. I clutched it and flipped it around to see my name scrawled on the front. Before I could ask her about it, Sarah cut me off.

"I'm the daughter of a board member of the Captrix Council."

My head made a sharp turn up from the envelope. I had heard of the council in passing and knew it was a governing body of Captrixes. As far as I knew, they handled their placements, and that was about it. I probably should have contacted them when my mom passed, but I didn't know who to call.

"They tasked me with finding Atalanta and getting to know her."

My eyes bugged.

"Once I found you, I was then ordered to watch you and report back to the council."

"So, they sent you to spy on me?" I asked. I wasn't sure how I was supposed to react, but all that I felt was numb.

"It's not that simple," said Sarah.

"Simple enough to me," said Tristan. He crossed his arms in front of him.

"So, what is this?" I held up the envelope.

"I'm not sure. They gave me this to give you after I had to tell them about Artemis. I've had it for a week or so because I had to work up the confidence to do this."

She appeared like she was going to cry but held her head high. I looked at Bridgette and Tristan, appalled at what was occurring. Bridgette held out her hand to take the envelope from me, but I shook my head. If this was for me, I needed to be the first person to see the contents.

Flipping the envelope over, I slipped my finger under the edge to separate the seal. I pulled my finger down slowly to avoid a paper cut and to prolong not having to see whatever this was. The seal of the envelope broke, and I pulled out a small, folded piece of paper that looked like the writer ripped it from an office notepad. I unfolded the note and read the words before dropping it to the ground.

We will be seeing you soon.

316

LOVED THIS BOOK?

Leave a review on

amazon

or

goodreads

Reviews help authors more than you know!

LOVE THE CAPTRIX WORLD AND CAN'T GET ENOUGH?

Be the first to know when the next book is coming +

Short Story From Bridgette's POV

Behind-the-Scenes Details

Book Soundtracks

Merch Discounts

And More!

SIGN UP FOR MY NEWSLETTER:

www.shelbymccraley.com/members

ACKNOWLEDGEMENTS

Thank you for reading *The Broken Huntress.* Can you believe we're here again? This book has been over a year in the making and I'm so excited I get to share it with you. However, this book wouldn't be successful without the people mentioned below.

Shawn, thank you for supporting me through all the steps of creating this book, because I know it felt like forever for us both. There's a reason I have a chair in my office and it's because you make it home when I'm working on my novels. Also, thank you for allowing me to use you to choreograph fight scenes. I'm sure it was loads of fun getting to pretend to swing a pipe at my head.

Thank you to my beta readers, Melanie and Chelsea, also known as the most helpful hype squad. I appreciate your time and attention, especially when you get some ROUGH drafts.

A big shout out to my mother, Tammy, for proofreading the final copy and for being my biggest promoter. I'm pretty sure she's shared my first book with everyone she knows and is a direct correlation to why some of you are here for book two.

Finally, I would like to thank my editor, Whitney at Whitney's Book Works, my book cover designer, Stone Ridge Books, my friends (Katya, Tay, Dani, Glory, and Chelsea), and my online community. Thank you all so much for your support.

And as always, thank you to my dogs, Kayla and Tilly, for your endless tail wags, visits to my desk, and for always being there when I need you.

Here's to seeing Atalanta journey continue in book three.

ABOUT THE AUTHOR

SHELBY MCCRALEY lives in coastal Georgia with her husband and two rescue dogs. When she's not writing or spending time with her family, Shelby loves watching a good fantasy movie or playing video games. Her favorite things are a good cup of coffee on a rainy morning, dog snuggles, and pasta with red sauce. Before publishing her novels, Shelby has been the author of a writing blog called *The Writing Addict* since 2017, where she shares writing tips, book recommendations, and some of her shorter works.

Get first looks of her upcoming books and behind the scenes content by subscribing to her newsletter:

shelbymccraley.com/members

instagram.com/shelbymccraley
tiktok.com/authorshelbymccraley
facebook.com/thewritingaddict

www.ingramcontent.com/pod-product-compliance
Lightning Source LLC
Chambersburg PA
CBHW031937210726
48290CB00006BA/1644